# The Little Red Book of

# Holiday Homicides

*To Nancy*
*Happy Holidays!*
*MJ Daspit*

A Collection of Short Stories

by

## MJ Daspit

Spoke Publishing

ISBN 978-0-9860017-9-6

# Table of Contents

At Yuletide, a Cinderella story unfolds in the post-WWII San Francisco of Dashiell Hammett's famous detective, Sam Spade. Spade's secretary Effie Perrine is out in the cold. Evicted by her stepmother and canned by her boss, the stalwart Girl Friday won't give up her dream of becoming a writer, even if it means confronting a villain who has eluded Spade for years.

# The Shoe Santa

INT. DETECTIVE'S OFFICE - NIGHT

DETECTIVE SAM SPADE

eyes the fetching female client and suavely lights a
cigarette as he leans back in his desk chair.

CLIENT RITA DAHL

sits opposite and arranges her splendid legs. So slick,
so cold. She's a road covered in black ice. He's afraid
of losing it on the curves, but he puts the pedal down,
betting he can ride out the skid, reach out to save her
the way he reaches out to all the lookers who ankle
into his life asking to be heard, believed.

THE MACHINEGUN STACCATO of the keys
stopped as she considered how to begin the dialog. The
phone—not the one in the story, but the one in the house—rang
with shrill insistence, echoing through the stillness where all were
in bed save the writer.

Mother poked her head out around her bedroom door.
Dentureless, with her pin-curls swathed in a blue hairnet
and her spidery form wrapped in a quilted blue bathrobe,
she blinked at the cone of light over the dining room table.
"Feona Elaine!"

Effie had already gone to silence the disorderly party.
"Hello?"

"Hello, Precious."

"You woke Mother again."

"Listen, a mug named Spofford may call by tomorrow. Tell him Santa Barbara. Got that?    Santa Barbara. Wait a second. Somebody's at the door."

A clunk on his end. She waited for a shot or a scream. Then he was there again. "That was Spofford. I told him myself. Go back to bed."

Dead air. She put down the receiver, feeling like a chump.

"Who's that?" the old puss demanded, her thick Irish speech sloppy with her nightly tot of Jameson's. "Not that so-called boss of yours, I hope."

"It was an emergency."

"He takes advantage, calling at all hours. 'Tisn't proper."

"Yes, Mother, but I need the job. Besides, it's only temporary. Just until I get someone to buy my screenplay." She returned to her typewriter.

"You'll be sure and let me know when you'll be off to Hollywood to hobnob with all those movie people. I'll need to rent out your room."

"You needn't make fun just because I have a little ambition," Effie said.

"Ambition, says you. Wool-gathering, says I. You'd be better off learning to cook and sew. Then you'll have something to offer when the right man comes along. And you might not be so tetchy when someone offers you a suggestion." Effie's step-mother pulled her head back into her room and shut her door emphatically.

Effie lit a cigarette. She shot back the platen return and set the typewriter keys clacking.

CLOSEUP - DAHL AND SPADE FACE TO FACE

> DAHL

I'm afraid, Sam. I can't face this alone anymore.

> PRECIOUS (V.O.)

Spade looked like he was going to unhinge his jaw
and swallow her head first.

CAMERA PULLS BACK to reveal Precious standing by the door.

> PRECIOUS

> (coughs)

Will that be all?

> SPADE

> (eyes still on Dahl)

Sure. I'll buzz if I need anything else.

Precious leaves Spade's office and CLOSES the DOOR behind her.
Spade grabs Dahl's arms and pulls her closer.

> SPADE (CONT'D)

I said I'd help you, but you've got to give me the
straight story. I won't play the sap for you.
Understand?

Spade kisses her long and hard. Dahl closes her eyes, looks like she
might swoon. The kiss over, Spade pushes her away and smiles
coldly.

> SPADE (CONT'D)

Now that's out of the way maybe we can get down to
business. I want the truth about you and this Profes-

sor Smith. What kind of phony name is that, anyway?
You ought to use some imagination. Makes the story
sound more authentic.

#### DAHL

His real name is Fritz Arnheit. He's my uncle, my
mother's brother. He told me not to let anyone know
because it's dangerous for us to be associated.
But I trust you.

#### SPADE

Sure, sure. I'm a real boy scout. So it's safe to say he
never left you at the altar. I figured that was all hooey.
You're the type to leave, not get left.

#### DAHL

He's a chemist at some dusty college in San Jose.
We visited him a time or two when I was a kid, but
I never knew him really. He was all about books and
molecules.

#### SPADE

Get to the point.

#### DAHL

When I came out here to live my mother insisted
I call him. Once a month on a Sunday I'd talk to
him for ten minutes. He always asked if I could
use a few bucks. I usually said yes.

#### SPADE

A regular sugar daddy.

DAHL

No, it wasn't like that. He was kind.
He never wanted anything in return.


SPADE

But the last time you called for a bump to your bank
account he didn't answer.


DAHL

I checked with the college. They said he'd gone on
sabbatical, that it had been arranged months ago.


SPADE

Go on.


DAHL

A couple of days ago I noticed someone following
me. Then my apartment was broken into -- all the
drawers turned out, everything upside down! Sam,
I'm so frightened! Who would do such a thing?


S HE LAY ASLEEP with her head on her arms on top of
the typewriter, vaguely aware of voices calling, "Effie!
Effie! Wake up!" She opened her eyes to see her stepsisters Gloria
and Carmen giggling over a page of her manuscript. Carmen read,
"The lovely Miss Dahl chewed her lower lip and looked even
more vulnerable as Spade moved closer, seeking a truth in the
depths of her violet eyes."

Effie sprang out of her chair and lunged for the page. "Give
me that!"

Carmen danced out of reach and hid the page behind her back. Effie grappled with her only to realize Gloria was holding the sheet over her head and laughing. "Come and get it!" Gloria taunted.

Effie leaped to grab the piece of paper but Gloria pushed her off balance. Effie landed hard in an armchair and squealed in pain. She reached under her and came up with a ball of yarn with knitting needles stuck into it. "Who left this knitting on the cushion! These darn needles are sharp!" She heaved the knitting at Carmen who dodged it but bumped against the end table and upset the lamp. The crash as the lamp hit the floor brought Effie's stepmother on the double.

"What's all this rumpus?" she demanded.

The stepsisters scampered away leaving Effie to answer. She smoothed the creases out of her typed page as Mother surveyed the breakage. "So, Fiona Elaine, don't you know better than to rough-house in the front room? I can't have this behavior!" She thrust shards of ceramic into Effie's face. "Well, what have you got to say for yourself?"

"I'm sorry, Mother. I'll replace your lamp."

"No, you won't. It was an heirloom all the way from my family's house in Cork. You'll pay me, though, as soon as I get an appraisal of what it was worth. Then you'll be moving out. I'm fed up with you and that's the truth."

"Oh, no, please, Mother. I've nowhere to go. It wasn't my fault. Carmen and Gloria were teasing me. They ruined a page of my work. Just look." She held out the crumpled page.

"It's no use your crying about it now. My mind's made up."

"But it's nearly Christmas. How am I going to find a place with the holidays and all?"

"I'll give you till the new year out of Christian charity, but that's it. After that you're out on the street, typewriter and all. And good riddance!"

The hall clock struck nine as the stepmother left to get a broom to sweep up. Effie grabbed her things off the dining room table and made for the stairs. "My God! I'm so late!"

Thirty minutes later she stepped off the street car and shouldered through a tide of shoppers lugging bundles. The department store windows glittered with Christmas decorations. As she hustled down the sidewalk she tried to ignore the elaborate scenes of mannequin families gazing with rapt expressions at piles of wrapped presents. "Some holiday," she muttered as she reached the door of the office building that housed Sam's rooms on the top floor.

At the pebbled glass door labeled Samuel Spade Detective Agency in gold lettering, she stooped to pick up the newspaper off the carpet. She let herself in, threw the paper on her desk and hung up her hat and coat on the rack in the corner by the door. She filled the vacuum pot with water from a pitcher and found just enough ground coffee to make a pot. Once it was set up on the hot plate, she dropped into her desk chair and opened the section of the paper with the classified ads. She chewed the end of a pencil as she ran her finger down a column under the heading "Rooms for Rent." The telephone rang but before she could pick up she heard Sam's voice answering from behind the closed door to his office. She got up and pressed her ear to his door to listen. At a lull in the conversation she cracked open the door.

Sam was leaning back in his desk chair with his feet on the blotter and a cigarette in one hand. He was still on the phone but signaled her to come in. "Hang on," he said. He palmed the mouthpiece and waved an envelope and a cleaning ticket at her. "I need you to mail this and pick up a pair of pants from Flint's." He put the items in her hand. "Now scoot. And take your time coming back. I'm expecting a client who thinks I work alone, if you know what I mean." He resumed his phone conversation. "Sorry Angel, but I really think you should come in."

At the post office Effie joined a grim mob carrying brown-papered parcels. The same dialogue repeated like a skipping record. "I can't guarantee it will get there before—" "Just stamp it fragile!" Clunk goes the box onto a heap in a big bin. "Next!"

She bought the stamp for Sam's letter and had just poked it into the slot marked "City," when an odd little man came in with a laundry basket full of shoes. He was short and chubby, without hat or coat, his scabby elbows hanging from a short-sleeved shirt. His white hair was shorn close, as if he'd had his last haircut courtesy of the state. Perhaps he'd come in a cab, she thought, but when she looked out to the street she saw no taxis. He dumped the shoes on one of the counters with cubbies full of postal forms. There must have been ten pair, all men's of a moderate size, all highly polished. She watched him unfurl some brown paper, scattering several labels covered with crabbed writing. A postman walked by. The man grabbed his arm. "Can I borrow some glue to … to paste the … the addresses on?" He spoke with an agonizing stammer.

The postman shook himself free. "We don't lend stuff. You gotta do all that at home."

"But the children ne … need their shoes," the little man pleaded. "Surely … you can spare some … some mucilage and a … a little twine."

The street door opened and a gust of wind blew one of the labels off the counter and swept it across the floor. It came to rest in front of Effie. She stooped to pick it up.

The odd little man raised his sky blue eyes and confronted Effie watching him as if he were an elf in a

Yuletide pageant. "What ... are you ... are you lo ... looking ... at?"

"Sorry," she muttered, and made for the door. She was too cowed by his glare to mention that she had one of his labels. Instead, she stuck it into her pocket and left for the dry cleaner's.

On the street, she turned up her collar and felt a pang of remorse for failing to return the label to the odd little man, so pitiful running around in shirt sleeves. Wrapped in warmth and guilt, she thought about his intense blue eyes, the hacked white hair, the shoes. Where would he be sending them? Surely not to children. They were all men's. She stood perplexed with her elbows on the counter after telling the story to Clara Simms, the clerk at Flint's.

Clara wrinkled her brow. "Maybe the little man has grown-up sons he still calls 'children.' Or maybe he's some religious type and means it like 'children of God.'"

"I didn't hang around to find out," Effie replied. "He gave me the creeps. Those cold, blue eyes. And running around with no coat."

"He must be nuts," Clara said. "So how's tricks, apart from getting crossways with some weirdo in the post office?"

Terrible. I'm in Dutch with my step-mom. She says I have to move out for breaking a lamp. Wants me to pay for it, on top of everything else. The new year's already ruined."

"She probably don't mean it. She's just steamed."

"I had any money I'd move out of there like that." Effie snapped her fingers.

"I can't believe she charges you to live in that little closet at the top of the stairs. Maybe your boss could lend you enough to get on your feet."

"I don't want to borrow from Sam," Effie said. "I got a script I been working on. I need to sell that. Then I'll be set."

"A script? Like a movie?"

"Yeah. I got to find some producer ..."

"Effie, listen." Clara put her hand on Effie's arm. "You're not gonna believe this, but we got an order in from the Taylor Street Hotel, a top coat supposed to belong to some movie guy up from Hollywood. He's scouting a location for a new Cagney picture. Name's Goldfarb."

"You're kidding!"

"Bellboy over there's friends with Chuck, our delivery man. Chuck told me all about it. And I checked the label in this guy's coat besides. Beverly Hills."

"Oh, my God."

"He's a big shot, I tell you." Clara lowered her voice and leaned closer to Effie. "And I shouldn't do this, but since you're a friend of mine and you're in a jam ..."

"What? What are you saying?"

"The coat's cleaned and ready to go on the rack for delivery. But I'm gonna hold it out and let you take it to the hotel so you can meet this guy. You take your script with you and get him to look at it. See?"

"Oh, Clara!" Effie leaned across the counter and hugged the other girl. "That's the nicest thing anybody's done for me in ages."

"Okay! Jeez, don't get carried away." Clara broke from the hug. "Take your coat off. Let me see what you got on."

Effie did as she was told with sagging spirits. The best that could be said of her skirt and blouse was that they were serviceable. Her shoes were badly scuffed and run over at the heel.

"We got our work cut out," Clara said. "You got any credit at Spiegelman's?"

"Not enough for a whole new outfit. Besides, I can't run up a bill with Spiegelman. I'd never be able to pay him back."

"That's no way to talk. You're gonna sell a script, remember?"

Effie brightened. "Yeah, that's right."

Clara thought for a minute then slapped her forehead. "Effie, we're such dolts. Look around. We're surrounded by clothes. There's gotta be something here you could wear."

"Clara! I couldn't!"

"You borrow a dress to wear for a couple hours. Bring it back in the morning. We press it and put it out for delivery. Nobody's the wiser."

"But my shoes," Effie said with a look down at her battered pumps.

"Don't worry. I'll let you borrow a pair I got for my sister's wedding. They pinch, but your feet are smaller than mine. I'll go home at lunch and get them."

With Sam's pants tucked under her arm, Effie left the cleaner's buoyed by the sort of faith that only youth and inexperience can inspire.

That evening she turned a few heads as she crossed the lobby of the Taylor Street Hotel with her coat open to reveal a midnight blue number with a scoop neck, a fitted bodice and a full chiffon skirt that swished and swayed like a million bucks. Even the snooty desk clerk who wanted to appear too busy to notice didn't quite pull it off. "Delivery for Mr. Goldfarb," she said to him, tilting her head toward the coat on a hanger that she carried over her shoulder.

The clerk phoned the suite and a minute later Effie was on her way up to room 315.

Goldfarb opened the door wearing a silk dressing gown. He was a fat guy with thinning hair combed over, glasses, a pencil thin mustache and garters holding up his black socks. She thanked god she wasn't his blind date and put on an engaging smile. "Your, coat from the cleaner's, sir. Where would you like me to put it?"

His words fizzed out like soda from a siphon. "Anywhere. On the couch."

"I'd better hang it in the closet so it won't get wrinkled," she replied. "Where is it?"

He pointed through the interior doorway. "In there. Where do you think?" He watched her walk into the bedroom and out again. "I guess you want a tip now."

Effie shook her head. "I couldn't," she said. "It's all part of the service."

Goldfarb smirked. "What service is that? You're pretty dolled up for schlepping dry cleaning."

"Actually, I ..." There was no graceful way to put it, so she just took the script out from her pocketbook and showed it to him. "I was hoping you might look at something I wrote."

Goldfarb grasped his head in his hands. "Oh for crying out loud!"

"Oh, please, sir. I know you must get dozens of scripts, but if you could just read one page, just take five minutes."

"If I had a nickel for every tootsie who shoves a script at me I'd have a pile I could climb to the moon!" He shook his head at her, but held out his hand. "Give it here. Take off your coat and sit down in that chair."

"Oh, thank you, Mr. Goldfa—"

"Yeah, yeah." He thumbed the pages. "What's your name, anyway?"

"Fiona Elaine Perrine. People call me Effie."

He tucked the screenplay under his arm and jerked his thumb toward a bottle of scotch and a bucket of ice on the sideboard. "Want a drink?"

"Sure." She followed his every move as if she'd never seen anybody slop scotch over ice before. "Would you like me to tell you something about the—"

"Be quiet," he said. He put the drinks on the coffee table and dropped his bulk into the chair next to hers. He took a drink and finally pulled the script out from under his arm and unbent it. Much to her alarm, he opened to the middle. She gauged that he was looking at the scene where Spade is on stakeout in a seedy industrial part of town.

A taxi pulls up and Precious jumps out. After dispatching the cab, she climbs into Spade's front seat on the passenger's side.

CAMERA MOVES INTO THE CAR.

SPADE

I told you to go straight home and stay
with Miss Dahl.

PRECIOUS

Sam, she was gone when I got there.
Packed up lock, stock and barrel. She's been
playing us for suckers.

SPADE

What do you mean?

PRECIOUS

I think Arnheit's on the run from her. He's not her
uncle and I'll bet my last nickel she never wanted us

to find him -- just his formula for synthetic gas.
And we led her right to it. Now she's going to sell
it to the highest bidder.

                    SPADE

How do you know that?

                    PRECIOUS

I searched her room and found a section of the newspaper in the wastepaper basket. There was a piece
torn out of one page -- the list of ships arriving and
leaving the port today. The only ship leaving tonight
is the Kobi Maru bound for Tokyo.

                    SPADE

You're saying she's going to Japan?

                    PRECIOUS

It makes sense. The Japanese are just starting up
their auto industry and can design the cars
and the factories from the ground up. Detroit would
never invest in cars that run on synthetic gas.
It would be too expensive for them to retool.
And the oil men in this country would never
sit still for it either.

                    SPADE

So Dahl is in bed with the Japs!

                    PRECIOUS

We need to get to the pier before nine and see if
someone fitting Miss Dahl's description is
booked on the Kobi Maru.

SPADE

But what about Arnheit? We gotta save the chemist,
don't we?

PRECIOUS

There's no time. We have to get to the pier.

SPADE

(looking at his watch)

I make it twenty till. I'm going in.

PRECIOUS

(grabs his arm)

Sam, be careful. Whoever Dahl hired to take care of
Arnheit won't mind killing a nosey detective.

SPADE

You saying you care what happens to me?

PRECIOUS

Don't be stupid. If you don't know how
I feel by now —

Spade pulls Precious to him and kisses her.


G OLDFARB CLOSED THE script and peered at Effie.
"First rule of good writing is to write what you know.
It won't be convincing otherwise."

Effie tried to keep the disappointment out of her voice.
"For instance?"

"That bit about synthetic gasoline. Why should I believe you
know what you're talking about? You're just a dame with a big

imagination. Nobody's going to risk a wad of dough on this loony story. The Japs? How dumb do you think I am? Everybody knows the Japs couldn't make a good tin can. Their stuff is cheap junk." He laughed. "Japanese cars!"

"But I've read about—"

"And that love scene. It's weak. You're cautious. You hold back. It's a big scene, the pay-off for following these two chumps while they chase their tails all over town. And you give it one lousy action line. What, you don't know how people make love? You never been there?"

She felt the blood rush to her face. "Of course I have."

"Yeah? Show me." Goldfarb was all over her quick as a sprinter out of the blocks. He smothered her with his mouth and shoved one hand down the front of her dress.

She pulled away and yelled, "Let me go!" Then she cracked him a good one across the chops. "I said let go, you fat old masher."

He wound up sitting on the coffee table massaging his jaw. "Get out," he said, without looking at her. He hauled himself to his feet and grabbed her coat, her purse and the script. "I said get out, you cheap little tramp. Get out before I call a cop!" He went to the door and flung her stuff into the hallway.

Effie scrambled after her things, crouching in the threshold to gather them. He slammed the door into her and sent her sprawling. As she fell forward there was a loud ripping noise. She staggered to her feet and turned to see that the door had closed on her skirt. "Mr. Goldfarb!" she called. "Mr. Goldfarb, open the door. My dress is caught!"

"Scram!" he yelled back. "I'm calling the cops."

She pulled at the skirt fabric and managed to widen the tear. Seeing it was ruined anyway, she gave it a good yank and left a chunk of chiffon behind as she ran for the stairs.

In the lobby she stopped to pull on her coat, then raced outside to flag a cab. "Horrible man," she muttered, wiping tears away with the back of her hand.

The cabbie who picked her up seemed concerned. "Say, doll, it's none of my business but are you all right?"

Effie managed to get herself under control before she answered. "Thanks. I'm okay."

"You run out of the hotel like the devil was on your tail," the cabbie continued. "I seen you's all dressed up. Must have been some wild Christmas party going on in there. Happens a lot this time of year. Guys go to those parties an' get a little tight an' before you know it they're puttin' their hands where they don't belong. Well, don't you worry; I'll get you home. Then you'll get yourself a nice cuppa cocoa. Chalk it up to experience."

Effie didn't reply. The cabbie kept talking.

"You girls today take too many chances, wanderin' around the city alone after dark. You're askin' for it, is what I say. My daughter Louise is just like you, traipsin' all over town all hours of the night. Leaves a big basket of stockin's at home needs darnin' all for her mother to do. Louise says all the kids go out. She says it's modern. I say it's spinach."

He was still yammering as he drew up in front of Effie's house. She was glad when he pulled away, even though she had to negotiate the icy path to the house in the dark. She unlocked the back door and stepped into the kitchen. The squat forms of the stove and the refrigerator were visible in the gloom. She felt something underfoot as she crossed the room to reach the wall switch, something soft and sticky. Groping, she flipped on the light.

From the looks of the kitchen, Mother had spent the afternoon baking Christmas cookies, drinking Jameson's all the while. Cookie sheets blackened with the corpses of cookies forgotten in the oven stood stacked in the sink. The floured counters were littered with dough-caked bowls. Much of Mother's holiday shortbread had dropped raw to the linoleum. Clara's fancy heels were caked with sugary muck. "She's going to kill me." Effie whispered in horror. She took off the pumps and tiptoed to retrieve the Jameson's from the top of the fridge. An inch showed at the bottom of the festive green bottle. She carried it upstairs to her room.

She put on her nightgown and drank the bottle dry as she sadly surveyed the ruined dress and the crusty shoes parked on top of a magazine with a sumptuous decorated Christmas tree on the cover. *Make your own ornaments this year! Yeah, sure.* She doused her light and thought about what Goldfarb had said about the love scene. *He's wrong. Anybody who knows Sam Spade would get that. With Sam you'd be lucky to get enough romance to complete a sentence.*

The next morning she was out of the house before anybody was up and around. She went straight to the It's Tops Coffee Shop where Mavis Lamont was serving the counter. As Effie plumped onto a stool, Mavis filled her cup. "So what's up? Still waitin' for your life to start?"

"What's that supposed to mean?"

"Sorry, I was just jokin'. Want your usual?"

"No, just toast."

"What's wrong? You look all in. Oops. Wait a second. I got an order up." Mavis pirouetted away. Effie watched her perky double-time efficiency and wondered if maybe she should consider waitressing. *But how would you ever think straight with all the plates clattering and the cook yelling at you?*

Mavis came back and planted her elbows on the counter in front of Effie. "Okay, spill it. What's so tragic?"

"Don't make fun."

"Boy, you really are down."

"I'm in a huge jam."

Effie explained the Goldfarb fiasco. She nodded at a shopping bag on the floor next to her stool where the dress and shoes were bundled. "Clara will probably lose her job," she concluded, close to tears.

"Hang on," Mavis said, "your toast is up." She brought a plate with two thick pieces heavily buttered. "Here's some boysenberry jam, too. It'll make you feel better."

Effie dabbed at her eyes with her napkin. "Maybe I should just give up writing. Go to steno school. Get a real job."

"Don't talk like that. You'll sell a story. You'll see."

"That doesn't help me with the fix I'm in right now. Mother's making me move out on top of everything else."

"What a rum deal. Your father's probably spinning in his grave."

Effie sniffed. "Thing is, I wish I could move out. My stepsisters are so mean and they're always leaving their knitting in the chairs. I'm sick of getting poked in the backside with knitting needles. Who needs to knit when they have perfectly good socks at Woolworth's?"

"Oh, I don't know," Mavis said. "It's kinda fun. You should try it sometime."

"It's a menace! Why's everybody so hot for me to take up needlework?"

The cook yelled, "Eggs up," and Mavis left again. She came back with a copy of *The Chronicle*. "Look here," she said, pointing to a column-inch of print on the front page of the City Section. "I just remembered I saw this piece about a Christmas story contest yesterday. See, it says they're giving a fifty dollar prize."

Effie read the small print inside the box. She frowned. "Says it should be heartwarming and reflect the true spirit of Christmas. I don't write pap like that!"

"Seems like you might try," Mavis said. Annoyed, she folded the paper and shoved it under the counter. "I swear Ef, you're your own worst enemy."

"Even if I could write something like that, the deadline's Friday close of business!"

"Okay, so drop it!" Mavis took her rag and started wiping the counter. "Look, I hope it works out. I gotta go now and make up a BLT. I got a new regular, this cop Steve Murphy. Says I make the best BLT in the city. My secret is, I make the sandwich ahead and wrap it up. The tomatoes and lettuce soften up and the mayo soaks in and the whole thing mooshes together so it don't fall apart when you eat it."

"You know a cop?" Effie's brain spun like a roulette wheel. "Could you ask him a favor?"

"Depends. What you got on your mind?"

Effie gave Mavis the run-down on the guy from the post office. "It's somebody I might be able to write about," she explained. "For that story competition at the *Chron*. But I need to find out where he lives so I can interview him."

"He'll do it," Mavis said. "For me."

Effie slipped a quarter under the edge of her saucer, slid off the stool and grabbed her shopping bag. She made it to work before Sam. The office was dark with only a pale blade of daylight cutting through the soot-caked window. She took the dress out of the bag and hung it on a hanger on the coat rack. It looked fine from the front. She hung up her coat next to it and went to the desk where she spied an envelope on her blotter. She picked it up and found writing on the flap side—Sam's rough printing in pencil. "Gone to Pasadena for Xmas. Will call next year if I need you. Check want-ads in meantime. Drop key through mail slot. Spade."

She fingered the worn-out bills that accounted for the last two weeks of her life and thought of her words to Mother. "It's a temporary job, all right. At least I can sleep here on the couch a few nights till he gets back."

The phone rang. She thought about not answering, but finally picked it up.

"Effie where are you?" It was Clara, hissing into the phone, trying not to be overheard. "I need that dress back right now."

"It's here at the office," Effie said.

"Fat lot of good that does me," Clara snapped. "What if Mrs. Wynan comes in for it?"

"Call her and tell her there's been a delay. The dress got torn and it needs to be mended."

"Torn! You've gotta be kiddin'! She'll have a fit! You bring it over here right—"

Effie moved the receiver away from her ear while it was still spewing Clara's angry words and quietly hung it up. She laid her head down on her folded arms and closed her eyes, suddenly very tired. She thought of Rita Dahl and the synthetic gasoline caper.

INT. WAREHOUSE - NIGHT

Precious comes into the cavernous, dark space on the first floor. Stiff with fear she calls out to Spade cautiously and gropes forward through the dark.

PRECIOUS

Sam? Where are you? We've got to get out of here.

CAMERA follows her movements.

Precious walks through something sticky.
She taps the sole of her shoe on the floor, feeling the gooey substance underfoot.

Suddenly the scene is bathed in light. Precious finds herself standing in a pool of blood next to a corpse and SCREAMS in terror.

POUNDING. EFFIE'S BRAIN registered pounding before she raised her head. There was a man's silhouette visible through the pebbled glass of the outer door. A fat man with a fedora.

Effie called out, "Who's there?"

"Detective Malone. Open up."

She went to the door and cautiously opened it a couple of inches. The fat man sported a light colored suit and a flashy tie. "Yes?"

Malone pushed the door open wide. "That's no way to welcome an officer of the law."

He sashayed in and parked one cheek on Effie's desk. "How 'bout a cup of coffee," he said.

"We're right out," she replied. "No grounds."

"Sounds like the last time Spade tried to talk me into arresting somebody."

"I didn't know cops were so funny," Effie said.

Malone smirked. "What you don't know would fill the yellow pages. I want to talk to Spade. Where is he?"

"Out. Why do you ask?"

"I got a call from a dry cleaner complaining that somebody came in and stole an expensive dress. They said to check a certain address. It's an address I know by heart." He smacked the desk with the flat of his hand. "This address."

"Sam's got nothing to do with it."

Malone cast up his eyes to heaven. "For the love of God, I ask myself, why do the dames always stick up for Spade?"

"I'm not sticking up for him. I'm just telling you the plain facts." She nodded toward the coat rack. "There's your stolen goods right there. I saved you the trouble of locating them."

Malone grinned. "I like your style, girlie girl." He sauntered over and examined the dress. "It's not in such good shape. There's a big rip in the back of the skirt. Looks like it might have got hung up on something. You wouldn't know anything about that, would you? Any chance there's one of Spade's dames running around in a bra and panties?"

"How would I know?"

"Oh, I figure you know plenty. Otherwise how come this dress is hanging here in your office? You gotta know something about it."

"It was there when I came in this morning."

Malone inspected the skirt fabric. "If it weren't for that tear, I could just take the dress back to the cleaner's and no one would be any the wiser. You handy with a needle, girlie girl?"

"Not so's you'd notice."

"Too bad, because if you were, you could save yourself ten bucks."

"What do you mean?"

"That's what it'll cost you for me to take this piece of goods home to my wife, who is an excellent seamstress, by the way, and have it put right."

"Ten bucks! That's robbery!"

"Well, like I say, you'd be better off if you learned how to sew instead of sitting here minding the store for Spade. Not only that, you could whip up a dress like this for yourself in one afternoon instead of working three months to buy it—make that four on what he pays you."

"Why is everybody always harping on needlework? I'm sick of hearing about it."

"Do we have a deal?"

"Sure. For ten bucks you make this dress thing go away. It stinks, but it's a deal."

"What's your beef?" Malone came back to perch on the desk. "Ten's little enough for what needs to be done. The waist seam has to come out so the skirt can come off in the back there. Then that part where the hole is gets cut out and the skirt gets sewn up again, a nice straight vertical seam. The gathers are redistributed, the waist seam is resewn and the hem is put back neat as a pin."

"You sound like you know all about it."

"I seen my wife take skirts off dresses a thousand times."

"I bet you don't even have a wife, Malone. I bet you bought your own Singer machine so you can turn your collars yourself."

"Don't crack wise with me, girlie girl. You're the one wants a favor here."

"Sorry. I lost my head."

"Yeah, that's the trouble with you dames. You all lose your heads around Spade."

"Why are we talking about him again?"

"Because dames fall for Spade faster than the mother of us all fell for that snake in the garden of Eden. And once they fall they don't get up again."

"That supposed to scare me?"

"You might want to consider what happened to Brigid O'Shaunessy. He set her up to take the rap for plugging Miles Archer. Maybe that was before your time."

"I know about it. She did it, cool as peppermint ice-cream. I'd have turned her in if Sam hadn't."

"Sure you would, because you want Spade for yourself. You fell for him soon as you first sat down at this lousy desk and started lapping up his guff like it was ambrosia of the gods."

"Cut it out, Malone. I don't take guff from anybody. I'm not about to take a fall, either."

"Not even for Spade?"

"Especially not Spade."

"So you'll tell me then."

"Tell you what?

"Tell me what's he want with Myron Childres again after all these years."

"Who's Myron Childres?"

"The guy Steve Murphy was askin' about this mornin', sayin' if anybody knew where this bird lives they should call your office number."

"You know Childres?"

"Sam and I had our eye on him when we was with the Pinkertons. We couldn't pin anything on him except for a car theft. He went up to Vacaville for a few years."

"You got unfinished business?"

"Yeah. You could say that. I don't want Spade grabbin' headlines on this one. I've been keepin' tabs on Childres for quite a while now. I could get a big promotion if I bring him in."

"Why? What's he done aside from annoying the clerks at the post office?"

"Never you mind, girlie girl. Just tell Spade I'll have him up on obstruction of justice if I find he's nosin' around Childres."

"I tell you Sam has nothing to do with this. Murphy asked about Childres for me. I'm the one who needs to find out about him."

"Oh, so you're the private dick on this case?"

"Relax, Malone. I'm no private dick. I'm a writer. I'm doing an article for *The Chron.*"

"So you're a writer! I don't remember seeing your by-line in the paper.

"You'd have to look somewhere besides the comics page to find it, Malone."

"Oh, funny. You're a comedienne, too. Well that's good, because if I got wind you were investigating a case without a PI's license, I'd have to run you in. A sense of humor comes in handy in the slam. Jail's an ugly place any time of year, but especially at Christmas. It's cold and there's not enough mattresses to go around, so the new fish have to sleep on the linoleum. I wouldn't want to think of you curled up on the floor without even a blanket, girlie girl."

"Don't worry about me, Malone. Like I said, I'm no detective. But I do want to know where Childres lives. So are you going to tell me, or do I have to call Steve Murphy and get him to spread the word about how you like sewing dresses?"

"I can tell you where to get in touch with Childres' landlord."

"Childres' landlord? How do you know him?"

"Met him years ago at a gin-mill on Ellis." He paused. "But first I think you meant to give me the ten bucks to take care of the dress."

Effie pulled two fives out of the envelope Sam left her and slapped them into Malone's palm. "Who's this landlord and where do I find him?"

"His name is Larkin. Orville Larkin. He holes up at John's Grill every afternoon from about three to five. You'll find him in a booth at the back. Buy him a beer and a bump and he'll tell you whatever you want to know. Buy him two or three and you'll get his life story. Any more than that he won't say another word; he'll just sit there and cry."

"Thanks for the advice."

Malone smiled and folded the bills into his pocket. He walked to the door and took the dress off the coat rack.

"Oh, you mind taking the shoes back, too? In the bag there. Come on, for ten bucks—"

Malone picked up the bag and tipped his hat. "Anything for you, girlie girl."

Effie locked the door behind Malone before she darted into Spade's office and started going through his files. "Myron Childres..." Finding nothing, she slammed the last drawer shut and started through the desk. She had no luck there either, except for a little white sack half-full of ballpark peanuts that came in handy since the toast hadn't stuck with her and she was starving.

John's Grill was the kind of place Sam favored, dark as a raven's gullet, smelling of roasted meat and whatever they used to mop up. She felt stares slide from her shoulder to her heel as she asked the bartender for Larkin.

He nodded toward a booth. She crossed the floor slowly, hoping the measured clack of her heels would do for a show of confidence. The man smoking in the booth didn't get up. Larkin smelled of cheap aftershave, in spite of having ignored the exercise implicit in the term. His shirt hadn't seen a laundress since his last meal with brown gravy. Effie sat down and gave him the rundown on the little man in the post office. Only after the bartender brought over a beer and a bump did Larkin open his mouth. "Myron Childres. Wife's Blanche. They keep quiet and pay their rent on time. No dogs, no kids, no complaints. Way I like it."

"You're their landlord?"

"My old man died and left me the building at 355 Taylor." He downed the shot.

"I saw Childres trying to mail a whole bunch of shoes," Effie said.

"Childres got a trade in the joint. Fixes soles and heels."

"So all those shoes he was mailing, he was probably just returning them to customers?"

"In general how it works when you drop off shoes is you leave the goods and you get a claim ticket. You bring back the ticket and pay the tab, you get your shoes back."

She tried again as Larkin slurped his beer. "When's the last time you were in the place?"

"Never. Last I saw him he was on the street, bringing in groceries and papers. Blanche wears the pants. She don't do errands. Now unless you wanna go again, I got an appointment."

She watched him shamble off. "Tight-lipped SOB … and talk about shoe leather…" She stuck her foot out and surveyed the heel of her pump, all run-over on one side. She thought about job interviews, looking good … then it occurred to her: two birds with one stone.

On her way to the apartment house on Taylor there was a Woolworth's. She stopped to pick up a bottle of mucilage. At 355 she heaved herself up the steep steps of the stoop and rang the buzzer opposite 'Childres.' When the door clicked open, she nipped inside and climbed two flights. She knocked, breathing in the reek of boiled cabbage as she listened for a footstep. The door cracked open. A little man squinted out. "Are you from the ... the post office?"

"No, no—I mean, you saw me there, but I'm not *from* there. I was talking to one of the postmen ... you know, about the shoes. Anyway, he said you repair heels. He gave me your house number. See, my heels are shot. I thought I'd just drop over and see if you have time to..."

Childres eyed her footwear.

"If it isn't too expensive, I mean."

"Come ... in. Sit there, in the ... in the slipper chair and let me lo ... look at them. I'll take your ... your coat." She slipped it off and sat down. Childres laid the coat across a stack of newspapers on a dining table crowded with all kinds of groceries in neat ranks. He pulled over a low cobbler's bench with an inverted shoe-lathe and sat astraddle it in front of Effie. He took off her shoes and examined them. "You're hard on your footwear."

"I know," Effie said. She took in the dead plants on the window sill, the lack of heat in the place. "So, I hear you live here with your wife."

"Blanche? What about Blanche?" In his alarm he had lost his stammer.

"Nothing! I'm just talking. What else do I do, sitting here in my stocking feet?"

"Blanche isn't home right now. If she were, I wouldn't have an ... answered the door. She wouldn't like me talking to you. She tells me to button my lip. That's what she says." A creepy grin lit his face. "But she isn't he ... here, so she can't tell me anyth ... thing."

Effie felt the hair on her neck stand up. "When will she be back?"

Childres continued to grin, enjoying an inside joke. "Oh, I ... I don't know. Not for some time, I sho ... shouldn't think. She went to visit her sister."

"Oh, how nice. Where does her sister live?"

Childres giggled. "I don't re ... remember the name of the place. It's cold, though."

"The shoes," she said. "Can you ..."

"You need new top lifts and half soles," he said. "Let me see if ... if I got what I need to fix them."

He took her pumps and vanished into the next room. From the low upholstered chair where she sat, Effie peered at the odd collection of items on the table. She counted nineteen jars of Postum, twenty-two boxes of cornflakes, eleven jars of Ovaltine, and too many cans of soup to keep track of—or, make that soup *cans*. The tins were without lids. All the jars were empty. Probably the boxes, too. Souvenirs? She was on the point of sneaking over for a closer look when Childres came back into the room. "I don't work on ma ... many women's shoes, but I ... can use the lifts off my ... my wife's spectators."

"Your wife won't mind?"

Childres sat at the bench, inverted her shoe and took up a small square-headed hammer. "Oh, my ... my wife is gone," he said with a glint of glee in his eye. "We don't... don't li ... listen to her ... anymore."

"We? Do you have a pet?"

"A ... pet?" His little hammer went tap-tap-tap as he grinned. "You might ... say that."

It didn't square with what Larkin had said, but considering the landlord didn't check on his tenants, he wouldn't know the latest. "At the post office," she said, getting down to the reason she'd come, "you were mailing several pairs of shoes."

"Eleven pa … pairs. I had the … addresses and the paper and all I ne … needed was some twine and what-not, but the po … postmaster wouldn't give me anything. They used to. I never had any … any trouble … before."

"You mail shoes every year?"

"Oh, no, Blanche … wouldn't hear of it. I used to send little gifts…before I …met my wife, but she made me stop. I …I fooled her, though. I was out one day and I saw a sidewalk sale outside an apartment house where someone had …had pa … passed away. They were selling his clothes and his … shoes. I brought the shoes … home and hid them where … where Blanche couldn't find them. She … was … a la … large woman with a … a bad back. She … never liked to look into the … back of the closets … on the floor."

"Was?" Effie shivered. The room was cold, especially the bare floor through her nylons.

"Oh, she's not … not so bi … big anymore." He switched shoes and started tapping again, smirking all the while. "Did you know … I was … in prison? Grand theft auto. Sometimes I … I think people can … te … tell."

"No, no. Not at all. So how long did it take you to repair eleven pairs of shoes?"

"Oh, a … long time. The children have all grown … up."

"These men, they're your children?"

"Of course … mine," he said. "You … don't forget a … a child just because he's gone."

She felt a tug of sympathy assail her heart. He had nurtured this love of his children in spite of a selfish wife, giving it expression only at Christmas when he somehow found the means to give a pair of shoes, lovingly restored, to each of the men he would always think of as a little boy. It was as if she'd found Santa Claus in a dingy apartment, shivering in his shirtsleeves, tapping with his little hammer. She watched as he applied the polish to her shoes and massaged it into the uppers with his fingers. *This story's going to be a real tear-jerker. It'll write itself. I'm going to win that fifty bucks!* She couldn't wait to get to her typewriter. "Are you almost done?"

"Pu … put them on."

After she had slipped into the shoes, he propped one foot then the other on his bench. His polishing rag snapped back and forth and made the leather glow with a deep, warm shine.

"Wow," she said. "It's like magic. They're good as new. Better!"

"Twe … twenty-… twenty-five … cents," he said.

She reached for her handbag and got him a quarter. "You did such a nice job, I was thinking maybe I could help with mailing the shoes to the children. The office where I work has lots of mucilage, so …" She pulled the bottle of glue out of her bag with theatrical flair. "I thought it was kind of raw the way that postal clerk treated you."

It warmed her heart to see his face light up with pleasure.

"Wait!" He jumped up and disappeared into a back room. When he reappeared he was carrying the laundry basket full of shoes, brown paper and the white slips on which he had written addresses. He carried the basket to the table and began the job of wrapping each pair.

"I can paste the addresses," she said. As he finished wrapping the first bundle she began going through the labels. Jimmy Rogers, San Antonio, Texas. Charlie Pike, Detroit. Jimmy Peterson, Elmira, New York. Peter Daltry, Utica, New York. Stevie Young, Odessa, Texas. Michael Riggins, Duluth. Timothy Kerr, Watkins Glenn. Henry Wheeler, Salinas, California. Chuck Carter, Gilroy. Nick Severn, San Louis Obispo. "All different last names," she observed.

"They were ... chil ... children ... of friends," he said. Their eyes locked for a long second. Then Childres' face broke into a grin. "I still need twine. I can maybe unwrap something el ... else and use that twine."

"Sure, I don't see why not."

"Okay. Wait here. I have to go to the freezer."

Effie realized they were a label short and remembered the one that had blown over to her while she and Childres were in the post office. She went to where her coat was lying on top of a stack of newspapers and fumbled in the pockets to find it. When she drew it out she read the name and address, Matthew Jeffries, Burlingame. She was about to toss her coat down again when she glanced down at the headline of the newspaper on top of the pile. **Search for Matthew Jeffries Continues. Child Abducted Five Days Ago Still Missing.**

She stood frozen for a second, then slowly drew her coat on. She turned to see Childres standing in the kitchen doorway, watching. "Is something wrong?" he asked.

"I just realized what time it is. I'm meeting someone for dinner. I have to go."

"You're me ... meeting someone?" A sly look crossed his face. He wasn't buying it.

"My fiancé. I can't be late. He worries about me if I'm late."

Childres held up a package about the size of a loaf of bread wrapped in white butcher paper and tied with string. "Before you go, could you help me untie the knots? I got no fingernails. Blanche was always on me about biting them but I told her I been a nail-biter since I was a kid. Things that happen to you when you were a kid ain't that easy to forget. Me, I got nervous because of my childhood." He held up a hand to show her the nails, bitten out of existence. "You got nice nails." He moved to the dining table and put the package down. "Light's better over here.

Don't you want to know what happened to me to make me so nervous?"

Effie stepped over to the table and began working at the two knots on the package, looking up every couple of seconds to keep an eye on Childres.

"You want to know what happened to me that made me like I am?" He sidled closer.

"Yes. What happened?" Her fingers trembled as she worked at the knots.

"There were six of us kids," Chlidres said, inching closer. "Mother raised us. The old man was only there once in a while. He lived on the road. Sold bibles." Childres giggled.

Effie managed to loosen one of the knots around the package. She rested one end of the package on the table as she worked on the second knot. "What's so funny?"

"Him, sellin' bibles, what with the way he was."

"How was that? Was he mean to you?" She made a mental note that he wasn't stammering anymore.

"Oh, no. He loved us kids. Me most of all. You know how I know that?"

"No, tell me." She tore at the second knot.

Childres edged closer. "One day right before school started he showed up out of a clear blue sky to buy all of us kids new shoes. I remember my mother sayin' that—out of a clear blue sky. He took the three oldest kids out first. Then he brought them home and took the next two. And when he brought them home he took me. But he never brought me back. He said he liked me best. I was six."

Effie was desperate to keep him talking. The knot was beginning to loosen. "You went on the road with your father?"

"Yes." Something in his voice made her look up at him. His face had turned ugly. Childres screamed, "He took me!"

The knot broke and the package dropped to the table. The white paper unfurled. An adult foot, severed at the ankle, rolled out onto the table. Effie made a break for it.

Childres pulled a long knife from behind his back. He lunged after her. She fumbled at the door lock. He raised the knife and slashed down at her back. She pulled open the door and twisted away. The knife flashed through her coat. She pounded toward the stairs. Childres raised his knife again and came after her. Her toe caught a rent in the carpet. She went down, crouched in a tight ball, braced for the end. He tried to stop but couldn't, stumbled over her, pitched headlong into eternity. A moment later, after the thudding on the stair had stopped, she stood and looked down. His inert body lay crumpled, his neck bent all wrong. She screamed.

One of the other tenants called the cops. Relieved of the coat sliced open at the back, Effie found herself bundled in a blanket under an umbrella outside the Manning Arms. She registered a drenching rain, streams coming off the hat brims of curious people who had gathered on the water-glazed street in the headlights of the police cars. Malone was barking in her ear.

"Seems like Childres won't be bothering any kids ever again. Still, you're lucky it turned out the way it did. I'd stick to answering the phone from now on if I was you. Let Spade handle these loony birds. Let me get somebody to run you home before you drown."

Another detective approached Malone. "You might want to come upstairs, boss. There's a body in the freezer—in pieces—all wrapped up in butcher paper and tied with twine." He nodded at Effie, couldn't resist the wise crack. "Your little man wrapped a nice, neat package."

"It's Childres' wife Blanche," Effie said to Malone.

Malone frowned. "What do you know about it?

"Judging from the potted plants, I'd say she's been gone two weeks or so, and I don't mean in the Bahamas. See if I'm not right."

Malone hustled into the building, having forgotten to tell somebody to take Effie home. She sighed and started toward the bus stop, looking mournfully at the puddles on the sidewalk. *And I just got my shoes all fixed up.*

A reporter pounced on her before she'd gone ten feet. "Are you Fiona Perrine?"

"That would be me."

"Miss Perrine, what did you see up there?"

"A lot of empty cereal boxes and Ovaltine jars."

"Come again?"

"Never mind."

"Miss Perrine, what made you go looking for Childres? Did you have a line on him from Sam Spade's case files?"

"I just saw him in the post office day before yesterday trying to mail shoes. I thought it would make a good Christmas story."

"Missing boys a Christmas story?"

"Yeah, funny, huh. I had him all decked out in a Santa hat and everything."

"Decked out?

"In my imagination. I was going to call the story 'The Shoe Santa.'"

"So you really didn't suspect him?"

"Not at first. Not until I got that feeling, when the hair on the back of your neck stands on end."

"When was that?

"When I saw he'd kept souvenirs of each child."

"What kinda souvenirs?" The reporter's puppy-eager hands, padded and penciled, were poised to get it all down.

"Look, I'm getting wet here."

"There's a coffee shop around the corner. I'll buy you a cup and we can talk." As they started to walk he took her elbow. "So how long have you been a private dick?"

It was on the tip of her tongue to deny the assumption, to say she was only Spade's secretary, but instead she said, "Oh, not long. This is my first case."

"Wow and right out of the box you crack a case that the cops have been trying to put down for fifteen years. This is going to make you famous."

"I'd rather be the one with the byline," she said. But as they walked, she knew that part of her life was over, the white page rolled into the typewriter waiting for the next lines of cheesy dialogue and pat metaphor, the stack of manuscripts cringing on the closet shelf, each one a candy apple red convertible with no engine. She'd never met evil, the real thing, before and now that she had, she couldn't face the math. Her brain had gone deaf, the cacophony of phrase-making dead quiet. A silent movie unreeled: she sitting there shoeless while Childres worked with his hammer, a subtitle reading "Tap, tap, tap." Stocking-footed, witless. How easily he could have taken his hammer, dashed out her silly brains, and stashed her, disarticulated, in the deep freeze next to Blanche. The scene shifted to a montage, a runaway merry-go-round flashing the faces of anonymous little boys. She was undone by the delicate, pale faces with their long-lashed, clear eyes. She wondered if she would ever again come to the gift-giving time of year without dreaming of missing children, Myron Childres, mashed cookies, and Sam with his iron guts and his grass snake smile, saying Merry Christmas.

Our story for the first month of the year takes place on January 6th, also known as Twelfth Night. The eve of the twelfth day after Christmas is traditionally a night of masked revels with costumed "mummers" (from the French "momer," meaning to wear a mask) cavorting in the streets and knocking on doors of strangers asking for wassail and other seasonal food and drink. Accordingly, guests attending Lord and Lady Montfort's Twelfth Night party came in fancy dress. Men dressed as women, women as men and the high-born came as humble folk, while the lowly dressed as gods and goddesses. With everyone so conveniently disguised, it's no wonder the evening's revels provided the perfect camouflage for a murderer.

# The St. Nicholas Abbey Rum

C OLLET WAS HER Ladyship's personal maid, a tall, dusky woman of brooding looks, handsome, correct in every detail. But there was something else, something slightly off-putting, a reptilian coolness, as if she apprehended the world with a forked tongue, or a chameleon's panoramic vision. Seated next to Collet, waiting to go into the library, Gwen found herself anxious, nattering.

"Vernon was Elizabeth Bennett because I'm not much of a seamstress but it was too easy to make a Regency gown out of an old night dress and then put some blond ringlets on his head. The vicar's so fresh-faced it rather suited him. Naturally, I came as Darcy." Gwen pulled off the wig of short brown curls that she'd worn to complete her gentleman's disguise. "Sorry, I'm rattling on. This seems to be taking an extraordinarily long time."

Collet swiveled her eyes down to the carpet. "I'm sure Detective Inspector Busby is trying to be thorough. You must be very tired. Would you like me to get you a cup of tea?"

"That's terribly kind, but no. Thanks." Gwen looked at her watch and saw that it was nearly four hours since the police had descended upon the manor and told all the guests to stay on the premises until they'd been specifically told they could leave. "He's saving the colonial for last," she said, and saw a sympathetic spark in Collet's eye.

"Indeed." Collet said it with a barely noticeable smile, one non-European to another. She and Gwen both knew the term. Pronounced with a certain inflection, it was meant to describe all that was wrong with them, a defect as incurable as a weakness in the bloodlines of a hunter.

Gwen rose stiffly and put her wig down on the table next to a vase of Christmas lilies. "Wish they'd get on with it."

As if on cue, the pocket doors of the library parted. Captain Wooley, head of the cricket club, and his wife—they had come to the party dressed as a naiad and Neptune respectively—emerged from the interrogation room. Collet rose to show them to the door and help them don winter coats over costumes that consisted of little more than some netting strung with strips of paper kelp and strategically placed scallop shells.

Detective Inspector Busby called out, "Mrs. Wickersham? Come in. Close the doors."

Irked by his bossy tone, Gwen complied, but crossed her legs casually when she sat down to demonstrate that he didn't scare her one bit.

"So, Mrs. Wickersham," he said, peering through his monocle at the tight scribble in his notebook, "tell me; is there anything in particular that you remember of the evening's festivities? Anything odd?" His manner reminded her of a certain grade school teacher who would quiz students in this way. "There were seventeen guests at dinner, were there not? Eight couples and the child, Alice. She was the only child present. Is that not odd?"

"No, not really. She's the daughter of the house—was."

Busby frowned. "Well, then, did you find it odd that she was packed off to bed before any of the guests had taken their leave, before the charades—I believe that was the amusement that engaged everyone shortly before midnight."

"Yes. That is, yes, we played charades, but no, I didn't think it odd that Alice went to bed. She came around to everyone and said good night around 11:00. I suspect she was bored, being on best behavior all evening." Gwen was sorely tempted to add, *I know I was*, but resisted.

"Was anyone absent after Alice went upstairs?"

"I couldn't say. If any of the guests slipped out of the drawing room I didn't notice."

Busby frowned at his notes and snapped the little notebook shut. "All right, you may go," he said, as if she'd proved to be a terrible disappointment. "If we should need to ask any more questions of you we'll call by the vicarage."

She crossed the room and let herself out of the library to find Collet gone. She wandered through the downstairs rooms, feeling shaky, hoping to encounter someone who could say where she might find her husband but seeing little more than the remains of a spirited party that had come to a tragic end. She felt as if the festivities had been interrupted in full stride by a death ray from outer space that had vaporized all the guests, leaving as the only evidence of the lively scene a few warm cocktails, cigarette ends, and the odd lipstick-printed napkin. She wanted to be gone from the depressing scene, and wondered where on earth was Vernon.

She came at length to a corridor with a closed door at its end and two closed doors to either side. "Like a rat in a maze," she muttered, as she began discreetly knocking twice then opening each successive door. Behind the third door were three maids clearing up party detritus and chattering, oblivious to the lady peering in at the door. "I can't see why us chambermaids should be used to clean the parlor," a lean girl with a sharp nose was saying, as she emptied ashtrays into her dustbin. "No one from the scullery ever turns a hand."

"Because there's one more maid now than need be," explained a maid with a streak of gray at her temple. "You know when Her Ladyship brought Collet with them from Barbados, when they came back from their vacation, Mrs. Fast had a fit. One more on housekeeping staff and short-handed in the kitchen. I heard from Mr. Miller that Spence and Fast, old biddies as they are, went at it like cats on a fence. And that's why Iris ended up in the scullery."

"Iris already moved up to Fast's assistant and here I am still emptying out ashtrays."

"You'd best not complain or you'll be the first one to go. Remember Collet is Her Ladyship's particular favorite, so when it comes time to cut the household expenses it'll be one of *us* who's sent packing, don't you doubt it. Best make yourself extra useful."

"What's so special about that Collet anyway? She's a shifty type if you ask me. Always so quiet, like she's scheming. What is she, do you think, part gypsy?"

"I reckon it's something to do with them wanting another child, some fertility thing."

"What on earth do you mean?"

"I've heard they practice a kind of heathenish folk medicine out there in those islands."

The older maid laughed dismissively. "I should think if they wanted another child Her Ladyship would let her husband into her bed now and then."

Gwen interrupted to preempt further discussion of the Montforts' marital relations. "I seem to have misplaced the front door." The maids turned toward her, faces bland as milk.

"I'll see you out, madam," the senior of the three said, stripping off her rubber gloves. "It's like one of those old knot gardens they used to make of hedges. They had one on the estate where my mum was in service. I got lost there a hundred times." She walked quickly, taking two turnings, and with a curt nod that spoke volumes about her opinion of the helpless upper classes, left Gwen at the entry to the foyer. Gwen crossed the marble tile and peered out the window flanking the door. There was the car, where Vern had parked it the previous evening, but not a living soul to be seen. "Where can he be?"

She turned and started back through the rooms that had been so bright with celebration only a few hours before. Peeking into the dining room, she saw Mr. Miller, the butler, and Mrs. Spence, the housekeeper, standing near the sideboard. Mr. Miller had his arms around Mrs. Spence. She was weeping into his shirt front. "Oh, how shall we ever get over this?" she keened. "What sense does it make? Oh, Sam. If it was an illness as took her I could see it as God's will, but how are we to understand this? When was there ever a reason to murder a child?"

Gwen's step caused a board to creak. Mr. Miller straightened his spine as if he'd been stung and let go of Mrs. Spence. He quickly found his handkerchief so the housekeeper might dry her eyes. "Please forgive us, Mrs. Wickersham. I was just telling Mrs. Spence about the many times I passed by the door of the master's study of an evening and stopped to peak in at His Lordship reading a bedtime story to Alice. He'd be sitting in his favorite wing chair with his glass of rum on the table close to hand. The little girl would be nestled on his lap with her head resting against his shoulder, her eyelids drifting down as she nodded off. I'd knock and just put my head in to see if he wanted anything before I retired downstairs, but he never did. As long as he had his tot of rum and his little girl there with him he needed nothing from me."

"I'm so sorry to interrupt." Gwen blushed with sympathetic embarrassment, having intruded on such a private moment. "I can't find the vicar. Have you seen him?"

Vernon was at that moment in the company of the mistress of the house, Lady Sibyl Montfort. Even though he'd donned his black overcoat and stuffed his blond curls into his pocket, he still felt distinctly foolish dressed as a woman in a white eyelet frock. Lady Montfort looked up with muddy eyes that bore no resemblance to those of the celebrated beauty whose annual Twelfth Night party had been the event of the season ever since she had married Sir John twelve years ago. His second marriage. The first had ended in divorce. It was said the first Lady Montfort had drunk herself into a breakdown and spent her married life in a succession of sanitariums. The vicar wondered at the evil luck that dogged the master of Burridge Down. One wife gone mad, and now the second was surely headed down the road to Bedlam as well.

Sibyl had doffed her party costume—she'd been Daddy Warbucks to her husband's Little Orphan Annie—and now appeared soberly clothed in gray flannel slacks and a beige sweater. She wandered to the window seat and sat down, clutching a crocheted wrapper around her shoulders, holding it close at her throat. "What am I to do?" she asked. As light paled the sky, she studied the snow-shrouded shapes outside her window, the crescent of the bluestone drive, the statuary, topiary and fountains, the things that had not changed.

"You must try to rest," the vicar said, drawing from a stock of platitudes that had gotten him through disasters in the past.

"The guests? They've gone?"

"I would think so." He considered the gaunt hollows of her face. "Perhaps I should send for the doctor to see you again."

"But what about Alice? Surely he needs to see to my daughter." She clutched the shawl tighter around her neck and shrank into it. "She's asthmatic, you know, at risk of asphyxiation if she exerts. And allergic to certain strains of pollen. Her system is quite sensitive."

The vicar stiffened. "My dear Lady Montfort, you must try to come to grips with the fact that Alice is with God."

Sibyl Montfort went to the mantle and with trembling fingers took a cigarette from the box. The vicar quickly produced his lighter and ignited it for her. After a long drag she spoke again. "I'm a religious woman. I believe God acts through people, much as he acted through the Virgin Mary when it pleased him that she should bear his son on earth. We are taught to believe such things." She turned her vaguely puzzled gaze toward him. "Through whom might God have acted in this case? What was God thinking?"

"You must sit down," the vicar said. He gently took her arm to guide her toward the sofa.

She pulled away from him. "No. Please leave me alone. There's nothing you can tell me." She turned to stare once more out the window at the winter blankness. The hollowness of her voice struck the vicar as he left the room. The doctor had given her a sedative, he reasoned, and now it was kicking in. As he descended the stairway he considered how queer she was acting. *But what's normal when a child dies?* He'd had only one prior experience. The mother had come at him with her fists. A swimming pool drowning. *Where's the why of that?*

On the main floor of the hall, he looked into the great room where a massive Christmas tree stood with ornaments shining in the first spears of dawn light slanting through the windows. It was time to take the decorations down. He wondered how long it would be before any of the staff would have the heart to see to it. The butler appeared at the other end of the hallway.

Mr. Miller," the vicar said to the senior staff member, "I wonder if you've seen the Detective Inspector."

"In the library. I'll see you in."

"Don't bother. Please, go on with what you're doing," Wickersham said. "I'll knock."

"Oh, no, sir. No bother. It's the proprieties that help us keep our balance in these times. They must be observed. Oh, by the way, Vicar, Mrs. Wickersham is looking for you, Sir."

"I dare say she's ready to go home," the vicar said.

Miller led him into the dim room smelling of foxed paper where the policeman sat with a distracted look on his face. "Detective Inspector Busby, the vicar wishes a word."

Busby rose and greeted the clergyman.

"Sorry to disturb," the vicar said. "Long night."

"Indeed," Busby replied.

"I've just seen Lady Montfort and I was alarmed by her demeanor. I wanted to make sure someone stays with her." Wickersham knew he had failed to communicate the extent of his worry, but he didn't know how to speak of it.

"Miller, have Collet see to her mistress," Busby said. "Now if there's nothing else…"

Mr. Miller saw the vicar to the door. "We'll see to Her Ladyship," he said.

"Good man," Wickersham replied. He left the house with heavy feelings of misgiving and walked across the drive to his car. The sky was white and thick with fine snow. The world, hushed and drained of color, was a silent movie, slightly out of focus the way shrubs, walls and cars were softly mounded. Thinking of a new grave, he stood and breathed in the sharp air, trying to shake off the bone-tiredness before it deepened into depression. He pictured Lady Montfort's dull eyes and had the thought that every grief, like every snowflake, is different. Strange, he reflected, that no one had suggested that John Montfort might look in on his wife to try to give comfort. An instant before he climbed in behind the wheel, he heard himself hailed.

"Vernon! Wait!" With her coat tails flying, his wife came trotting down the drive like a schoolboy just released from a Latin recitation. She was panting, a patch of rose on each cheek and her hair all awry, unruly whisps floating around her face. "I've been looking all over for you. Where have you been?" She called to him loudly, in her brash New York accent. She seemed like a cartoon to him, her words captured in vapor puffs felted on the gray air.

The delay seemed to intensify his discomfort as he stood there with his feet pinching in his Mary Janes, already soggy from the snow, and a cutting breeze blowing up the back of his skirt. "Please, Gwen, get into the car. You can't be galloping and bellowing about."

"You love it that I gallop and bellow." She opened the door and plopped herself into the passenger's seat.

He slid behind the wheel and leaned over to kiss her cheek before turning the key in the ignition. "I'm freezing," he said with a shudder as the engine came to life. "Don't see how you women manage in frocks. And these torturous shoes!"

"And you call us the weaker sex!"

"You'll never again hear that from my lips."

She cuddled up next to him as the car started to roll away from the grand house. "What a night! No one would tell me anything about what happened. Not that they ever talk to me in any case. So give."

"Terrible business," he began. "The police don't understand any more about it than they did ten minutes after they were called. They have to wait for the coroner's report to be absolutely sure, but it seems the child may have been poisoned."

"Do you mean intentionally?"

"Oh, surely not. I can't imagine it was anything but a tragic accident." He patted her hand. "And what do you mean no one ever talks to you? Everyone is very fond of you."

"Parties remind me of losing at Musical Chairs."

"Oh, darling," he said, "you're just tired. Everything will seem better once we've had a sleep." He slowed down at the end of the long driveway and stopped to wait for a lorry rattling down the road toward Wellington. "What's wrong with this damn heater! My feet are like ice."

He chanced to glance into the rearview mirror and caught sight of a figure belting down the drive, waving his arms and shouting. "Is that Miller?" He turned to peer out the back window and waited for the butler to draw near.

When he reached the car, Miller leaned down to speak through the driver's side window. "Please, sir, we need you to come to the kitchen at once. Iris says she wants to confess, but before she'll speak to the coppers she insists on having a clergyman beside her."

"Hop in," Vernon said to the panting man. As soon as the butler was in the back seat, the vicar turned the car around and returned it to the same space where it had spent the night. He and Gwen then followed Miller to the servant's entrance at the side of the house and stepped into the mechanical region below stairs that breathed life into the great dwelling. They passed through a catacomb of storage spaces, down a narrow corridor past the boiler room and the laundry and through the kitchen to the servants' dining room where the staff had assembled, standing expectantly. At the long trestle table, like a plump bird ready for the oven, sat Iris. She held a handkerchief in one dishwater roughened hand, pressing it tight against her mouth as if she wanted to tamp down some terrible truth that was on the verge of tumbling out.

The cook, a spare, graying dame with large-knuckled fingers twisting a dishtowel, was speaking to Detective Inspector Busby. "This is Iris Trent." Her eyes, as fierce as a harrier's, cut toward the distraught figure at the table. "We've kept her here to make sure she didn't scarper."

"Thank you, Mrs. Fast." Busby drew his notebook from his breast pocket and flipped it open to his most recent entries. "Iris works for you, I take it."

Mrs. Spence, the housekeeper, stepped forward to correct his assumption. "She does not. Iris is a housemaid. She works for me, but was lent to the kitchen as extra hands was needed during the holidays. Never mind that my staff had been polishing all the floors and furniture and putting up the decorations without any extra help. Why, it would never occur to me to ask."

Busby glanced up at Miller and the Wickershams. "Ah, Vicar. Glad we caught you before you left. Sorry to delay your breakfast."

The vicar took off his overcoat and folded it across the back of the chair next to Iris where he sat down. She met his steady gaze and waited for her fate to unfold. "Now then, Iris," he began, "I understand you have information about the death of Alice Montfort."

Iris nodded.

"Don't be afraid." Wickersham looked pointedly at Busby. "As long as you tell the truth before God all will be well."

Busby cleared his throat. "Please tell me your story leaving out no detail whether you feel it is important or not. Take your time. I am in no hurry."

Iris began to speak in a voice that wavered slightly at first but gained confidence as she went on. "There had been such a fuss all day below stairs. Cook was barking orders like a sergeant major: That's not how you make a roux! Yes *all* the knives. If you'd use the steel on them every forty slices you wouldn't have so much work to do now! Hurry up! Don't you know what it means to sweat vegetables? Do it properly, then!"

Mrs. Fast's face broke out in red blotches. The kitchen girls smirked. Iris went on.

"Poor Lily was so jittery, she cut her thumb chopping onions and bled everywhere. Cook said it was bad luck and sent her to lie down. That's why I had to help with the Baba au Rhum."

"The dessert that was served at the Twelfth Night dinner," Busby said.

"Yes, sir. That's what killed her. Little Alice."

"In good time I expect I'll see how you came to that conclusion," Busby said. "But let's not get ahead of the story. Let's go back to the beginning. At what time did you start the preparation of the Baba au Rhum?"

"Cook likes to serve them warm so a bit after six we started the yeast to raise the dough."

He made a note in his little green notebook. "Tell me more about that."

"Well, you heat the milk until it's lukewarm, then you dissolve the yeast into it and stir in some flour. That's the sponge. You add more flour and butter and sugar and eggs to the sponge. That's the batter. You spoon it into the molds and let it rise. Then you bake them and when they're nicely brown you unmold them onto the dessert plates and pour the syrup over each one."

Here she faltered, but collected herself and went on. "There were seventeen for dinner, counting Alice." Tears sprang to her eyes at the mention of the child. "We made three recipes of the dessert. I remember Cook saying it was a bother, since there was only one too many guests for a double recipe. Cook said when she was growing up the children never ate with the adults. They always had their dinner in the nursery with the governess."

"So there were seven extra portions of dessert. What happened to them?

"We ate them below stairs. We all got a half except for Mr. Miller. He got a whole one."

"Did everyone on staff eat some?"

"Oh, yes, sir. You put a tablespoon of rum and a big dollop of whipped cream on each dish right before it's served. It's quite a wonderful treat. No one would want to miss it."

"So every guest and every one of the staff ate the dessert, yet only Alice Montfort became ill."

"Yes, sir. You see, after we'd put the Babas in the oven and the syrup was made, Cook was called upstairs. His lordship likes to introduce her to the guests and they all clap for her and then he pours her a bit of wine and they toast her health. I don't think she likes it actually, because she's always called away just as she's getting the dessert on."

"What exactly did you do?" Busby asked.

"I made the servings just as she'd told me. But right at the end when there was but one more bowl to finish, I ran out of rum. And the pantry was locked. I couldn't think of how to find Mr. Miller to get the key since he was in the dining room with Cook."

"So what did you do?"

"I put out the seventeen desserts for upstairs, making sure one of them was the one that lacked the tablespoon of rum. You see, sir, I thought like as not that dish would go to a lady or perhaps to Alice and they wouldn't care if there was rum on or not. And even if it was noticed, the dinner guests wouldn't complain whereas downstairs if you shorted anyone a tot of rum there'd by hell to pay."

"I see," Busby said. "So you arranged the one unfinished dessert to go to the dining room."

"Yes, but then it occurred to me that I might have time to get some rum from the bottle in His Lordship's study. You see, he has a decanter there that's for his use only. It's a special kind of rum from St. Nicholas Abbey on Barbados. He gets a bottle each year for Christmas. No one else dares touch it. I took a tea cup and fetched a spot of rum from that bottle and added it to the one dish that needed finishing before anyone was one wit the wiser."

Busby frowned. "So when the tray with the seventeen portions of Baba au Rhum went to the dining room, there was one dish—and only one—that had that special rum."

Iris nodded.

"And am I right in thinking you had no idea to whom this different portion would be served?"

"None at all," Iris said, "until I heard the child had died of poisoning, and then I knew she was the one who'd got it."

Busby narrowed his eyes. "I'm sorry, miss. Are you saying you knew the St. Nicholas Abbey rum was poisoned?"

"Sir, I didn't! I swear! Not at the time. But later on as I thought about it I knew because I'm a housemaid, not a cook. It's the silver, you see. Any silver that's kept in the kitchen for use at table is polished by the scullery maids. But any odd bits of silver upstairs that's never used in the dining room is the responsibility of the housekeeping staff. Well, sir, it was me who polished the silver neck band on the rum decanter in his lordship's sitting room—when I was upstairs, before I came down to the kitchen. That's how I knew the rum was there in the first place."

Busby's expression indicated that his brain was racing, trying to get on the same train of thought as Iris's. "So you are saying the poison came from silver polish?"

"I knew when I heard the body smelled of bitter almonds." She dissolved into tears.

The cook stepped in to elucidate. "It's common knowledge there's cyanide in silver polish. It's why you have to be so careful to wash it off the plate and not get any on your hands."

Iris spoke again. "I reckon I left some polish on that bit of silver on the decanter. That's how the rum got poisoned." She broke down again, but continued speaking through her sobs. "I didn't never mean to hurt that child, sir. Please, as God is my witness. I never meant no harm."

"When did you serve dessert?" Busby asked the cook.

Mrs. Fast answered without hesitation. "At nine-thirty, Sir. Same as every year."

Busby then asked to be shown to the room where the decanter was kept. "I need to collect it and test for cyanide." He motioned toward a uniformed underling skulking with the kitchen staff. "Charles, get this girl down to the station."

Iris turned panicky eyes toward the vicar. "Oh, sir! Don't let them lock me up. I didn't mean no harm."

Wickersham laid his hand on Iris's arm. "You did right to come forward with this information, my girl. Have faith that things will come right. Do as you're told and trust to God."

The girl hung her head as one of her comrades went to fetch her hat and coat.

"Come my dear," Vernon said to Gwen. "We must be getting home."

They walked arm in arm to the car. This time Gwen was careful to hold her tongue until they were inside the vehicle. "I don't understand," she said. "Does that cop really believe that a little silver polish on the outside of a decanter could contaminate the rum inside?"

"I don't know what he believes," Vernon answered her. "The laboratory results will tell the tale." He frowned. "I see what you mean, though."

After a few minutes of silence during which they managed to negotiate the deep ruts in the snow and get out onto the roadway, Gwen said. "Lady Montfort's maid Collet...she's ... what, Caribbean?"

"From Barbados."

"How did she come to be here in Somerset?"

"Montforts had a sugar plantation on Barbados ages back. Most of the property was sold off long ago but they kept a small plot with the house for vacationing. Sibyl's family live on the island full time to this day. Anyway, she and John met while he was visiting and they tied the knot on the island. I believe Collet was Sibyl's maid before she married. Why do you ask?"

"Just curious. She seemed friendly, within the confines of what's considered proper for a servant in a stuffy old British household. So that's the reason for Lord Montfort's special rum."

"Yes. The owners of St. Nicholas Abbey have old family ties to the Montforts. The rum's frightfully expensive. Special customers get their own numbered bottles refilled every year."

"The freight alone must be a nightmare." Gwen laid her head on his shoulder. "It would make a bit more sense if it were Montfort who was dead instead of Alice."

"It's all speculation until the lab report comes back," he said. "Meanwhile I have to christen the Burkett's baby in—" he took a look at his wristwatch, "—about three hours. Just enough time for a hot tub and some breakfast, if my wife would be so kind."

"Only if you say you love me," she said.

He smiled. "To a fault," he replied.

She made them a meal of egg and chips, finished with strong coffee. The telephone rang as Vernon was swallowing his last bite. She left the table to get it and after a moment returned with a look of regret. "For you, I'm afraid. Detective Inspector Busby would like a word."

Vernon wiped his mouth and rose to take the call. Before she'd finished stacking the dishes in the sink he was back for his last sip of coffee. "I'm off," he said. "The autopsy confirms cyanide as the cause of death. It was found in the rum." He rolled down his shirt sleeves and buttoned the cuffs before donning his jacket. "The girl is being charged. I'm going to stop by the station to see her before I go to the church. Busby has dispatched a car to collect me." He settled his hat on his head and shuffled into his coat. "Sorry, darling, but I'm not sure when I'll be home. Hate to desert you. Do take the car if you feel like getting out to amuse yourself. And try not to worry about all this." He pulled on his overshoes then opened the door.

"Wait!" Gwen came to where he stood by the open door and reached for his pocket where a ringlet of the blond wig was hanging out.

"You won't be needing this, I expect."

He planted a gentle kiss on her forehead. "What would I do without you." He kissed her again and hurried off.

She tossed the wig on the table and got on with the washing up. Every so often she found herself staring into space with a soapy plate in her hands. It was the Alice Montfort business. What bothered her was the notion that some stray bit of silver polish on the neck band of a decanter had poisoned the child. "How in the world does that make any sense?" she asked herself out loud. "The poison was *in* the rum."

After she dried the dishes, she stretched out on the couch under a lap robe and opened a book on the Tudors that invariably caused her eyelids to grow heavy, but her mind would not stop pressing the point that no matter how one might hold the decanter it would be almost impossible to slosh rum across the neckband while pouring it into a tea cup, much less contaminate the rum inside the bottle. Had Iris taken the top off the decanter and allowed some polish to drip inside?

It was by then mid-morning. The sky had cleared and sun sparkled the snow, beckoning her to take a drive into town.

Thinking of the situation at Burridge Down, she came up with a perfectly good reason to make the trip. She checked the cupboard to make sure of her ingredients, then got her purse and bundled herself up against the cold.

"Ah, now would you be wanting the Muscat or t'other?" Mrs. Wembly at the grocer's asked, when Gwen said what it was she needed.

"Whichever's best for raisin cake," Gwen said. "It's for the Montforts."

"Ah, as it's for them I'd recommend the Muscat," Mrs. Wembly said. "Oh, it's an awful business. That poor little Alice. I don't know how her parents will survive such a tragedy." She shook her head. "Couples never get over it, do they. Some it brings together and some it splits apart, but none are ever quite the same. Think of the overwhelming blame you'd feel. Wouldn't you spend all the rest of your days going back over all your memories with the child, wondering where you went wrong, what you failed to teach, how you failed to protect." She wrapped Gwen's raisins while still preoccupied with the thought, or perhaps a memory. "How can one spouse hope to penetrate that pain, reach through it to the other, make himself seen at all?"

"You're quite right," Gwen said, taking some money from her purse.

"But as it was an accident, perhaps it will not be so hard to bear as if there were malice aforethought," Mrs. Wembly added.

As she left the grocer's shop Gwen pondered how quickly the word of a fatal *accident* had spread through the village. That was the crux of it. Was it accidental? And if it wasn't, then what was the motive? Who would ever have wanted to kill Alice Montfort? Her way home took her past the library where, on impulse, she stopped in.

"Ah," the librarian said, as she stepped out from behind her high desk and started walking toward the reference volumes. "I've been expecting a spike in interest in poisons, but so far you're the first to inquire." She pulled a thick medical tome off the shelf and carried it to one of the study tables.

"Ta," Gwen said. She took off her coat and found an old shopping list at the bottom of her handbag for notes: *may be derived from pits of stone fruits such as apricots, corpse exudes bitter almond aroma—skin a blue color—when administered in quantity, fatal within thirty minutes.* She sat with the revelation for a moment. *Iris is innocent.* It had to be, but then how had the child been poisoned and by whom?

The librarian spoke when Gwen stood. "Did you find what you were looking for?"

"Oh, quite," Gwen said. She closed the medical text and rose from the table. "Thanks awfully. I have to hurry home, now."

As Gwen drove back to the vicarage with her raisins, a dozen questions bubbled in her brain. Who was the last person to see the child alive? Who might have benefited from her death? What if the cyanide that killed Alice was meant for someone else?

Upon arriving home, before she did another thing, she telephoned the church and left word for Vernon to call her back. "Tell him it's urgent," she explained to the volunteer who was working in the office. "Oh, and if he can't reach me at the vicarage, then tell him to call Burridge Down and ask for me there."

She put the raisin cake together with such deliberate speed that she was afraid of a poor result. But when it came out of the oven it looked absolutely perfect. It didn't even stick when she turned it out of the pan onto a pretty plate. Vernon would never believe it, she reflected, wishing she could somehow save him a piece.

The aromas of ginger, cinnamon and cloves hung in the air as she found a box that would do to carry the cake. Once it was packaged, she rushed upstairs to put on a good dress. She had to walk more quickly than was prudent with snow on the ground and her arms full, but managed to make it to the car without a pratfall.

As the vehicle lumbered along the road ridged and humped with snow, she considered the matter of who to talk to, how much to reveal and what questions to ask. It was a delicate thing, detective work, a matter of inspiring confidence, making others feel it was safe to share secrets—something of which the likes of D. I. Busby knew nothing whatsoever.

Mrs. Spence answered the door.

"I brought a raisin cake." Gwen entered and put the box on the table in the foyer.

Spence opened the lid and clasped her hands. "Oh, how lovely! And so kind of you to think of us. Her Ladyship has barely nibbled a biscuit since it happened, but this will surely tempt her. I can't thank you enough."

"Would it be possible to peek in on Lady Montfort?" Gwen asked.

Mrs. Spence shook her head ruefully. "I don't know … I'm afraid she's lying down now. Oh, we've been in such a state around here! The poor woman has had no sleep at all. Downstairs has been in a tizzy getting Lord Montfort ready to go to the continent and—"

"He's gone?"

"You just missed him. He left a few minutes ago for the train station. He's going to London and then on to France. Mr. Miller went with him, so I'm left to manage everything—even the funeral arrangements!" The poor woman broke into tears.

"There, there," Gwen said, as the housekeeper sniffled into her hankie. "The vicar will see to that."

"The house is completely topsy-turvy. It's lucky no one wants to eat a proper meal."

Gwen ventured a gambit. "I have a bit of good news that might make everyone feel a little less wretched. That's why I wanted to speak to Mrs. Montfort. I know it will cheer her."

"But what is it?"

"The dessert had nothing to do with Alice's death."

"But how can that be? Why did the police—"

"I'll be off to the police station after I've told Her Ladyship. I'll see myself upstairs. You run and tell Mrs. Fast."

"Oh, thank you, Mrs. Wickersham. It's to the left at the top of the stairs. I'll just ..." She rabbited off, leaving the thought unfinished.

Gwen took the cake out of the box and carried it to the door of Lady Montfort's sitting room. She knocked softly before entering. Sibyl was stretched out on a chaise longue by the window. Her head swiveled at the sound of the door. "Oh, hello," she said. Her dull eyes registered recognition, but little enthusiasm. "Gwen? What a surprise."

"Sorry to disturb." Gwen placed the cake on a side table near the chaise and then threw her coat on a chair. "I had to come and see how you're faring." She pulled off her gloves and tossed them on her coat. "The vicar and I have been so worried about you and His Lordship. Please don't get up. I won't stay long."

Sibyl swung her legs to the floor. "I must look a sight."

"Nonsense. Besides, it hardly matters between friends." Gwen sat down next to Sibyl and looked into her exhausted face. "How are you? Scraping along?"

Sibyl sighed. "Just."

"You must eat something. Look, I brought you a cake. It's raisin."

"Oh, I couldn't."

"Oh, but I made it especially for you. I need something to cut it with. I won't leave until you try a bite."

Sibyl smiled weakly. "I'll ring for Collet."

She hauled on the bell pull and a moment later Collet entered from the adjoining dressing room. "Good afternoon, Mrs. Wickersham." Her eyes moved to her mistress. "My Lady?"

"We'd like a pot of tea to go with the cake the vicar's wife brought," Sibyl said.

"I was just about to make it," Collet replied. "After your tea you must rest. I'm sure Mrs. Wickersham understands." She looked pointedly at Gwen.

"Yes, of course. I'll not stay long."

As soon as the maid had gone, Gwen placed her hand on Sibyl's and came out with her startling news. "Iris is innocent. If the dessert had been poisoned Alice would have died within thirty minutes of eating it, while she was still downstairs. But she didn't die until after she'd gone upstairs to bed. Nonetheless, it appears that Lord Montfort's special rum was poisoned, and not from any incidental contact with the silver neck band."

"I don't understand."

"It seems clear to me that Alice was poisoned accidentally, that the intended victim was your husband."

A shadow passed over Sibyl's face. It was gone in an instant, but was enough to convince Gwen that Lady Montfort already knew all of what she'd just revealed. Recovering herself, Sibyl wore a look of confusion. "John? Why would anyone want to kill John?"

The maid entered with a tray before the question could be answered. "Here's the tea, then, madam. Shall I pour out and cut the cake?"

"Yes, thank you, Collet." Lady Montfort seemed tense. She rubbed her fingers across her forehead. "I'm rather looking forward to a cup of tea," she said. "I'm feeling a bit rough." She took her cup and drank right away.

Collet gave each of them a slice of cake. "Very nice bit of baking, this," she said.

"Won't you take a piece for yourself?" Gwen replied.

"Do," Sibyl said. "Take the rest downstairs."

"You mustn't stay too long," Collet reminded Gwen.

"Give me ten minutes. I'll see myself out."

"You were saying," Lady Montfort said, as the maid left the room.

"You had asked me why anyone would want to kill your husband," Gwen said. She noticed that Sibyl had already drunk down her tea and slid the empty cup back onto the tray. "May I pour you another?" she asked.

"Oh, no. I never have more than one cup. You should drink it while it's hot," she said, nodding toward Gwen's untouched cup.

Gwen raised the cup to her lips, but didn't actually drink any of the tea before she spoke again. "I was thinking you might shed some light on the question of who might have wanted to harm Lord Montfort."

Sibyl picked at her cake with a fork, ate a tiny fragment. "Delicious. And such a moist crumb. You must tell me your secret."

"No, Sibyl," Gwen said. "You must tell me yours."

Again the shadow crossed Sibyl's features, this time it lingered longer than before. She dropped her eyes to her lap.

"I can't imagine what you mean." She put down her plate and reached for the bell pull. "I hope you won't think me rude," she said, "but I'm beginning to feel tired. I fear I must ask you to leave now."

"Why has he gone away so precipitously, without even waiting to attend his daughter's burial?" Gwen asked coldly. "Is he afraid to stay here? Afraid of the inquiry that will be resumed when the police figure out that their current explanation of the poisoning is utterly ridiculous?"

"I don't know. I don't know. Where is Collet?" Sibyl leaned back on the chaise. Her words were slurred, as if the lady were drunk.

Gwen watched her drift into a heavy slumber and, after a moment spent considering what she'd best do next, began pulling on her gloves in preparation for a trip to the police station. She didn't notice Collet, a shadowed figure standing in the dark doorway to the dressing room, until she reached for her coat. "Lady Montfort's asleep," she whispered. "I'll just be going."

The figure stepped into the light. Gwen started. "Oh, my," she managed to say.

It was a gentleman in traveling clothes, a Harris tweed suit and trilby. His olive face was dominated by a heavy mustache and horn-rimmed glasses. His hair was a dark mass of curls that Gwen recognized immediately. "So that's what happened to my wig," she said.

Collet smiled grimly. "Forgive me for taking advantage of your leaving it lying about."

"Of course. I see you've decided to go after Lord Montfort."

"I must make haste if I'm to catch him in Paris," she replied. "I may even be able to make the same Channel crossing if I'm lucky."

"Yes," Gwen said, "it would make things a trifle easier for you if he were lost at sea. I'm sure the police would content themselves with calling it a suicide, a man so desolate over the death of his child that he threw himself off the ship."

Collet held out her hand. "I'll be going now, if you'll just lend me your car keys and drink your tea."

"I'll have an answer to one question first," Gwen said. "I want to know if I got it right, the truth of this awful affair. It has to do with why Lady Montfort brought you back with her from Barbados. She needed your special skills."

"How clever you are, Mrs. Wickersham. And how right. My special skills, as you say, I learned from my mother. She was a servant in the house where Her Ladyship grew up. She was a maker of herbal cures, nostrums for the belly, spirits to quicken the bowels, poultices to draw infection, hot wraps to cure aching joints, potions to induce sleep…"

"Never-ending sleep," Gwen said.

"Yes." Collet said. "That, too."

"Go on."

"As you know, the Montforts had a plantation on Barbados. The young master met my lady and they fell in love and married even though Madam's parents had reservations. There were rumors about John Montfort, things whispered in the servants' quarters."

"What rumors?"

"That he liked sex with very young children." She stared woodenly as she said it, but came quickly back to her purpose again. "But Madam was in love and love is blind. So they married and soon had a baby girl. Every year at about the time of their wedding anniversary in late November they came back to the house on Barbados. They would go to St. Nicholas Abbey and the master would get his decanter filled with the rum that was only his to drink. Every year the child grew taller and more beautiful. Then only two months ago, last November, when madam came to the island, she sought me out and revealed to me an awful truth. She said her husband had a custom of reading to Alice in his study before she went to bed. When she went to sleep in his lap, he would carry her into her room which was just the next door down the hall and he would tuck her into bed. What alarmed Madam, the reason she came to me, was that he stayed a very long time in the child's bedroom. And it began at about this time that John Montfort lost interest in his wife, as if he had taken a mistress. My poor lady remembered the rumors from before she wed and realized she had made it perfect for him, for this—pedophile."

"Yes, I see," Gwen said. "So when Sibyl came to the island last November she asked you to come back with her for the sole purpose of getting rid of this threat to Alice. And you did it by the most obvious means, by poisoning the rum that only he was allowed to drink. You put the poison into the decanter sometime after dinner?"

Collet regarded the clock on the table next to the tea tray. "About ten o'clock. It seemed like such a good plan. I had no idea anyone else would touch his special decanter. But he must have accustomed Alice to taking some of his rum before bed, to make sure she was too drunk to resist. She must have poured some for herself last night. That's the only way it makes sense."

"Yes. I agree. It makes sense entirely." Gwen sighed heavily and stood. "My dear Collet," she said. "I wish we could talk longer, but you must hurry. You need to make that Channel crossing." She searched her coat pocket and came up with the car keys which she pressed into Collet's hand. "And I must drink my tea."

When Gwen woke she was in a ward, her throat was terribly sore and her dear Vernon was sitting on the bed clasping her hand. "Gwen? Darling, can you hear me?"

"Hello, my dear. Oh, lord. Talking feels like the devil. Why am I in the hospital?"

"We had to get your stomach pumped. Someone tried to poison you."

"Oh, Vernon! I hardly think that was necessary. It was only a sedative in the tea. Collet had been giving Lady Montfort the same concoction to make her sleep—unlike the concoction she put in Lord Montfort's rum. You've figured it out by now, haven't you?"

"Yes, darling. We worked it out. Several hours after you did, it seems. But where is Collet? She seems to have made off with our car. Do you remember if she said where she was going? I know I shouldn't ask you any more questions. My poor darling! You've been through such a nightmare! Are you really quite all right?"

"Shhh! Not so loud. Sick people. Someone will think you're a Yank."

"That's enough out of you," he said.

She mouthed something in response that made him smile.

"Yes," he replied, "to a fault."

Our holiday for February is Presidents' Day, which we commemorate with a story that takes its inspiration from Thomas Jefferson's taste for wine.

# The Jefferson Bordeaux

ACCORDING TO THE *Wine Spectator*, it was a marriage made in heaven: young Russian River winemaker to the stars, Chad Sturgess, partnering with wine dealer and internationally syndicated critic Frederick Church. When their new urban winery opened in the Gaslamp near the ballpark where the Padres were getting ready to turn in a winning season, San Diego real estate prices climbed through the roof. But then Sturgess wound up under the Coronado Bay Bridge with a crushed skull and an empty wine bottle stuck up his ass. Not just any wine bottle, either—a bottle once owned by Thomas Jefferson and insured for seven figures before it was emptied and used as a suppository. That's where I come in. I'm an insurance investigator. The home office wanted answers to some pointed questions before they paid the claim.

Frederick Church pursed his lips whenever I asked him a question. The shutters at the cellar windows were half closed against the sun. The pale, smooth fat man was cast in light and dark stripes like a toadstool behind bars. His mouth was puffy like a catcher's mitt. I wanted to stick my fist in it. "Your accountant said your capital's running thin. Was Chad skimming?"

He gave me that look of injured innocence most people save for IRS auditors. "The architect's design, the build out, the equipment—all very expensive. Why, the cooperage alone!" The way he wrapped his fat lips around the word, it was obvious he loved saying it instead of 'barrels.' "But we're well financed. It's merely a question of adjusting our business plan."

"Still, you and Chad had your differences."

"I didn't kill him. The suggestion's absurd. I was in Seattle. Besides, I revered him as an artist. His palate was unparalleled—except for mine. Where am I going to find another Chad?"

"Shouldn't be too difficult for a guy with a gold-plated wine collection insured to the hilt. Incidentally, when were you going to report the Jefferson Bordeaux stolen?"

His index finger stroked his billowy lip. I couldn't watch. He was making me insane. I studied the brickwork arches that marked the caves lined floor to ceiling with wine bottles. The Caves. That was the name of the joint, pronounced the French way like a baby cow.

"I didn't know Chad had taken it until I saw the story on the news."

"Where was he taking it?"

"To settle a gambling debt," Church said. "Chad favored a floating crap game. Literally. A high stakes game aboard a yacht. The Calysta."

"When's the last time he went out to play, apart from the night he died?"

"You might check the calendar on his computer," Church advised. "The police have it."

Church wasn't telling me anything I hadn't seen in the police report, so I headed to the waterfront to find out about the Calysta. The concierge at the Marriott had told me about a fish market where they make a mean crab sandwich. Most places put in too much celery and crap. But a good crab cake, fried crisp and slipped onto a sour dough bun is worth standing in line for, which is what I did. When I got to the cashier I asked, "You know the Calysta?" He jerked his head toward the Navy carriers tied up at North Island. "Moored near the channel. Black hull and white up top. Can't miss it." I headed outside with my sandwich and a beer. He was right. It stuck out like an eagle in a duck pond.

I ate listening to the clank of sailboat rigging and watching the pelicans take formation drills. Seagulls screamed and fought, much to the amusement of the war-mongering humans who tossed French fries and laughed at the battles their leavings provoked. It put me in mind of my time in Afghanistan, but only for a second. A fishing boat pulling into the marina saved me from going back there.

A deck hand tied her off to a cleat, then got busy tossing silver-sided fish onto the pier. Day sailors staggered off the boat looking ragged, either from the ocean chop or the margaritas. The skipper came down from the fly bridge and clambered to the foot of the gangway to collect his tips. I finished my beer and went to have a word. "I'd like to arrange a trip," I said.

His eyes peered from slits in a beefy face adapted to the glare off the water. "Fishing?"

I nodded toward the Calysta. "Know anything about her?"

"Belongs to some Tijuana cartel that runs an offshore card game."

"La Familia," I said.

"Yeah. The ones kidnapping Mexican police and leaving their heads rolling around on the Avenida Revolución. No thanks."

"How 'bout I double your normal fee?"

"What, you think I want to get my nuts shoved down my throat?"

I strolled to my car to call Gillian Dickinson, my contact at the SDPD. She'd met me at the airport and given me the lay of the land. Not bad looking for a homicide detective. "So how's America's Finest City treating you?" she answered.

"I need more sunscreen," I said.

"Can't help you there."

"Maybe you can check Sturgess's appointment calendar for the dates and times he visited the Calysta. Thought I'd bounce them against his bank account. See how much of a hit he took."

"No problem. Anything else?"

"Yeah. I need a record of his phone calls for the past month or so."

"Cell or office?"

"Both. Anything new on your end?"

"The ME confirmed the bottle was the murder weapon. Blunt force trauma. Insertion was post-mortem. No indication of where the murder occurred or where the bottle was emptied."

"Except we know neither of those events occurred where the body was found."

"Bingo."

The body was found in Chicano Park, my next stop. I parked on National Avenue. A fresh breeze picked up a flattened paper cup and cart-wheeled it along the base of a graffiti-covered wall. I don't have much Spanish, but I was able to decipher 'abajo Mexico' and 'parque de putas'. As I approached Logan Avenue I saw the priest in front of the massive ramps curving like petals of an Easter lily leading on and off the Coronado Bridge. Murals on the supporting pylons flashed bright swatches of color against grayness on a non-human scale. On the ground beneath the bridge grass struggled to grow in the perpetual shade of the massive roadbed. Under the freeway, the temperature dropped with the onshore wind ducting under the concrete. The wind noise was doubled by the roar of traffic overhead.

Father Hernandez greeted me under a painting of a prison scene. "This one is called Voz Libre," he said. "It depicts the life of Don Pedro Gonzalez. He established the first Spanish radio station in California. They sent him to San Quentin on false charges.

I took a course on graffiti art at SDSU." He must have been quite the campus crush with his dark eyes and pony tail. Even in middle age his classic Latino good looks were not quite lost in the graven lines on his face, the sad aura of the devout.

"Thanks for meeting me," I said.

"I cooperate whenever possible. Detective Dickinson is a good cop. She often contacts me when crimes are committed in the barrio, to see what I've heard." I fell into a gait that matched the priest's loping stride. "His body was found near the Kiosk." He led me to a spot of ground like any other once the crime scene tape had been removed. There was no blood, no sign of violence. I crouched and poked around but there was nothing to learn. I got to my feet. "Why do you think the body was left here?"

"This is a place where families bring little children to play. The church is holding summer camp. It's a message, I think, to the church, to me, not to interfere with the business of La Familia."

"You're saying La Familia killed Sturgess?"

He looked uncomfortable with my conclusion, but didn't contradict it. "I work with a non-governmental organization called HumanKind," he said. "It fights against human trafficking—the sex trade. Chad Sturgess contacted me about rescuing a woman. He wanted help to return her to Mongolia."

"Mongolia?"

"Mongolian women are incredibly beautiful. The night he was murdered I was waiting for him to bring the girl to an apartment on Broadway. He never showed. I assumed he backed out."

"Did he say where this woman was being held?"

Hernandez shook his head, lying reluctantly, if I'm any judge of faces. I said goodbye and handed him a business card. He gave me one of his under the aegis of HumanKind. I plodded back to my car, trying on different scenarios. It went like this: *Chad Sturgess takes a priceless bottle of wine out of his partner's cellar with the intention of a) settling his gambling debts, or b) buying a girl's freedom. Sturgess is jumped by muggers.* I visualized the taunting, the game of keep-away with Sturgess lunging this way and that after the prize until one of his tormentors cracked his skull with it. *When they work out the cork and find the wine tastes like vinegar they vent their frustration on the corpse.* But how had Chad run afoul of the punks in the first place? Hadn't he arranged his usual transport to the yacht? It didn't make sense unless Sturgess had been set up. Maybe that's where the priest came into it, wittingly or not.

Back at my hotel room, I drew the drapes against the blazing sun and tried to take a nap. But crime scene photos of Sturgess kept popping into my head, alongside postcard images of deeply-tanned, scantily-clad people riding bikes, jogging, and zooming around on jet-skis. After ten minutes I sat up and called Dickinson's number. "Got it solved yet?" she asked.

"I need to get out to a yacht in the harbor. You know the Calysta?"

"I've got a surveillance file two inches thick on it, but no case. We've never been able to come up with probable cause to go aboard."

"You got a number for the vessel?"

"You gotta be kidding."

"Thought I'd angle for an invitation to visit," I replied.

"I think you're crazy," she said, but she gave me the number.

"Say, you got Sturgess's phone records yet?"

"I'm working on it."

After that I called my assistant at our home office to get some information on La Familia, HumanKind and Mongolia. She told me the remaining bottles of Jefferson Bordeaux had roughly doubled in value since the one belonging to Frederick Church had been destroyed.

I didn't lie once I got the captain of the Calysta on the line. I told him straight up who I was and why I wanted to come out for a chat. He took my number at the Marriott and said he'd call back. When he did, he told me to be at the ferry pier at the foot of Broadway at 9:45. He advised against packing heat.

At quarter to I was waiting, as directed. The launch showed five minutes later. When we came alongside the Calysta, somebody on deck yelled something in Spanish and lowered a Jacob's ladder. The launch skipper translated. "He says I should pick you up in twenty minutes." I started climbing. The launch pulled out from under me and vanished leaving only a white arc of wake.

Once I heaved myself onto the deck a thug pointed an Ouzi at me while another one patted me down and relieved me of my cell phone and flask. "Standard procedure," he said. The discharge end of the weapon prodded me toward a hatch that opened into a salon with a curving bar of bird's eye walnut, black leather chairs and white Berber carpet. There were platinum records in frames, a bronze ballerina—undoubtedly a Degas—and a painting of sunflowers that looked a lot like a Van Gogh snatched from Amsterdam some years back. A tall, slender woman drifted toward me with two glasses of bubbles. She was delicate as a child with skin the color of caramel, dark heavy hair and eyes as black and shining as the road to perdition. Her curves, less pronounced than the arc of the bar, but a lot more interesting, were upholstered in black leather, same as the chairs. The yacht's owner had obviously had her decorated to match. She smiled. "I'm Jasmine." In spite of her name she smelled of gardenia. "This is a sparkling wine from Limoux in the south of France." Her little finger grazed the heel of my hand as she passed me the glass. "I'm quite partial to it." She raised her flute and sipped.

"What about Chad Sturgess? Were you partial to him?"

"He was a client. I did not know him well."

"I hear he'd fallen for you—hard. A priest told me Chad intended to take you away from all this." I pulled out the HumanKind business card and laid it on the bar. "Heard of these folks?" Before she could say, the boss showed up. She palmed the card as he came to greet me. He was a barrel-chested hulk with a grin like a picket fence in need of a coat of paint. "I am Ramon Vasquez."

"Also known as The Surgeon," I replied. According to underworld lore, Vasquez removed certain body parts from his victims and kept them in specimen jars. The surgeries were never performed post-mortem and there was no anesthetic involved.

"You want to speak to me about the murder of Mr. Sturgess," he said.

"The night he was murdered he was on his way over here with a very special bottle of wine, one insured for a considerable sum by the company I represent. Maybe he wanted to settle a gambling debt. How much was he into you for?"

Vasquez shrugged. "He owed me something on the order of four hundred thousand. If we suppose that he was coming to repay me, it makes no sense that I would kill him."

I did the arithmetic. Clearly Sturgess had planned to use the balance of what the bottle was worth to buy Jasmine. "Maybe you wanted to send a message to anyone who thinks he can welsh on a note," I said. I really didn't think that, because, brutal as it was, the Sturgess murder wasn't Vasquez's MO. Jasmine shifted her molten eyes to the bubbling surface of my flute, as close as she could come, perhaps, to begging me to shut up.

"In any case," Vasquez continued, "Sturgess never arrived here that night. I was greatly disappointed, like an ugly girl sitting at home on a Friday night." He fiddled with one of Jasmine's dangling earrings. She cringed like she expected him to tear it off and the ear with it. "Even if you suppose I dispatched Mr. Sturgess, you must know I would never have destroyed that particular bottle of wine. It was one of a case Thomas Jefferson bought in France when he was the American ambassador, a 1787 Château Lafite. Only four bottles of that case survive today. Now only three. Something like that is priceless to a collector, which, in case you hadn't noticed, I am. I would have preserved it at all cost."

"Unless it was a fake."

Vasquez smiled. "Surely your company verified its authenticity before insuring it for millions?"

"We did. The expert that verified Church's Jefferson bottle in 1998 was Christie's top appraiser. But he died a couple years back so we can't very well ask him now if he was sure. We can test the traces of wine left in the bottle to see if it's really over two hundred years old."

"Really?"

"Ever heard of that little bugaboo DNA? Yeast has pretty simple DNA to code, apparently. Geneticists have been playing around with yeasts for twenty years. It's easy to tell if a strain was around during the French Revolution. If it's a more modern strain, such as what's used to ferment wine today, my company will refuse to pay the insurance claim. We'll know soon whether that bottle was phony or not."

"I wish you well in your search for the truth." Vasquez glanced at this wrist. "And now I believe your launch is here to take you back to the city."

I gave Vasquez my card with my hotel phone number scrawled on the back. The guy with the Ouzi materialized at my elbow and prodded me out of the salon. My ride was waiting alongside the yacht, according to plan. Before I started down the ladder, the Calysta boys gave me back my cell phone but not my flask. Thirsty bastards. Maybe they were the guys who'd emptied the 1787 Château Lafite.

I got back to my hotel, got a beer out of the mini bar and drank it. Then I got another. I lay down and nodded off. Next thing I knew my phone was ringing. The clock showed a little after 3 AM.

I answered and heard a female voice, breathless. "It's Jasmine. I need your help."

"Where are you?"

"An apartment on Broadway. I came to meet Father Hernandez. He was going to take me somewhere safe. When I got here I found him dead."

I wrote the address on a slip of paper—2550 Broadway #24— threw on a windbreaker and grabbed the keys to the rental car. In no time I was at the intersection of Broadway and 25th where the barrio faces off with white middle-class suburbia, a mishmash of restored Victorians housing law offices cheek by jowl with taco joints, pawnbrokers, and Mexican markets.

It was a run-down square of flaking stucco that used to be a motel. The wind ripped at cascades of bougainvillea climbing the fence where a security gate was broken off its hinge. I dodged fast food leavings and beer cans as I rounded the corner of the building, listening for the footsteps of a tail under the canned laughter of late night TV coming through the flimsy doors of the apartments. At 24 light shone at the edges of the window curtain. I stood and listened at the door. I knocked. Jasmine opened up wide enough to see my face and then stood aside as I entered the living room. The priest was sprawled on the couch. One arm hung off the side. The sleeve was rolled up, showing needle tracks, and below his slack-fingered hand there was a syringe on the floor. I felt for a pulse though I already knew he was gone.

Jasmine stood with tears running down her face. "It's my fault. I'm so scared. I don't know where to go. If Ramon finds me he'll kill me."

I gripped her arms. "Forget Hernandez. Listen to me. Did you touch anything in here?"

She shook her head.

"Come on. I'll take you to my place."

In the car she shivered all the way back to the hotel. "Ramon's men got him," she said. "It's my fault. I should never have tried to get away. They're too powerful. They have their hooks in everyone."

"You'll be all right if we use our heads," I said. "Right now they don't know where you are. So you're safe." Heavy drops of rain pelted the windshield as I made the turn at the foot of Broadway. I remembered hearing something about weather moving in, the fringe of a hurricane off Baja. I parked near the elevator and stripped off my windbreaker. "Put this on." The big jacket and her oversized handbag made her look skinny as a wet cat. "In the elevator turn away from the security camera."

We made it into my room without running into anyone in the hall. I got her a towel. She wiped her face. Her lips left a red smear. Our eyes locked. She came into my arms and whispered, "I'm so cold."

"There's a robe on the back of the bathroom door. Wrap up and get a brandy from the mini bar. I'll be back in an hour, two max."

She looked stunned. "Where are you going?"

"To see the cops about the body. I'll say I was meeting Hernandez. I'll keep you out of it."

All the way back to that apartment, I imagined warming her up skin to skin. I parked and called 911 on my cell. A black and white rolled up. I took the cops to the body and floated the story I'd cooked up while I was waiting. "He told me to meet him here. I think he wanted to give me something on the Sturgess case. This is how I found him." One of the cops called Dickinson. She came with the ME. We stood around the doc like guests circling the bean dip at a dull party. "Looks like an OD," he said. "We'll know more once I get him on the slab."

Dickinson waltzed me toward the door for a private word. She yelled over the rain pounding on the tin awning over the entry. "How does Hernandez play into the Sturgess murder, apart from the fact that the body was found in his parish?"

"He knew more than just where the body was found. That's why he wanted to see me."

"Did you know he was a junkie?"

I remembered our meeting, the long-sleeved cassock. "I guess the tracks speak for themselves."

"So you buy the OD thing?"

"I didn't say that. I think somebody got to him and stuck him with a lethal dose so he wouldn't spill what he knew about who did Sturgess. That's all I know. I swear."

She gave me a look that could have peeled paint off a car. "I'll need a statement in the morning."

I told her to call me if any interesting trace evidence turned up and left before she could take another run at my story. I calculated the new day would dawn in a couple hours, not that there was any sign of light in the storm clouded sky. I was almost to the street when Dickinson called after me. "Wait a minute!" She trotted up and thrust a rain spattered envelope at me. "Those records you wanted."

I drove back to the hotel mentally unwrapping my bathrobe from the long, lithe form of Jasmine. I wanted to make her trust me with her sweet body and all its secrets. I wanted to hear every rotten detail of her life as a sex slave. I wanted her to cry in my arms. I wanted to save her.

As I came out of the elevator onto my floor the lights in the corridor began to flicker. I was ten paces from my door and had my plastic key in my hand when the power went out. Only ten paces from the girl, a nightcap and a good bed. I hated to wake her, but I had to get her to let me into my room. I knocked softly at first and called to her, so she'd know it was safe. She didn't answer. I knocked louder. I wondered if she'd taken a sleeping pill. As I started down the nineteen flights to the lobby my imagination went wild on the dark side. Maybe the goons from the Calysta had run her to ground. I burst out of the stair well and ran full tilt for the front desk. The chandeliers in the lobby flickered on. "The power's back?" I asked idiotically.

"No, that's our emergency generator," the desk clerk replied. "May I help you?"

"Thanks. I'm good." I ducked into the elevator and pressed nineteen, wishing what I'd said was true.

The girl was nowhere to be seen. My bathrobe hung on the back of the bathroom door just as I'd left it. The brandy in the mini bar was untouched.

My mind raced with dire possibilities: she'd been snatched as soon as I'd left her alone. I'd underestimated the Mexican mob all along, probably because I was a racist and didn't think they were as smart as white guys like me. Jasmine was going to pay the price. Stupidly, I kept looking around the room as if I might find her in the closet or under the bed. For a second, it seemed like I might have imagined the whole thing. Except that I was soaking wet because I'd given her my windbreaker. My windbreaker. It hit me that I hadn't seen it anywhere in the room. I looked around again to make sure it wasn't there. Neither was the towel I'd given her to dry her face. I remembered the lipstick stain. She'd taken with her any shred of evidence that would prove she'd been with me. It felt like she'd played me, but why?

I tore into the envelope Dickinson had given me. She'd printed out Sturgess's appointments for the four weeks prior to his murder. On both the day he was killed and fifteen days earlier he'd made the same entry: "Water taxi, 11:15P." Those were the dates he'd gone to the Calysta. I checked his cell phone records for those same dates starting a few minutes after 11:00. When he was onboard the ship two weeks before his death, there was a call of nine minutes duration to a number I had for Frederick Church at The Caves. Immediately after there was a five-minute call to the number on the priest's HumanKind business card. Since Sturgess would have been required to give up his phone when he boarded the Calysta, it meant someone else had made those calls on Chad's phone, someone who knew Sturgess would be coming back to the yacht in fifteen days, someone who wanted him killed for a bottle of wine.

I had the whole case figured out by the time I got to my car. I sped through the canyons between the tall buildings, following my headlights along streets black as a raven's eye, racing toward Jasmine, hoping I wasn't too late. In ten minutes I was parked outside The Caves. The electric mechanism that operated the gate at the delivery entrance had been switched over to manual operation because of the power failure. I heaved it open wide enough to slip inside. I followed the emergency floodlights to the winery and found myself in the deep shadows of the barrel room. Two hushed voices sounded unnaturally loud in the cavernous space where the noise of pumps and vent fans had fallen silent. I heard the words "wire transfer" and "off-shore account." "It's ready to execute," Church said, "but I can't send until the network comes back up." They were huddled at a counter cluttered with blending apparatus and a laptop.

I stepped into the light and walked toward them. "I wouldn't do that if I were you," I said.

Church looked up from the computer. "What are you doing here? What do you want?"

"Your gate was open, so I figured I'd drop in and let you know it's probably not a good idea to pay her off, even though she's kept her end of the bargain."

"What bargain?"

"Don't play the innocent. You're too ugly. It doesn't come across. I know you two were in it together from the start. It's all about collecting the insurance money on the Jefferson Bordeaux. What's her split? Thirty percent? Fifty? You're probably paying her out of a corporate account, right? What's the expense code for 'Murder'?"

"I don't know what you're talking about."

"I'll spell it out for you. Sturgess took the Lafite to cancel his gambling debts and buy Jasmine away from Ramon Vasquez. But Jasmine discussed a different angle with you. She offered to have Sturgess killed and the bottle destroyed in exchange for a piece of what you'll collect on the insurance."

Church bristled. "That's absurd!"

"I have the phone records to prove it. You got a call from Sturgess's cell phone fifteen days before Sturgess died. The call was placed from the Calysta while Sturgess was embarked for a gambling cruise. Only I happen to know cell phones are taken from passengers at the brow. Only a member of the crew would have had access to his phone at that time. Jasmine made the call." She looked daggers at me. I knew I'd hit the nail on the head. "It took care of two problems for you, Church. It got rid of a gambling addict who was spending you into the ground and it liberated cash locked up in a collector's bottle of wine so you'd have enough working capital to stay solvent until the urban winery started earning. You'd be the sole owner of a business with all the earmarks of a cash cow. And you were hedged away from all the risk. If things went sideways you could say it was all Jasmine's doing. Your hands were clean."

"How interesting." The fat man chuckled as if he'd never heard such a loony idea.

"It gets better," I said. "She used a priest named Hernandez as an unwitting accomplice. She called him with some hooey about how it wasn't safe for Sturgess to come aboard the Calysta that night. She asked Hernandez to waylay Sturgess before he got on the launch and tell him to go to another spot on the waterfront. She couldn't let that bottle of wine get to the yacht, you see." I looked at the girl. "This starting to sound familiar?"

"You can't prove any of it," she said.

"But it all fits. Hernandez was asking questions about why you'd had him short-stop Sturgess, wondering if it had anything to do with the murder. You offered to meet the priest at that dive on Broadway to explain it all, but you slipped a needle into his arm instead. So now you're almost home free. Only Church can still swear that the whole scam was your idea. Oh sure, you think since you have as much on him as he has on you, you're both safe. But he doesn't know about the DNA test, does he."

Church frowned at the girl. "DNA? What's he talking about?"

She shook her head. "He's just trying to make trouble."

"That may be," I said, "but before you effect that wire transfer into Jasmine's offshore bank account, you'd better consider that right now my company is studying the DNA of the yeast found in traces of wine on the murder weapon. For years there's been a lot of back and forth among wine experts about whether the so-called Jefferson bottles were genuine, but nobody was willing to destroy their investment to find out. The DNA will tell us how old that wine really is and if the age is less than a couple hundred years then the policy is fraudulent on its face and the company won't pay. As soon as I told your girlfriend here about that, she started making her move to collect her part of the dough."

"There is no test," Jasmine snapped. "He's bluffing."

"My home office will be open in an hour," I countered. "You can call and verify what I just said."

"We'll wait as long as it takes for the network to come online; not a second longer," she said.

I knew she'd pull a gun as soon as she felt Church's allegiance waiver. Even though I knew it, I hadn't yet figured out what to do about it. A big part of the calculus is whether or not you think the person with the gun will really use it. Another consideration is clear lines of fire, whether you can take cover before you catch a bullet. The biggest consideration, though, is whether you feel like it's one of those days when God is on your side or one of those days when the son of a bitch feels like fucking with you.

In the end, all it takes is just a twitch for all hell to break loose. But Church did more than that. He grabbed the laptop and threw it at her. I dove behind a barrel. She squeezed off a shot that hit a stave and threw splinters into my eyes. Church grabbed her gun hand and they wrestled. Another shot went off. My vision was still blurry, but I could see the two of them standing there, like dancers waiting for the music to resume after it had abruptly stopped. Then I saw her slide to the floor. Church was left on his feet. I took the gun away from him while he was still gawking at the red smear down the front of his cashmere sweater. "You saw it. It was self defense. I had to do something!"

"That's for the DA to decide." Somebody must have heard the shots and called the police. I could hear the sirens approaching.

"But you'll back me up."

"Sure, right after I explain how you arranged to have your partner killed."

"But I saved your life."

"Saving people is a risky business," I said. "Look where it got Sturgess and Hernandez." I could have added my name to the list. There was still a faint scent of gardenia on my clothes from that moment in the hotel when she'd let me take her in my arms. As soon as the cops were through with me I went to the nearest bar to see how much booze it would take to wash it away.

Our story for March takes place in San Diego in 2003, the year before the city's beloved but hapless Padres moved from Jack Murphy Stadium to their downtown home in Petco Park. The occasion is Major League Baseball's opening day. We join two long-time friends at the ballpark for the home opener. What ensues is a contemplation of how life imitates the pastoral game, even in the case of an unsolved murder.

# Feldman's Obsession

IT HAPPENED DURING the sixth inning of a sublime home opener as the Padres faced the Giants at the Murph. Per long-standing tradition, the Pads were scoreless, having left seven men stranded on base through the bottom of the fifth. The home team's starting pitcher had been pulled for James Slattery, a wily middle reliever who majored in English, causing batters to splinter the lumber and chop the ball, giving the infield plenty of opportunities to look like golden glovers. The fans got into the act, catching more than the usual quota of balls lofted into the stands. Like the rest of the faithful, Satchel Terry socked his fist into his mitt and waited for the next pitch. The count was three-two with two outs. As he shook off the sign, Jimmy Slats had them on the edge of their seats. Terry's happened to be on the left field line just above the visiting team's dugout and, as fate would have it, just beyond the edge of the net behind home plate. Slats let fly with a nasty sinker that the batter, a leftie named Mendoza, managed to take the other way into right field. Incredibly, the right-fielder muffed the ball and the Giants had a man on first. Next up was Romeo "The Kiss" Fortuna. He got his nickname from the paparazzi who made a lot of hay out of snaps of Romeo locking lips with fabulous blondes. Satch saw Jimmy's jaw tighten. "This is where it gets personal," he said to his pal, Dan Feldman. The pitcher glared in and let go a first pitch strike. He followed with a dying swan that had the batter swinging before it was half way to the catcher's mitt. "He'll waste one," Satchmo said as the pitcher went into his wind-up. These were the last words he ever spoke to Feldman.

On the next pitch, a ball low and away, The Kiss, a righty whose moniker would soon transmute into "The Kiss of Death," hit a rope-line foul down the left field line where it homed in on Feldman's right temple, clobbering his melon with sufficient force to knock him into next Tuesday. Feldman was carried off in an ambulance. Satch Terry, full of faith in modern medicine, stood in the waiting room of the hospital and watched the final moments of the game on the wall-mounted TV. Despite the brilliance of the San Diego battery in the last three innings, the Padres lost, having failed to score any runs, not a headline. The headline was this: Fortuna's Foul Fells Fan. Comatose at press time, Feldman lasted long enough on life support to let the brouhaha over ballpark safety die down before expiring, whereupon a snippet documenting his end appeared on the second page of the sports section to the right of that day's box score.

It fell to Satch Terry to see to his friend's funeral, settle his meager affairs and receive his worldly goods, several boxes of baseball memorabilia, clothes, and three file folders bulging with notes on two cases that stood like bookends at opposite ends of the deceased detective's dossier. Terry thumbed the cold case files that had haunted Feldman down to the day he was fatally beaned. It was unsettling, all that unfinished business. He worried that Feldman's soul might be wandering the ozone in agony because of Acosta and Heinz, the two names inscribed on the tabs of the manila file folders. Try as he might to avoid the thought, Terry concluded a true friend would try to put Feldman's spirit to rest. Fortunately, there was a cosmic loophole of sorts, a way that might allow Terry to avoid this obligation. Feldman was Jewish, and to the best of his knowledge, Jews didn't really believe in an afterlife. So how could Feldman's soul be in agony? This rationale provided Satch with enough peace of mind to shove the cardboard box with the files to the back of his coat closet. To be sure, he decided to consult a rabbi.

From the phone book Satch chose a rabbi named Solomon, feeling that if life was anything like baseball, there was something in a name. The rabbi turned out to be younger than Satch expected, with thick-lensed glasses that magnified his brown eyes and made him look even more like a fresh-faced child than his mere youth might suggest. But youth notwithstanding he seemed to know his stuff. "We consider that the soul of the departed will be at peace as soon as the body is properly buried according to our laws," he explained. "Time is of the essence. We believe that any delay of the burial is a humiliation of the dead." He dropped his eyes to his desk calendar. "Fortunately Passover doesn't start until April 16 this year, so there's ample time to see the deceased properly buried as a Jew before the holiday. Also the burial cannot take place on Shabbat; that's Saturday. Does Mr. Feldman have a plot?"

After all the business of the arrangements had been discussed (turns out there was a group called the Chevra Kaddisha that was specifically organized to assist with burial rites) Satch made out a check to secure a plot, a plain pine box and a shroud. The rabbi leaned back in his chair. "Now tell me about your friend Daniel. What manner of man was he? What were the milestones in his life? Did he have a wife, children?" He hastened to add, "It's for the eulogy."

For all the years he had spent as Feldman's partner on the force it seemed Satch knew precious little beyond a few basic facts. "Well, let's see. I think he was born in 1945. He was from some little town in Pennsylvania. Maybe had a year or so of college. I met him here when we were green detectives. We partnered for fifteen years. I never knew of a wife or kids. Then he moved up to Oregon, little town called Bradford. Worked as a detective up there till just last month when he retired. Came back down here because we like hanging around together and going to baseball games. Loved his baseball. Good fan. Good man."

The rabbi's eyebrows raised above the black frames of his glasses. "That's it?"

Indeed it was not, but Satch had chosen to omit the part about Feldman's scandal-tainted resignation from the SDPD, all that business with the Acosta case.

Apart from these suppressed and sordid details, there was still a significant part of Feldman below the surface, like the bulk of an iceberg. When Satch considered the underwater part of his friend's life, what he'd come to call Feldman's obsession, he felt less sanguine about whether his soul would ever rest in peace, the Jewish burial notwithstanding. In the days and weeks that followed Feldman's interment, the notion clarified in Satchmo's mind that it was incumbent upon him, Satchel Paige Terry, to do whatever he could to get to the bottom of both cases: Heinz and Acosta. Acosta and Heinz. He decided to tackle the Heinz case first, as its bulk came to roughly half of the mass of the Acosta documents. Having come to this decision, he put off actually opening up the Heinz file for two weeks before his guilty conscience finally drove him to it late one Thursday evening after the Diamondbacks defeated the Padres in a dismal dust-up made even worse by the empty seat next to his, the one Feldman should have occupied.

Back at his Hillcrest apartment, Satch got himself a beer and settled onto the couch. With a heavy feeling of dread, he spread open the file on the coffee table in front of his knees. He pawed through the crime scene photos showing the shattered chest of the corpse, the post mortem, the ballistics report, statements from everyone remotely connected to the production—the wardrobe mistress, prop builders, cast, running crew, director and other members of the company who had known Heinz personally. There was so much information, a cacophony of shock and grief poured out over the pages of the file, a haystack hiding the apocryphal needle.

He got through all of it and then started over again, this time organizing everything chronologically. The salient points scribbled on a pad amounted to these:

- ✍ *Heinz murder—27 Mar 2002, 1ˢᵗ night Passover during Rogue Rep performance of Trojan Women Hecuba costume (brooch) explodes. C4. FBI links murder to pro-Hezbollah Bradford resident/activist Salim Khoury (jailed last year $ laundering)*

- ✍ *Heinz mother Edith Heinzelman lost overboard (suicide? murder?) 15 Sep 2002, 1ˢᵗ day Yom Kippur—last seen on promenade deck Panamanian registered vessel Calavera Catrina at 10 pm (waters off Antigua)*

- ✍ *Feldman notes "Murders were timed to make it look like an Arab-Israeli thing, but it isn't. It's just murder."*

- ✍ *Any names in common between Troj Women audience and ship's manifest?*

- ✍ *Feldman note on inside front of file folder: "1980 Old Globe performance of Salesman, Woodson pipped by Heinz. Motive!"*

It was the last item on his list that gave Satch Terry hope that he might be able to dig up a lead. Doubtless it was the reason Feldman had come back to San Diego, wasn't it, love of his old friend and the old ballgame notwithstanding.

The next day Satch headed to Balboa Park to visit the Old Globe Theatre. He left the Capri in a little lot in a eucalyptus glade behind the botanical garden and made his way toward the Prado. After four on that early spring day the foot traffic was sparse; a few dog-walkers, a tour group of camera-toting Germans sussing out one more museum to visit by consulting their maps near a reflecting pool of water lilies. A security guard in a blue blazer and tie poked his head out from the door of the Art Museum and then retreated back into the dim, archival depths.

Satch had developed an affinity for the park during his years on the job. With its cool shadows and antique buildings, a haven from the brutal realities of law enforcement, it had become his place to walk and puzzle things through in his head. Most of the structures had been erected for the Panama-California Exposition of 1915. Even back then, it seems, San Diegans were determined to fight the image of their city as one defined only by its beaches and the Navy. So they hired a New York architect. He came up with long arched collonades, echoing the galleries of the monastery in Majorca where Junipero Serra had taken his vows before coming to the New World. Satch glanced up at the stone figures of armored heroes standing in niches and bare bosomed ladies holding up the eaves and wondered if Padre Serra would find anything about the place in keeping with the monastic life.

Between the Art Museum and the Museum of Man, the Old Globe complex occupied a sedate courtyard set back off the main drag. Given the feelings of the Elizabethans toward the Spanish, it was appropriate that the Tudor-style theater kept its distance from the Prado. He noted the rep season offerings on a sidewalk billboard, particularly the opening date, about three weeks away. In the run up to the premiers, the theater would belong to the technical crews coaching the actors on hitting their spots. He paused before the shuttered box office and considered his chances of getting anybody to talk about an incident from twenty-three years ago. His musing was interrupted by a rack of costumes trundling toward him without benefit of human guidance. He trotted out to meet the runaway wardrobe, just as its rightful owner bolted to the rescue. "You need chocks for this thing," Satch said, as he grabbed hold.

"Sorry?" She shook her corkscrew tresses to indicate she didn't get the flight-line lingo, in spite of her suede bomber jacket, a baby blue article that matched her fingernail polish. Satch couldn't decide whether it was more of an insult to cowhide or aviation. The rest of the package consisted of black stretch pants with lace-trimmed white anklets ending in gold lamé sneakers. But the clothes be damned. She was tall, lithe, and smooth as a conman's come-on with huge eyes in a face that struck him as Somali.

"Chocks—things you put under wheels to keep them from rolling." He smiled.

"Oh, yeah. Thanks so much for helping me. Don't know what I would have done if all the rags for *Shrew* got dumped into the flower bed." She grinned back.

"Happy to help," he replied. "Where were you headed before they escaped?"

"Just over there." She nodded toward the doors at the back of the Cassius Carter, an indoor alternative to the Elizabethan Stage.

He fingered a sleeve. "Beautiful work. You make any of these?"

She laughed. "Oh, no. I'm a wardrobe assistant, not a seamstress."

"And what does a wardrobe assistant do? Aside from the fifty yard dash."

"Oh, you know. We help with changes, make sure everything is clean and ready for performances, right costumes in the right dressing rooms—like that."

"So what's it like, working backstage? Lots of egos to contend with, I imagine."

She rolled her eyes. "Tell me about it. They need nannies, not dressers."

He assessed her age at about thirty, but thought he'd give his next question a shot anyway. "You ever hear of an actor named Woodson? Was in *Death of a Salesman* with Eddie Heinz in 1980?"

"Oh my God! We all heard about how Eddie Heinz died. So terrible."

"You ever work with him?"

"Once. He was here five or six years ago. Kind of a big deal since this is where he started. He had a birthday during the run. His mother gave a party for him in his dressing room. We all got treated to champagne and cake. I heard she does that every year wherever he's playing whether it's Moscow, Idaho or the real one."

"No kidding. So what about Woodson? Anybody around here who still knows what happened to him, where he is now?"

She shrugged. "I could ask around and call you. Do you have a card or something?"

He dug one out of his wallet and handed it to her. "Maybe I can buy you a drink after you get off work. There a gin mill you like around here?"

"How about Fifth and Hawthorne in about thirty minutes?"

She began to wheel the clothing back across the courtyard, but paused. "Oh, by the way, my name is Maude Jones."

"I'm Satch Terry. He watched her swaying caboose and found himself beginning to like gold lamé sneakers.

The bells in the tower at the Museum of Man chimed quarter to so he decided to mosey on over to Fifth and Hawthorne and wait for her there. One block west and four blocks south of the Laurel Street entrance to Balboa Park, Fifth and Hawthorne was easy to find. As he walked into the restaurant, a balding bartender stood halving then quartering limes behind a floral arrangement that consisted of ball-bat sized spears of red ginger and woody sprigs that resembled bed springs. There were only six stools at the bar. The two at the end were occupied by an elderly couple. Her makeup was valiantly applied to a face from which the features had faded over the years. He was florid and cherubic, making with the jokes. Finding they'd finished off a bottle of pinot gris, he ordered two glasses of champagne. Obviously planning on a taxi ride home, Satch thought, as he scoped out the dining area. Intimate and dimly lit, there were only about twenty-five covers. It had all the earmarks of one of those stylish places where the chef spent most of his effort decorating your plate with squiggles of balsamic drizzle. The walls were lined four rows deep with actors' headshots. He settled onto a barstool.

The bartender slapped a cocktail napkin on the polished granite by his elbow. "What can I get you?"

"Bombay Sapphire martini, shaken with two olives."

"You got it."

"So this is an actors' bar?"

"Sure. We got all the Old Globe regulars and other celebrities, too, going back thirty years. Carol Channing, Robert Goulet, Merv Griffin—they all come here."

"You ever heard of Michael Woodson?"

"Woodson's famous for two things," the barman replied. He stuck out his index finger. "The gig where he broke his leg and Eddie Heinz starred in the role of a lifetime." The middle finger joined the index. "And the gig where he had a walk-on in that show where Dick Shawn dropped dead. It was some sort of comedy revue at the UC San Diego Theater."

"Dick Shawn? Who's Dick Shawn?"

"A comic. He was in *The Producers*, the production with Zero Mostel and Gene Wilder."

"Oh yeah? So he was major league?"

The bartender waggled his hand in a so-so motion. "More a Dave Magadan than a Tony Gwynn. When he collapsed, people thought it was part of the act because he did physical comedy. Looked like a pratfall. There was a flap over how long it took to get an ambulance."

Confusion and delayed response, Satch mused. Good to keep in mind if you planned to stage a murder.

"As a kid Shawn was signed by the Chicago White Sox but he got drafted and had to go into the Army."

"That right." Satch mulled the intersection of baseball and theater with sip of his martini.

The barkeep craned his neck to see if the couple needed a refill on their champagne. "So you in here hoping to catch a glimpse of King Lear or Maggie the Cat?"

"I'm having a drink with a dresser."

"I take it you don't mean a piece of furniture."

Satch imagined the perfect comeback, the line he would have laid on Feldman if the two of them had been sitting there. *"No I mean a piece of—"* And Feldman would have cut in with, *"You eat with that mouth?"* Satch sighed and made nothing of the bartender's opening. Instead he said, "You have a picture of Woodson?"

The bartender pointed past Satchmo's left ear. "Right there by the door. That's Woodson. Second row down."

Satch turned his stool around and panned down along the doorjamb until he came to the one he thought the bartender was talking about. "Any idea if he's still around here?"

As the bartender shook his head in the negative, Maude Jones slid onto the stool next to Satch. She gave the bartender a dazzling smile. "Hey, Jimmy, have you seen a guy who looks like that handsome bailiff on *Night Court*?" She turned to Satch. "Oh, here you are!"

He grinned. "Nice to see you, too."

"You won't believe what I found for you," she said. "I should say 'who,' actually."

The barkeep slapped the obligatory napkin down in front of her. "The usual?"

"You know what I like."

"So?" Satch prompted, as soon as the bartender went to his work.

"Well, now," Maude said, "I think you should go first."

"What do you mean?"

"I mean I want to know the whole story before I spill. Once you get what you want you'll dash out of here and I'll never hear from you again."

Satch studied his drink, remembering Feldman's peculiar sense of obligation, the pained look on his face as he'd explained that even though the FBI and the state had chipped in their forensic experts and a bevy of blue-jacketed crime scene investigators, it was still his case, his to mull and to mourn in the hours past midnight. "Heinz was murdered during a performance of *The Trojan Women* on the first night of Passover," he began.

He went on to explain how Heinz had been a controversial choice to play Hecuba. Having built his reputation by wearing skirts and eye shadow and doing stand-up, there was a conspicuous lack of serious acting among his credits. There was the usual reaction of critics pro and con, those shocked at the latest assault on traditional theater by the Rogue Repertory's new Artistic Director and those ecstatic over his bold disregard of convention. That spring had been an unusually rocky one in the continuing saga of Israel vs. Palestine. With the jailing of Bradford philanthropist

Salim Khoury on charges of money laundering to fund Hezbollah, there was heightened sensitivity among the locals on both sides of the Settlements question. Many saw a clear anti-Israeli message in Heinz's death, as it had occurred on a Jewish holiday. It had been a cold and drizzly Tuesday at the end of March, early in the Rogue Rep season. Speculation was rife in the blogs that tuned in to theater doings that Eddie's murder was a surgical terrorist strike, an act so intimate and immediate as to be truly terrifying.

"I read about that staging," Maude said, "the all male cast. I remember thinking Euripides' famous indictment of war has been stirring up controversy since 415 BC. Eddie as Hecuba would have pleased the playwright to no end."

"The bomb went off when Heinz/Hecuba was on stage with the women of Troy. They're lamenting the death of Hecuba's grandson. The Greeks threw the child off the top of the city walls because they were afraid he'd grow up and whip some Greek ass as payback for Troy being sacked. On stage his little body is laid out on his father's shield. The Greek soldiers are digging a grave off-stage. Hecuba takes off her scarf and covers the child with it. Then she reaches for a piece of jewelry to place on the body, a big old silver brooch. Bang! Everybody in the theater thinks it's a gunshot. Nobody saw a muzzle flash, mind you. Still, all the witnesses say it's a shot." He paused, thinking of the irony of eye-witness testimony, so many eyes, all focused on one event—and all of them wrong.

"Crime scene showed up and found out it was a bomb. Heinz was blown up in front of an audience of two hundred people, most within ten yards. A dime-sized wad of C-4 stuck to the back of the brooch. Heinz detonated it when he opened the fastener."

Maude looked puzzled. "How does Woodson figure into it?"

Satch sighed. "I don't know. My partner originally worked the case. Never said how he put Woodson in the frame. All he left was a note about Woodson getting pipped by Heinz."

She wrinkled her brow. "Pipped?"

"It's an expression from baseball. This guy Wally Pipp was a first baseman with the Yankees. He sat out a game one day because he had a headache. Lou Gehrig took his spot. Pipp never started again."

"Oh, I get it. So Mike Woodson got pipped because he broke his leg and Eddie Heinz famously took his role in a landmark production and became a big star while Woodson faded into oblivion."

"Yeah. So it figures Woodson had a motive to kill Heinz. But there's some tie-in with the way the mother died, too. I haven't figured that part out yet."

"Heinz's mother? What happened to her?"

"Eddie's mother was on a Caribbean cruise and went overboard in waters off Antigua this past September 15, was never found and is presumed dead. It's officially classified as death through misadventure, possibly suicide."

"But you think it's murder?"

"My partner did. But the only conjecture the Feds care to make relates to how the Heinz and Heinzelman murders laid out on the 2002 calendar: the murder of the son on the first night of Passover, March 27 and the murder of the mother on the first day of Yom Kippur, the Day of Atonement, September 15. The whole wacky terrorist scenario. You ask me, the murderer did that on purpose to disguise the real nature of the crime."

"Smart," she said. "But that means Heinz was killed the day after his birthday, the day after there was a big party in his dressing room."

"You know Heinz's birthday?"

"Same as mine, it turns out. March 26. So there's a lot of people and hubbub. Woodson slips behind the rack where all the costumes are hanging and plants the explosive on the brooch. It's rigged to blow when Heinz yanks it off during his next and last performance. It wouldn't be hard with a party going on."

"Makes sense."

"Maybe Eddie's mother saw Woodson at the party, asked him if they'd met before because she thought he looked familiar, so he had to kill her, too—albeit six months later."

"Could be. We won't know unless we manage to get the truth out of him. So did you find anybody who knows what happened to him? Where he is now?"

"Well, maybe. There's a seamstress who knew Woodson pretty well. They were an item, it seems. She's retired now and lives in Golden Hill. She may know what happened to him.

"You got a name and a number?"

"She said she'd rather contact you. I spoke with her and gave her your info. She promised me she'd call you in a day or two."

They filled in some of the blanks in each other's resumes and ordered another round. After an hour or so, Satch rose to leave.

Maude wrote her number on the inside of a matchbook and passed it to him. "You can call me," she said, "and I hope you will."

He used his phone to take a picture of Woodson's headshot on his way out. Maude seemed really nice, but he had made it a rule long ago not to get involved with anyone who figured in a case he was working, however peripherally. It was a lesson learned at Feldman's expense, one that Satch would never forget.

That night he couldn't close his eyes and kept going back to the Heinz file, reviewing the details of the witness statements, looking for something he couldn't name. He finally fell asleep for a few hours and woke to the sun blazing at the edges of the drape pulled across the front window. Unshaven, tied loosely in his bathrobe and slouched across the couch, Satchmo looked like the aftermath of a three-day bender. The glare from the TV played across his slack features. A panel of four sports writers wrangled with each other about Kobe and LeBron against a background of intense blue spanned by the eye-shocking red ESPN logo.

The ringing of his cell phone jolted him out of the basketball narrative. He fumbled in the folds of his robe hoping he might have had the presence of mind to put it in the pocket. No dice. Four rings. He bounded off the couch and grabbed his jeans from the pile of clothes he'd cast off the night before. Five rings. *Shit.* He lunged toward the kitchen counter, under the vague impression that he'd dumped his wallet and keys there. No joy. Six rings. The ESPN boys broke into gales of raucous laughter that drew his eye to the tube. There it was, on top of the set next to the VCR remote. He grabbed it just as the seventh ring became history. "Hello?"

There was a momentary pause, as if confusion had set in on the other end of the line. "Is this Detective Terry?"

"Yeah. Who's this?"

"Deborah Raymond. Maude Jones gave me your name and number. Did you know you have a bullet hole in your front window?"

He moved the drape aside and looked out toward the street. A woman was sitting on the wall in front of the parked cars. She waved at him.

"It was there when I moved in."

"Nice neighborhood for a cop."

He hung up, unbolted his front door and poked his head out. "I'm retired," he said.

She dropped her phone into a large pink purse. Her blue-veined and crepe-skinned arms protruded from the sleeves of a ratty pink kimono worn over a tee shirt and jeans. She fingered the fringe of false pink hair that hung in a Dutch-boy bob about her heavily painted face. "You going to ask me in? I'm not as kooky as I look. Everyone who works around the theater develops a taste for make-up and costume, particularly those who never get to strut before the footlights. An actor off-stage looks about the same as the general public, but the stage hands and the scrim painters appear on the street as gaudy as flamingos."

He opened the door wider and stood aside. "Come in." He didn't know quite what to make of this punked-out doll and kept looking for a human trait that might suggest her nature. Her eyelids had green and silver tints that shifted chameleon-like to russet depending on the light. Her long, black pasted-on lashes and brows plucked out and redrawn as pencil-thin arches proved distracting as was the white foundation on her face, perhaps the rice make-up of a geisha.

She entered and plopped herself down on his couch. "I hear you're interested in Mike Woodson," she began.

Satch grabbed the remote and turned off the TV. "Maude said you might know where he is."

"I wish. He dumped me without a word and left town."

"When was this?"

"Last year around the beginning of September."

"Can you fill me in on his activities about six months earlier, around March?"

"Depends on how much cash you have in your wallet. The bum means nothing to me anymore. I'll tell you whatever you want to know, but not for free."

He didn't have to check to know he didn't have enough to buy a vowel. "There's an ATM two blocks away up on El Cajon. You wait here. I'll be back with the cash. How much?"

She looked appraisingly at his ratty furnishings, gauging the market. "Two hundred."

He pulled on a pair of sweats and a hoodie and was back with her fee in fifteen minutes. "Let's start at the beginning," he said.

She raised an index finger to signal a pause as she counted the twenties. Satisfied, she squared up the bills, shoved them into her pink bag and pulled out a pack of Winstons and a lighter. "You mind?"

"Not if it'll help you remember," Satch said.

"Okay, so we're talking twenty-some years ago," she said, squinting against the smoke as she lit up. "We're all pals, Mike, Eddie and me."

"So Heinz and Woodson got along?"

"Oh, sure. Even after Mike broke his leg and Eddie got his big break legging it through the role he'd understudied for Mike. It was toward the end of the run. There was a Hollywood type in the audience who needed to cast someone just like Eddie in his next blockbuster. Voilà—another Cinderella is born." She pulled the cigarette out of her mouth. "You got an ashtray?"

He gave her a saucer and she tapped an inch of ash off the end of her smoke. "It wasn't till later that Mike started to resent Eddie's good luck. See, he was always a good actor, but he got work based mostly on his looks. Once his hair started to thin and he got a gut he didn't work much. He went into the insurance and investment business. Got cozy with lots of little old ladies and insured them right out of their investments. But he never had a dime come time to pay the rent. I should have figured him for stashing the loot in an offshore account, but I was in love with him. Stupid comes with the territory. Meanwhile Heinz gets bigger and bigger. I don't know when the switch came over, but Mike starts talking about taking him down. You know, comeuppance, something really theatrical. He started planning, found out where Heinz was going to be working next, looked at the running crews, trying to find somebody he knew, someone he could talk to about the props and costumes, things that can be rigged."

"Didn't anybody think that was odd?"

She shrugged. "Who knows. Maybe he put it across like it was going to be a joke in a tech rehearsal or something. But then he got in touch with this guy he knew from his navy days. Mike was a sailor before he started acting, you know. This friend of his was in some job that involved explosives." She winked and nodded. "So that's the name of that tune."

"So he got a device that would work on a piece of costume jewelry that he knew was constructed in such a way. And he planted the explosive on the costume at Heinz's birthday party. Does that sound feasible?"

She gave him a dismissive wave of her hand. "Easiest thing in the world. So about the third week in March, Mike takes off on a driving trip, a few days of golf in Palm Desert, so he says. Comes home the day after Heinz is killed. Comes back without any tan, mind you."

"When did he leave town for good?"

"Beginning of last September. Left me his dead car in the driveway. I think he took care of separating one last widow from her cash and then went to join his bank account in some Caribbean country where there's no extradition to the US."

"You think that last widow was Edith Heinzelman?"

"I'd never bet against it. It would suit Mike down to the ground to live off what would have been Eddie's cash if he'd survived to inherit."

After the seamstress left, Satchmo sat on the couch and pondered what he'd bought with his two hundred. He got up and drove to the cemetery and stood on the fringe of a patch of fresh sod and confided to Feldman that the Heinz case had laid out just as Feldman had predicted. "I don't know how you knew it was Woodson," he said, "but you were right and everybody else with their terrorist bullshit, they were all wrong." With his thumb and index finger he framed an inch of air. "You got this close."

That night at the Murph as the sky turned lavender and the stadium lights came on, the batter stepped out of the box to kick the dirt and adjust his gloves. Satch looked for the evening star, thought about how it was a game of inches, and wondered if Feldman knew—or was it like that time he missed seeing a triple play because he'd left the seats to buy a hot dog?

Our story for April is set in the eco-conscious theater town of Bradford, Oregon where beloved boulevardier Red Baxter has died. The celebration of his life, held on Earth Day, unites members of his fiancée's family, many of Red's old friends, an unruly dog, and at least one murderer.

# A Naked Man Has No Pockets

RED BAXTER WAS smart, not one to show off what he had on the ball, but pretty much on the money when he did open his mouth. Nice, too, once you got past his crust. He drove an old red pick-up with a guitar in the front seat. He wore pearl-buttoned cowboy shirts, cut a little too slim for his paunch and faded to that pale color cotton gets when you've worn the daylights out of it. His straight, shoulder length hair was steel gray, with mustache to match. His eyes were green, and sloped down at the outside corners. They had a toper's look to them. He was one of those guys who could fix anything and got by doing odd jobs. People here hired him to change the batteries in smoke detectors, repair appliances, and get stains out of carpets. "Here" is The Manor, 'assisted living without leaving home,' as it says in the flyer. That means they hang lots of pictures of puppies and pastel landscapes in the hallways and talk to you as if you were a four-year-old who got separated from Mom at the grocery store. Don't get me started. Anyway, that's how I came to know him. He was always around, especially at meal times. People used to fight to have him sit at their table because he could entertain like a Vegas stand-up. All the women were sweet on him, even after he got engaged to Marjorie Maynard.

You can imagine the pall that settled over this place when we got the news that he'd died. That morning Herb, Phyllis, Dot and I met in the game room for coffee, same as always. Phyllis brings her copy of the Bradford paper. She used to teach third grade and likes to read aloud, and since it saves the rest of us buying our own copies, we sit there and listen.

Phyllis puts on her Walter Cronkite voice and reads every word. But this time, when she realized who'd been found dead, she stopped and took off her glasses and passed the paper around so we could read the article for ourselves.

**Bradford Man Found Dead by Janice Springer, staff writer.**

CHARLES BAXTER, 58, known to friends as 'Red,' was found dead in the basement of his home at 3535 Precipice Street in Bradford on Wednesday. Friend of the family Taylor Chambers stated Josephine Maynard, daughter of Mrs. Marjorie Maynard, landlady of the deceased, discovered Baxter's body some time after two o'clock on Wednesday afternoon. Bradford police stated Baxter appeared to have had an accident involving exercise equipment that was set up in the basement. The death occurred in the early morning hours. Pending completion of a toxicology report, the Jackson County Medical Examiner has pronounced a preliminary finding of accidental asphyxiation as the cause of death. Baxter was an interpretative dancer, poet, guitar player, and busker well known to residents who frequent Lithia Park and the bricks. Baxter had moved to Bradford from the Boulder, Colorado area in March of 2001 to audition for the Rogue Repertory Theater. He was engaged to be married to Marjorie Maynard.

After I passed the paper on to Dot I couldn't help thinking about Red and Marjorie, how I'd been shocked when I heard about their engagement. I harbored a secret wish that it might have been me he fell for, and if not me, then a much younger and more attractive woman. But Marjorie was neither of these. Some of my more cynical companions whispered that Red was after her money. It was a notion not easily dismissed.

A Baptist minister's daughter turned party girl, Marjorie had married a minor beat poet who turned out to be the heir to the Bloomburg fortune. Alan Bloomburg was an electrical engineer

from Cleveland who invented fiberglass-reinforced plastic
on a hotplate in his garage during World War II. He collected
a lot of patents, died childless and unmarried, and bequeathed
his considerable bank account to John Maynard, his distant
cousin. John married Marjorie, many years his junior, and died
shortly after.

But I couldn't hold her fortune against Marjorie. There was
something about her bracelet-ringed chicken bone of wrist and
the delta of veins on the back of her large-gesturing hand that
spoke of valiant striving against age and oblivion, a striving we
have in common. The first time I met her, I liked her right away.
Red had brought her to a New Year's Eve party at The Manor.
I'd been in residence barely a week. She was the first person I got
to talking to. When she asked how I liked Bradford, she reached
over and touched my arm, as if I might need reassurance before
hazarding an opinion. It seemed like a gesture of such genuine
concern that I was nonplussed when ten minutes later she asked
me the same question in exactly the same words and with the same
motherly touch.

"We should do something," Dot said when she'd finished
reading. "Flowers, perhaps?"

"Today most families appreciate a contribution to the
deceased's favorite charity in lieu of flowers," Phyllis said, in her
reading aloud voice.

"When is the funeral?" Herb asked.

"It doesn't say." Phyllis scowled at the column of print again
to make sure.

"A card, then," Dot said. "Have everybody sign it."

"A big card," Herb said. He's a retired accountant and takes
a practical point of view.

Dot's face broke into a huge grin. "It will be the biggest
card you ever saw!" Dot is an artsy-craftsy type who enjoys

scissors and paste. By the time she was done, the "card", a sheet of poster board festooned with keepsakes and photos of Red, was crowded with expressions of love and sympathy from over sixty residents. Dot, Herb, Phyllis and I were appointed to take it to Marjorie Maynard's house. So, on an early spring day when the air was needled with freezing fog, we paid a visit to the grieving lady.

3535 Precipice Street is one of the grand houses perched above the clouds on the flank of Mt. Bradford. Herb's old VW made slow progress getting around the hairpin turns going uphill, but once we were there, the view was worth it. We spent a few minutes gazing down at the mist-mantled town in the valley, picking out the theater, the high school and the plaza, before we climbed the front steps of the house and Herb rapped on the door.

After a bit, the deadbolt disengaged. Marjorie Maynard's face appeared in the few inches between the door and the jamb. As soon as she saw the card she threw the door open wide. "You must be friends of Red's. Please, come in." We stood in the foyer as our hostess peered at inscriptions and faces in the snapshots. "Tell the mayor and the city council I appreciate it."

"No," Phyllis said, "it's from his friends at The *Manor*—where he used to do odd jobs?"

I was taking in Marjorie's seedy bathrobe and worn slippers, wondering why the rags. The beast caught me by surprise. Suddenly face to face with a snarling giant who had his front paws planted on my shoulders, I didn't dare flinch.

"Clancy!" Marjorie grabbed his collar and hauled him off me. "Didn't we agree there'd be no more jumping on guests?" My hostess turned to reassure me. "He's just so excited to see people. Please excuse me for a minute. I'm going to put him in the pantry."

Normally I would have told her not to bother, that I love dogs. But Clancy was a canine on the order of the hound of the Baskervilles. I just stood there and tried to catch my breath till Marjorie reappeared to issue the all clear. "Red said he'd settle down as he got older but so far he hasn't, not one bit. Won't you stay for a cup of tea?"

We followed her through the black and white tiled entry hall into a large living room with three sets of French doors opening onto a large deck. It had the feel of a hotel lobby. The small tables and occasional chairs stood silent and expectant, waiting for somebody to tell a joke. Marjorie led us to a green marble bar that separated the kitchen from the living room. The four of us settled onto barstools while Marjorie filled a kettle with water for tea and opened up a bag of chocolate chip cookies. "It's so kind of you to pay me a visit," she said. "It's been too quiet around here. I've been considering renting out the downstairs apartment again. That's how I met Red, you know." Marjorie raised her hand and mimed four lines of copy. "Furnished one-bedroom basement apartment, kitchenette, no smoking, $550 a month, utilities included."

"Cheap," Herb said.

"Some folks don't like living in a basement, so you can't charge as much," Phyllis said.

"Red said he loved it. Said he wanted to be well grounded." Tears sprang to Marjorie's eyes. "What a wonderful sense of humor."

The kettle whistled and Marjorie got up to rinse the pot. "We were planning to be married this June," she continued, as she made the tea. "A short engagement. *Too short*, according to Joey. But Red and I spent every moment together from the first day. Plays, lectures, nature walks, gardening, cooking... making love." She cleared her throat. "And always we talked. Red wanted to know what I thought about everything. Wouldn't let me get by with saying something like 'it was a good play,' or 'I liked the performance.' He wanted to know in what way it was good and exactly what I liked about the acting."

She described her relationship with such fervor I felt envious. But I inferred all was not sweetness and light. "Who is Joey?"

She rolled her eyes. "My daughter. I suppose I shouldn't complain. She's only doing what she thinks best. But, she has me on a budget and monitors my credit card bills like a hawk. That's why the apartment. I insisted on getting the rent in cash and when she asked me about it I told her it was none of her business. Bugged the hell out of her. Crazy to let a stranger live in the house, blah, blah, blah—but she couldn't do anything about it. When I told her I was marrying the tenant, my God! You can imagine!"

"She didn't like Red?" Herb asked.

"Joey doesn't have much use for men in general, if you know what I mean." Marjorie twitched her nose. "But worse than that, she's a snob. Took one look at Red's smashed up cowboy hat and his country music CD's and decided he was a hick and a gold-digger. Pure poppycock. Red said I should set up an irrevocable trust so Joey could relax about her inheritance." She pulled a Kleenex out of her pocket and blew her nose. "He was such a good man. I don't have to tell you that, as many hours as he volunteered with the council."

Dot side-stepped Marjorie's confusion about our association with Red. "So how did it happen?"

"The police are calling it accidental asphyxiation, but I know Red would never have done what they say he did." She clamped her eyes shut and shook her head. "A hood—and a cable around his neck—it's unthinkable. I've told that horrible Lt. Warren a million times, but he won't believe me."

We eyeballed each other, exchanged discreet shrugs. Nobody dared probe for specifics. We drank our tea and ate our cookies and left as soon as politely possible. When we got back to The Manor I paid a call on one of my fellow residents, George LaMontagne. George isn't nearly as interesting as his name, but besides working part-time as consultant in his son's home security business, he's a retired cop—tuned in to the jungle drums of law enforcement. As soon as I asked what was meant by accidental asphyxiation he cocked his head to one side and said, "Oh, you're curious about the Red Baxter case."

"Case?"

"Also called autoerotic asphyxia. Has to do with oxygen deprivation," he said. "Some people claim it heightens sensation during orgasm. So they throttle themselves while in the act, so to speak. You see all kinds of elaborate strangulation devices, but they all have one thing in common—an escape mechanism. Trick is to release the throat ligature before you actually kill yourself. Plenty of teen suicides aren't at all—just a way to spare the family embarrassment. Corpse gets taken down and dressed, scene gets cleaned up of sex toys and porn before the cops arrive and you get a story about how the kid had been depressed when really he was just beating off while hanging from a beam in the garage and forgot to release himself or the chair he was standing on tipped over."

George was a cold fish, but I couldn't fault his information. When I checked online, I came up with plenty of graphic examples of exactly what he described. The first entry I clicked on featured a grainy black and white photo of a balding man suspended from a floor joist by a noose around his neck. His hairy, tattooed forearms dangled from the frilly sleeves of a wedding gown. I pushed the back button and selected the next site with a sick feeling in my stomach. There were lots of variations on the nude and hog-tied theme, all with grim descriptors of ecstasy gone wrong. The last picture I viewed was a naked man in a black hood trussed up like a Christmas turkey and suspended from the ceiling. There was a vacuum cleaner hose wound around him. I didn't need to read the caption to figure out why. I clicked off wondering if I'd ever get the ghastly image of the guy making whoopee with the Hoover out of my head.

I found the truth about incidents of 'accidental asphyxia' highly disturbing, but worse was the idea that Red must have been a victim of his own sexual fetishes. He just didn't seem like the type to die in some contraption involving black leather, cables and cuffs like the wretched creatures whose pathetic ends were plastered all over the Internet.

A couple of weeks passed and the weather got milder. I confess that I put the whole matter out of my mind until we saw the notice about the funeral. Phyllis had just finished reading an article about how the town's white marble statue of Honest Abe located near city hall had been vandalized for the second time. There was a picture showing a child's Hello Kitty ball atop the truncated neck where the sage head should have been. She prefaced the next piece with a sour, "Give me a break."

"What is it?" Herb asked.

"It's about Red Baxter's funeral." Phyllis read the announcement. "Marjorie Maynard, fiancée of the late Red Baxter, has announced a digging-in ceremony for the popular Bradford entertainer in conjunction with a variety of hands-on Earth Day events highlighting gardening and recycling. Red's friends are invited to participate in the happening." She read the address.

"That's Marjorie Maynard's house," Herb said.

"Hands-on events," Phyllis muttered. "The whole thing sounds very odd."

"We should call," I said.

Earth Day isn't an occasion that ever registered on my radar before I came to Bradford, but I learned, as I settled into my new community, that here in the Rogue River Valley it's a bona fide big deal. Last year a coalition of commercial and public entities sponsored zero waste stations, organic farming seminars, exhibits touting biodegradable utensils and alternatives to plastic water bottles, composting labs, demonstrations of humane ways to keep deer out of your garden, a sign-up campaign for a petition to ban GMO adulterated food, a bike swap and a clunker clean-up site for disposal of old cars. Little children dressed up as endangered species. Scions of local Native American tribes caught and cooked up local salmon. The resident poets and writers staged readings of their conservation-themed works. After I spoke with Marjorie, I found out exactly what she was planning to add to this year's festivities.

Dot raised an eyebrow. "She wants us to spade up her garden and clean out her basement?" She looked at Phyllis. "Am I the only one who thinks that takes a lot of nerve?"

"She mainly needs help getting the apartment ready to rent," I said. "It won't be much fun, but if you think of all the times Red helped us ..."

In the end, the only one I could shame into going with me was Herb. On that cold and damp Thursday, the two of us showed up at the house on Precipice Street in blue jeans and rolled-up sleeves under our rain gear. We joined a milling mob on the soggy lawn at the side of the house. Everyone was crowded around a blanket ringed with azaleas in nursery pots. In the middle of the blanket was a Buddha-like figure sitting in the lotus position before an urn that I presumed was filled with the earthly remains of Red Baxter.

She was dark, round and wore Indian clothes. On her palms were symbols painted in henna. Her huge eyes were outlined in black. She began to sway and chant.

The stranger to my right leaned toward me and whispered. "Isn't Sharmae Ananda wonderful? Such grace—like a Cambodian dancer. She has a way of communicating, planting ideas in your subconscious. Weeks later you wake up in the middle of the night with a phrase in your head. You think, yes, that speaks to me, and wonder for hours where you heard it. Then you realize it's her. Very powerful. Very spiritual. Know what I mean?"

Sharmae Ananda put her index finger into her mouth and held it up to the breeze in the back yard. Herb and I exchanged dubious glances at each other and then looked back at the heavily jeweled sausage pointing up to heaven. A breeze rippled the orange silk draped over her head. Its gold border lifted away slightly from the dark brown hair that lay marcelled close to her scalp. We waited, as if she might announce the second coming. "Ah, yes," Sharmae said with the precise consonants of Mumbai, "definitely there is a storm approaching." Her finger ticked back and forth a few times like a metronome. "Do not worry! We must turn our faces to the rain and let it wash away our tears. Why do we hide from the drops of water falling from the sky? Would we not welcome the cleansing water from heaven if not for our clouded perception?"

That and common sense, I thought.

"We will stay here in this position until the spirit ascends," Sharmae said. She fixed her eyes on the clay urn in front of her. "We will summon the spirit with chanting. There will be a green aura forming in the air here. It will surround all of us, being taken inside us with our inhaling and being brought out again until it is visible no more. When the green glow disappears, we may be sure the soul has migrated into its next form. Then we may bury the ashes."

I eyed the flowering ornamentals in their plastic nursery pots along with a bunch of shovels and trowels and deduced that each azalea would be planted with a handful of Red in lieu of bone meal. I gave Herb an elbow. "Let's see what's going on in the basement," I suggested.

Around the corner from the lawn where Red was ascending was a covered concrete patio with a trash can, some recycling bins and a bike. A sliding glass door admitted us to Red's apartment. It had that depressing smell of wet cement that sticks to most basements despite all efforts to remodel it away. The main room was proportioned like a bowling alley: fireplace with flat screen TV at the far end, couch along one wall opposite desk and bookcase, all fairly typical except for the eight-hundred pound gorilla sitting directly in front of the slider. It was a maze of white enameled frames, benches, stacks of rectangular weights and cables. Herb looked at the universal and then at me. "And she's worried about getting rid of books?"

We found some cardboard cartons waiting to be packed and got busy. I took the bookcase and Herb took the desk. "Nice computer," Herb said, regarding the new-looking laptop on the desk blotter. "Wonder if Marjorie would like to sell it."

"I'll bet she would if you offer cash," I replied. "She likes cash, remember?"

I was taping my fist box shut when Herb scrabbled a wadded page from the back of the middle desk drawer. "What is it?" I asked.

"A statement. Some kind of investment fund. Marjorie's been taking a bath."

"Like a lot of other people," I said.

"She sold a big chunk of AXP in June of last year." He pushed his glasses up on his forehead. "Funny," he said. "I don't remember the share price being that low at the time."

I took a look at the statement and saw a lot of minus signs in front of numbers big enough to provide an annual income for an average family of four. I was about to ask what he meant by AXP when Marjorie herself came bustling down the steps from upstairs. "Hello, everyone," she said, with an over-medicated lightness. There were paint cards in her hands. "I need your opinion on what color I should use down here. I feel like I need to lighten it up a bit, don't you?" She taped a few paint cards on the wall near the slider and stood back to consider them. "What do you think?" she asked me.

"I don't care much for the robin's egg blue," I said honestly. "Not unless you mean to replace the rug with something more neutral."

She focused bloodshot eyes on me. "But Red picked this rug out himself. I couldn't possibly get rid of it."

I should have guessed. The rug was richly, unapologetically red—several shades of crimson worked in a floral pattern. Marjorie left the paint cards and went to sit on the couch. "Maybe I should leave it all just exactly as it is," she said. A minute later she dropped her face into her hands and began to sob. Herb sprang up from behind the desk and rushed to put an arm around her. I tried to look less guilty than I felt, since I'd brought on the meltdown. A gray-goateed patrician in a blue blazer and khakis with a crease you could have used to slice salami loped down the stairs. "Oh here you are," he said, as he joined us. "Marjorie, Joey found a buyer—" He stopped short when he beheld her distress and instantly went to her side—the one not occupied by Herb. "Marjorie? What's the matter? It's Taylor. I'm right here."

Only then did I notice that Marjorie had something clutched in her hand. "It's Red's lucky nickel," she said. She held it out on her palm so we could all see. "It's an Indian head, painted red on the side that's tails. Red always carried it in his pocket. At night he laid it on his bedside table along with his watch and his glasses. He never would tell me exactly why he thought it was so special, just that it was a lucky piece. I was wondering what had become of it. It must have been under the couch all the time. Camouflaged. No one ever noticed it."

She looked from Herb to the other guy. "Don't you see? It means somebody undressed him out here and killed him and made it look like—an accident." She searched our faces for understanding but found none. "He always undressed in the bedroom, not out here on the couch." She nodded toward the door to the adjoining room. "All his clothes were in there."

After a few seconds of adding two and two I saw what she was driving at. Red was found naked hooked up to his erotic aid, so how had the nickel wound up under the couch? "A naked man has no pockets," I said.

"Exactly." She sighed heavily. "At night when he undressed he always left his clothes on the chair next to the bed. In the morning he came out and did his exercises, showered and then dressed. There's no way his nickel could have fallen on the rug unless it fell out of his pocket when someone else took his pants off."

"You should call the police," I said.

The dapper guy with the goatee noticed me for the first time. "And you are?"

Marjorie pulled herself together enough to make introductions. "This is my tax man and very dear old friend, Taylor Chambers. Taylor, these are friends of Red's from the city council."

"From The Manor, where Red used to work," I corrected.

About this time I saw a pair of black high-tops clumping down the steps. The figure that appeared was female, though the clothes and cropped hair were distinctly masculine. "Mother," she said, "Katarina Grossman from the gym is here to pick up the universal. She—"

Sounds of mayhem erupted outside. Chambers jumped up. "Who let Clancy out?" We all followed him to peer through the slider out into the yard.

Hackles raised and teeth bared, Clancy stood snarling and barking at a black lab holding the high ground on a pile of humus. I held my breath. The mulch was about to hit the fan. Clancy flew at the black dog with a furious bound. The two dogs crashed together in a canine train-wreck. The lab yelped and cowered under the wolfhound, but before he suffered any serious damage, Clancy cut short his attack as if an invisible hand had yanked an invisible leash. We watched in amazement as Clancy headed straight up the drive to where a slight, blond woman was getting out of a white van with 'Oak Street Gym' lettered on the side. Joey ran out of the house with an actual leash in hand, snapped it onto Clancy's collar and dragged him back inside.

"You should have told people not to bring dogs," Joey said to her mother after stowing Clancy in the bedroom. Her tone was more than impatient, almost cruel.

Taylor tried to lighten things up. "No harm, no foul," he said. "Why don't you take your mother upstairs and get her a cup of tea."

"Why don't you mind your own business," Joey snapped.

Herb and I stood there like a fifth and a sixth wheel up to our hubcaps in family conflict. "We should probably be going," I said.

"The desk drawers are empty," Herb told Chambers. "It's all in that box there." He motioned toward a carton on the floor. Not entirely true. That crumpled financial statement that he'd been intrigued about was nowhere to be seen.

That night I couldn't get the events of Red's funeral off my mind. Joey's unkindness, the crazy dog fight, Marjorie's fixation on the red nickel, the odd financial statement. God what a circus. I kept thinking of a bit of dialog long after I'd gone to bed. A subliminal suggestion from Sharmae Ananda? Hardly. I got out of bed to search my bookcase for *The Original Illustrated Sherlock Holmes*, all thirty-seven stories that had appeared in *The Strand Magazine* along with Sidney Paget's illustrations. I flipped through looking for one story in particular, and when I found it, read the famous lines over with great satisfaction.

The Inspector at the crime scene asks Holmes, "Is there any other point to which you would wish to draw my attention?"

Holmes: "To the curious incident of the dog in the night-time."

Inspector: "The dog did nothing in the night-time."

Holmes: "That was the curious incident."

The next morning I Googled the woman who had come to Marjorie Maynard's house to pick up the universal. The name Katarina Grossmann produced a bunch of hits, one on an S&M dating site called 'Beat Me Daddy Eight to the Bar.' I verified from the photo of her impish face, that Katarina was the woman who'd arrived at Marjorie's in the white van. I also found that Katarina had once been an Olympic hopeful. Subsequent years had not been kind.

An article from a Florida paper dated June of 1998 showed Grossmann being led by cops out of a Piggly Wiggly where she'd been caught shoplifting. Police confiscated items worth approximately $29: mixed nuts, biscuits, strawberry jam and vodka. Grossmann claimed she was on her way to the checkout, but had seen a child outside about to rush into traffic.

The article went on to detail Grossmann's disastrous career since being disqualified from the US Olympic team in 1980. Her teenage son OD'd in 1996, following Grossmann's bitter divorce from her Mexican-born husband Felipe Guerrero. In 1997 Grossmann was arrested for DUI. The same year she resigned her coaching position at a sports center in Jacksonville when faced with a wrongful death suit brought by the parents of Jaycee Ridgeway, 13, one of Grossmann's gymnastics pupils. The Ridgeway suit had been dismissed.

I printed the article and went down to breakfast hoping I'd see George LaMontagne. When I found him I sat down at his table and showed him what I'd found out about Katarina Grossmann. "Think she's been involved in anything shady since she's been in Bradford?"

He folded the sheet and stuck it into his pocket. "I'll see if I can find any dirt. Why?"

I explained all about the funeral, how Grossmann had shown up, the red nickel business. "Marjorie is convinced it's proof that Red's death was no accident."

"Sounds about like Marjorie Maynard," he said dismissively. "Crazy old dame. She's been burning up the line to the police ever since she moved to town. High on some kind of medication half the time. Mostly complains about the guy next door, some retired academic by the name of Lloyd Hatch. Says Hatch has had it in for her ever since she bought her place—beat him out with a better offer. Says he's been harassing her ever since."

"Has he?"

"Hatch filed a complaint about indecent exposure once," George replied. "Apparently Red liked to exercise in the nude around daybreak. Trouble is, he did it with his drapes open so he could see the sunrise. Lloyd Hatch said when his little granddaughters came to visit they'd be up roaming around at the crack of dawn. They could look across the yard and see more of Red than he wanted them to."

"What did the police do?"

George shrugged. "Not much. Told Hatch to supervise his grandchildren. So then Hatch started complaining to the city about Red's truck. Rattletrap old thing. Red parked it on the street.

Hatch claimed the truck was a public nuisance because it leaked oil that eventually ran down into the storm drain. Said it was an environmental hazard to the watershed."

"Sounds like he might have had a point," I said.

"Yeah, but while the cops were still looking into it, the truck rolled right through the barrier at the end of the street and piled into a tree. Marjorie Maynard claimed Hatch had tampered with the brakes. The cops found no evidence of mischief. They thought Baxter had just forgotten to put the emergency brake on. Anyway, that was the state of things when Red died." He shook his head. "Consensus is the old broad has a screw loose."

"And if you were interested in getting hold of her money that would work in your favor," I said, "the fact that the local cops would never believe anything she said."

"Well sure." He eyed me narrowly. "You mean you think somebody murdered Red Baxter because he and Marjorie were going to marry?"

"If you're Marjorie's only daughter that would put a monkey wrench in your inheritance plans, wouldn't it—especially since Red was considerably younger than Marjorie. He'd still be living on her fortune ten years after she was gone."

"There's your motive," George said. "Now all you need is evidence of foul play."

"I'd give anything to have been a fly on the basement wall the night he died," I replied.

"Too bad Red didn't have a night vision security camera installed," George said. He started to laugh but stopped short when he caught sight of my face. "What? What is it?" he asked.

"You son's company handle stuff like that?"

"Sure. We got the cameras, the PCI cards ..."

"What's a PCI card?"

"A thing you install on your computer so you can view and store video from the camera."

"I'll bet Marjorie Maynard would be very interested in a system," I said. "Do you think you could install a camera at her place?"

"Well sure, but isn't that like closing the barn door after the horse has run off?"

"Not if we do it the way I have in mind," I said. I explained my plan to George and he agreed to help me.

The next day I took Marjorie out to lunch so he could mount the night vision camera outside the basement apartment. When we came home we found a van in the driveway. George got out of the van wearing coveralls with the logo of his son's security company embroidered across the back. He handed Marjorie a business card with his own cell phone number penned on the back and explained that he'd come to collect on an account for equipment Red had had installed on a trial basis. "Said he wanted to catch your neighbor in the act of putting his liquor bottles into your recycle bins." He grinned. "Deal is that if you keep the equipment over thirty days, you bought it."

He walked us around to the patio outside the basement slider and pointed up the camera. Out of sight behind a roof beam, it had a clear shot of the entry to the apartment.

"Why I never even knew it was there!" Marjorie said, craning her neck to see the little device. "How clever!" With that she handed over her credit card and George charged about a hundred and fifty dollars worth of parts and labor. I was pretty sure that would get Joey's attention. Indeed it did.

Within twenty-four hours Joey was on the phone to George demanding that he remove the equipment and refund the hundred and fifty bucks. George told her that he could take the camera down since it was an outside installation, but he couldn't retrieve the PCI card since it had been installed on a laptop in the home. In the basement, to be precise. After he explained to Joey that the PCI card contained the video record of the past month, she broke off the diatribe and said she'd call back. With that, the trap was set.

I had to explain to Marjorie what we were up to, because the next phase of the plan involved a bunch of Red's friends from The Manor waiting in the basement apartment that night, all quiet in the dark, the way you do for a surprise party. Long after Marjorie had climbed the stairs to go to bed, I could hear a clock ticking somewhere in the house. About twenty-five of us were crammed into Red's bedroom with the door closed. George had linked his smart phone to the surveillance video camera so he'd get an alarm when it detected motion and activated. Around two a.m. George's phone buzzed. He silenced it immediately and showed me the image that the camera was seeing, a hooded figure unlocking the slider and pushing it open.

A few seconds after the figure disappeared inside, we flung open the bedroom door and poured out into the living room, linking arms in front of the slider and the stairway, blocking the exits. George flipped on the light then he punched a button on his speed dial and spoke to the police dispatcher. "We got a B&E at 3535 Precipice Street," he said. The figure in the hooded sweatshirt stood frozen for a second with Red's laptop under one arm. She tried to make a break for it but the wall of geezers held long enough for George to wrangle the handcuffs onto her wrists. He pulled off the hood of the sweatshirt. Blond hair tumbled to the woman's shoulders.

"Just as I suspected," I said.

Dot, who'd seen fit to join us on our nocturnal mission, spoke on behalf of the group. "You mean this puny little thing killed Red?"

"This is Katarina Grossmann," I replied. "She was once a candidate for the US gymnastics team. Based on that she taught gymnastics to young girls in Florida—until one of the girls died tangled up in the cables of a universal."

"I had nothing to do with that," Katarina snapped.

"No, but it was a case of so-called accidental asphyxiation, wasn't it," I said. "You saw how it was done. And you used the same set-up to make Red Baxter's death look accidental."

"Bullshit! You make me laugh. If you don't take off these handcuffs, I'll sue you for all you're worth, all of you!" Like a cornered animal she glared at the staring faces encircling her.

I continued calmly. "I never would have considered it a possibility until the day of Red's funeral when you got out of the van and Clancy trotted up to you as if he'd known you all his life. But Joey and Taylor Chambers gave the impression that you were a stranger. Obviously not true. Clancy isn't friendly to strangers. The first time he saw me I thought he was going to tear my throat out. Why, I asked myself, would Joey and Taylor pretend not to know you? And the answer struck me when Marjorie found Red's lucky nickel. She made the case that the nickel showed that he was strangled by someone who then undressed him in this room and put a cable from the universal around his neck to make it look like autoerotic asphyxia."

"But why?" Dot asked.

"After they became engaged to be married, Red began taking an interest in Marjorie's finances. When George unpacked Red's desk he found a mutual fund statement that showed a significant loss, one that didn't make sense to anyone familiar with the market. I think that statement and many others were falsified to disguise the fact that Joey and Taylor had been draining Marjorie's account for some time. That's why this rich widow was actually living like a pauper, with her daughter monitoring every penny she spent."

"Absurd! You have no proof!" Katarina scoffed.

"Oh, but I do. I have the surveillance video that shows you had the knack of breaking in through the basement slider. You had to come back to get the laptop because you thought it had thirty days of surveillance video—video that would show you broke into the apartment the night Red died, just as you broke in tonight."

Katarina appealed to one of the oldsters clamped to her arms. "She's lying. I was never here that night the old man died."

"Oh?" I said, with unadulterated sarcasm. "Then why steal the laptop?"

"It was Joey. She told me to come and get it."

"You did all the work and now you'll be taking all the blame while Joey and Chambers get off scot free with Marjorie's money."

"It was her idea. Joey's. She used me. I thought she was in love with me."

"So when she suggested you help her get rid of her mother's meddling fiancé you were only too happy. But first you had to make friends with Red's dog, so Clancy wouldn't raise hell when you came in that night."

Katarina hiked her chin, a proud gesture learned in better days. "It was nothing. Working with dogs is easy. My parents were breeders. I grew up handling dogs."

"I surmised as much even though your bio didn't mention it."

"What do you mean?" she asked.

"Take a look at *Silver Blaze* by Arthur Conan Doyle," I replied. "You'll have plenty of time for reading where you're going."

Mother's Day is celebrated on the first Sunday in May and provides the backdrop for a story in which a daughter is trying to reach the safety of her mother's home. But the girl becomes the victim of a random homicide, a Jane Doe found in a spot where human life is bartered on the cheap. The police investigating the crime may never identify the body, but thousands of miles from where the murder occurred, the dead girl's mother knows. She knows.

# Flying Home

THE PIECE OF pie came beautifully and cleanly out of the plate, as pretty as any picture perfect slice on a magazine cover. Shame that only Bette Walker was there to see it, Bette who seemed equally delighted with store-bought as home-made. The bottom crust was browned, the pastry layered, because of the way the butter was cut into the dough. Butter, not lard. Butter ice-cold from the freezer. And not too much water. It was something you got a feel for, how much was enough to make it workable but not so it comes out soggy.

"Lemon meringue!" Bette says when it's put down in front of her on the old kitchen table where the dough had been rolled out the evening of the day before. Have to take care not to overwork it. That'll make it tough. Sunday afternoon. Pretty time of year. Apple blossoms floating past the window over the sink. Soft air just the same as years ago when the children would get new coats for spring and stand by the forsythia bush to have their picture taken. It had got so big over the years they'd had to take it out.

"It's Ellen's favorite." Lemon curd is no trick to it at all, long as it isn't too sweet, but meringue is fussy. Weepy or rubbery or shrunk in from the crust so it doesn't look right. It's all about how long you beat the egg whites.

Bette sinks her fork down through the pointed end of her pie. "I remember you making it for her birthday. All the other children liked cake but your Ellen was different."

Bette chews loudly, smacks her lips, leans her elbows on the table, never bothers to put her napkin in her lap. Raised in a barn. Asks through a mouthful, "She ever coming home?"

That's why there was pie in the first place. The idea struck her in the middle of a sound sleep, made her sit up and look at the clock to see the hour. 11:47. A few minutes before midnight on Friday night. The idea that Ellen was on her way home. That she had to make a pie. She could hardly lie back down for excitement.

It was barely light, just that stingy gray at the window when she finally left the bed, made coffee and got started. Mixed up the crust and put in the icebox to rest then put on her clothes to go to the store for the eggs and lemons. Some fresh cream of tartar. There was a tin in the pantry, but probably too old to be any good. She got new just to make sure. Walking out to the car so early in the day it seemed the whole world was uncommonly alive, scent of lilac sharper in her nose, crunch of gravel underfoot more palpable, strange quiet that sounded in her ear like a rest between bars. Pinkish gleam on the edges of things, the yellow-handled rake leaning on the side of the garage wouldn't let go of her eye. And Ellen was on her way home. Just Ellen. It would be just the two of them again, starting over. Just as if she'd never left. Just Ellen. If Randall came along the two of them would have to find a motel. A doctor, but a lout in spite of his education, a snob and something worse, something that made her never want to be alone with him. This person, this life-form engineered from conception to be the wrong man for Ellen, the one Ellen would choose anyway. Had she done it for spite? Payback for a sin of the mother? Such a puzzle. Time was they'd been peas in a pod. Best friends. But then things went wrong.

She parked and went into the store, straight over to the produce section, anticipating those shriveled little things they'd had last time she was there, only to find these gorgeous lemons, smooth-skinned, gleaming yellow, scent like perfume. Just Ellen. She'll be coming alone.

She carried the paper sack out to the car and put it on the back seat. Got in behind the wheel and sat for a time. It wasn't true that she didn't know when it went wrong. She knew exactly. It was when they hadn't heard from her for a while, when she was in college. It was so worrisome when she didn't phone home. Worry isn't enough of a word for when you lie awake thinking your child has committed suicide, or been killed. Ellen was always overly trusting, meeting all kinds of men now, going who knows where with them. Doing who knows what. When finally she did call—a weekend in Rochester. Big deal. No reason to hang up. She pulled out of the parking space and made her way back to the house, determined to apologize this time. *When Ellen comes home I'll say it, admit I was wrong and then we'll say no more about it.*

Sunday, late in the afternoon, when she finally realized Ellen wasn't coming home, the pie was twenty-two hours old. She felt it as certainly and suddenly as she'd felt the opposite conviction thirteen minutes before midnight on Friday night. Sunday afternoon it hit her that she'd never see her daughter again, not in this world. Her glowing optimism, new leaf of a rosy dawn, had been superseded by another page, this one as sober and simple as a Western Union wire. Only there was no word. None at all. Only a day gone past without a taxi pulling up in the drive, without a call from the train station, without a knock on the door. And she knew Ellen would never come again. So she'd called Bette to come over and have a piece of pie.

"Got a card. Came yesterday morning," she says and gets out the one she'd received some years before. Sprays of forsythia on the front with the greeting, *With love to Mother on your special day.*

"Ah, she never misses a Mother's Day," Bette says. She chews up the last bite of her pie and scrapes the plate with her fork. "One of these days she'll be sitting right here at this table. I feel sure of it."

"She would if she could," Ellen's mother says. "It's all right. I understand."

* * * * *

"LESTER BREEN," I told him. No skin off my nose. He scribbled my name into a little notebook. "I'm here at the junkyard Monday through Friday ten to six, Saturday ten to two. We're closed Sundays."

"How long you been working here?" he asks, impatient like most cops, as if they have something else to do, some other jerk's face to get into.

I told him about a year and before that the King County Boys' Camp. That got his attention. He perks up, like, and asks, "What charge?"

"Missed some court dates for driving while suspended then I got pulled over for something else. Then while I was inside I lost my place 'cause I couldn't pay the rent, so when I got out I came south. I got a buddy lives around here. I'm staying with him till I can get my own place again." I was kinda chatting him up since they usually don't think you're withholding stuff if you're all friendly and shit.

"One thing leads to another," he says, sort of wise-ass but not half as wise-ass as before I'd mentioned my jail time. Respect, isn't it. "Tell me how you found her."

*How?* What kind of dumb-ass question is that. I was hanging out on Friday waiting for a vineyard crew up from California. We let them sleep in the junkers for a couple bucks a head. After the driver paid me a fight broke out near the back of the lot. Some of the new arrivals were duking it out over a pair of boots like they were the ruby slippers or something. Women fighting. I watched for a while. Then I saw her in the backseat of the car with her head twisted around cockeyed.

But I wasn't going to mention that. So I said, "I walk the yard every morning as soon as I unlock the office and punch in." The office. That cracks me up. Shack with a telephone, a money box, a kitchen chair, and a coffee pot with a padlock on the door, as if there was something in there worth locking up. Sign on the wall says *Rust in Peace*. Comedian who owns the place is a fence, uses the yard to off-load hot merchandise. We're just a stone's throw off the interstate. Transients lay by here, like I said, hook up with rides into Portland and Seattle; fruit pickers, mules, girls who want to trick at the city rate, mail-order babies—you name it. Local talent bring their johns over from the bar across the street. Get it on in the back seats just like when we were kids. Study hall in the parking lot. Couple of dealers hang out near the back fence, just like at school. Kind of nostalgic. I don't say that, of course. My whole job is to be the guy who hangs around to make it look legit, like you could actually survive in business more than a week if all you did was sell an old carburetor or a pair of hubcaps every other Tuesday.

"What time, about?"

"Eight-thirty, eight-forty-five. Somewhere in there. Anyway, I'm just looking around and I see this blond hair hanging out the back window of this '69 Ford Falcon. It's not a bad looking car. I've had my eye on it, thinking maybe my buddy and I could fix it up. The back rear window on the passenger's side is busted out, though. That's how come I saw the hair."

We walked over there and I saw this gray-headed guy, probably the ME, crawling around in the back seat with the dead girl. "You know her?" the detective asks me.

I watched the doctor guy putting plastic bags over her hands, but made like I was really trying to place her. She had nice hair, blond like I said, but not bleached. Shiny. But that was all she had going for her. Face was hard, thin. Body nothing special. Just an average chick you wouldn't give a second look. Course she'd had a pretty rough night. I was like, "Never seen her."

"Dumped or done here?" the cop asks the doc.

"Here, based on the lividity," the old guy says.

"Cause of death?

"It's kind of weird. Ligature mark across the front of the throat here suggests strangulation but it doesn't extend around the neck, which is broken, incidentally. There's a purse in the front seat. I'm betting he tried to use the shoulder strap to maybe asphyxiate her, but then gave her neck a twist instead. Thing is, I don't see any defensive wounds, so it must have been quick. Consensual sex gone wrong, maybe. I'll know more once I—"

"Yeah, yeah," the cops says, "I know. Once you get her on the slab."

Now that's just plain fiction. She was dead before anybody ever found the purse. She had it slung over her head underneath the jacket. It was only after they stripped her they found it. They took her boots before that. It was the boots that started them off stripping her. As long as she had her footwear in place nobody would touch her. But after the boots were gone it was like a feeding frenzy. Weird. They even took her underwear. The guy who unzipped her jacket thought he hit the jackpot with the purse. But there was no wallet, so he got pissed and threw the thing into the front seat. The women fought over the purse for a while till they realized there was no money, then they went back to the clothes.

The detective snaps on some latex gloves and paws through the purse. "No ID," he says. "Wallet's gone. Maybe some prints we can use." He shoves it in an evidence bag. "Any identifying marks? Tattoos?"

The old guy shakes his head. "Negative."

"Working girl?"

The doc shrugs. "Probably. I'll check for semen," he says.

I knew they'd think that because of the girls who come over from the bar. Like I said, there's nothing wrong with a back seat. Still, I hate it that they're so unimaginative.

"Time?"

"Some time last night."

Jesus, give the man a peanut.

So the detective says I can go back to the office, that if he wants to talk to me some more he'll look for me there. He starts yakking on his cell phone about getting a crime scene crew out to process the car. Good luck with that. Gotta give 'em credit for trying, but give me a break. They pretty much got everything wrong except the time part. Ask me, I'd put the time of death just after dark Friday night, some time before the real action gets started around here.

\* \* \* \* \*

THEY HAD SPENT the winter in a town where the churches open their doors to the homeless at night. But once the weather grew milder, they went out to the Greenway again and started gathering things for a camp. They chose for their site a pebbly beach at an elbow in the creek on the opposite bank from the path used by dog-walkers and cyclists and shielded from prying eyes by the concertina briars of raspberry bushes. Against a steep bank that sloped up to a junkyard on Route 99 they built a lean-to out of fallen branches and covered it with brambles. The junkyard was across the street from a convenience store, a video rental, a bar, and a bakery. Sometimes the guy who ran the video store would pay them under the table for cleaning up the parking lot or breaking down cardboard boxes. There was plenty of bruised fruit and stale baked goods to be had once they gained access to the trash enclosure, so it all worked out like a dream. Better still, they set up to deal dope at the junkyard after dark and made enough to buy beer and keep themselves high.

Things came to them, gifts from the universe, you might say. Once when the creek rose after a heavy rain, a bright blue tarpaulin floated downstream and caught in the top of an uprooted tree that lay across the water like a great sieve. They took the tarp for the floor of their lean-to. And consider all the things left along the bike path. Jackets, shoes—never a pair—balls, Frisbees, money, hats, a pair of dangly earrings made of puka shells. All you had to do was go out for a walk and look down.

The only fly in the ointment was the bikes. Silent and straight, wire-guided, on rails, they bore down on anything that strayed onto the pavement, as if bikes was all it was there for, as if they owned it. The bikes were arrogant, high-tech, light-weight, carbon fiber flash and dash, and sexy as sin. Nature abhorred them, sent tree roots out to booby-trap the path with lumpy cracked eruptions that if hit at speed would launch a rider off his saddle and into the briars as if he'd been shot from a catapult. The creek in flood undercut the roadbed, and frost deformed it into a washboard. But even all of that wasn't enough. Nature needed help to keep the bikes away. So they set about thinking how to make an obstruction there at the bend where the blacktop path copied the elbow of the creek. They used a length of nylon rope that had drifted down the creek in a great wad. Once untangled, strung between two trees and stretched tight after dark, it lay ready like the taut string of a bow.

It'll teach'em, they said, discussing the trap. Teach'em to respect the path, the other people who use it. They ride like they want to mow you down. Assholes. This'll teach'em.

The southbound rider struck the line at full speed as they watched from the other side of the brambles. It was like an animation, how the cartoon body was snatched back off the speeding cycle, like some cosmic thumb and forefinger had reached down and plucked this person, this pratfallen creature all unawares. *Oh no you don't!* The coolness of it. Monster cool. They rolled on the ground laughing.

The bike ran on for another twenty yards before it piled into a tree at the next bend. The front wheel continued to spin as the machine lay on its back, a glint of spokes moving through a patch of moonlight, gradually slowing. Their hilarity subsided as they watched the felled rider. The small crumpled figure hadn't twitched. They studied the heap of black clothing for some time, whispering to each other, decided without debating the issue, that it was a girl. What if she's hurt, needs help? What if she's like— dead? Finally, they came out from hiding and approached her, reasoning that the longer they waited the more likely someone else might happen along, grab one of their ubiquitous cell phones and summon the law. They felt a common sense of urgency to collect their snare and move the body lest the local plod get the gist of what had happened.

Black skinny jeans, black hooded jacket, black gloves, and this amazing pair of boots, tooled leather, all fancy like maybe she'd been heading out to a line dance to make every woman in the place jealous of her footwear. The pale moon of a face made paler still by stillness. Strange whiteness of the cheek, like the skin of a pearl, the wrong color for life.

They had never talked about what they'd do after they'd snared one, never dreamed it would be death they'd be dealing with, but reached a silent consensus as they came to stand over the body. Untie the rope, stash the guilty coil in the lean-to. Find her wallet. Get the money as long as she's dead anyway. She won't need it. One on each arm pull her off the path, over the creek on a fallen trunk. Don't let her feet slip into the water. Why not? I don't think wet shoes will bother her. No, I guess not. But the boots, they're so nice. You want'em? No, it's evidence. If the cops come... We should bury the wallet, too. Just keep the cash, no cards.

On the other side of the creek, they clambered up the bank with her, and pulled her through a downed section of cyclone fencing into the junkyard. The closest car has the door ajar and the seat pushed forward as if someone had just crawled out of the back. They push the body, try to get it all the way in. The hood works off. Hair spills out, sweet-smelling like a field of Timothy Hay on a hot afternoon. What is that? I know that brand. Shut up. Go to the other side and pull.

When they get her situated they start back to get the bike, but the one who'd caught the scent reaches a hand in through the window to rest a minute on her head then gently pulls a hank of hair out the empty back window frame to watch it loft on a breath of night air.

\* \* \* \* \*

MAYBE THE THING that took so long was admitting she was right. Mother knew from the first time she laid eyes on Randall that he was wrong for me. She didn't say so, but I knew she thought so, and she knew I knew. And I went ahead with it. Married him six years ago. A lifetime of wear, weariness, fear since then. I had to try to remember what it was like to feel capable, to have a sense of self-respect. Years of abuse had worn self-respect out of me.

It was so hard to keep to my plan through all the preparation, the waiting. Find a bike, get some money together, let the weather turn fine enough to ride at night. I got everything ready for the next time he said he'd be gone for the evening; checked and rechecked the bus schedule, the fare; made sure of my riding time to the convenience store where the bus stops; figured out exactly what to take in a tiny purse and what to wear. I had to wear my boots, the fancy western boots my mother gave me years ago with a strange almost apologetic explanation that she'd always loved tooled leather. She'd saved up nickels to buy them for herself when she still lived in Texas and kept them in a trunk, oiled the leather once a year till it was time to give them to me. Thought they'd suit you fine, she said. I remember putting on a look as if I had been given second-hand trash, never even tried them on in front of her, waited until I was alone to see how beautifully they fit, feel how they made me want to be larger than myself, more daring, conjuring all sorts of adventures for me to live up to. Why was I so afraid to let her see how much I loved them? Why would I not give her that small pleasure? I couldn't come up with an answer, only the firm resolve to put it right, to come into the kitchen with those fabulous boots on my feet, let her finally see that I was remade, the daughter to do them justice.

It was about eight o'clock on the first Friday in May when finally I stepped out of the house for the last time. I got my bike out of my neighbor's shed. She was kind enough to keep it for me, no questions asked. I took a deep breath and stepped onto the pedals, into the next part of my life. Once I found myself riding away it felt like the stars were aligned.

Stars. They made me think of Harriet Tubman as I set off, how she walked from tidewater Maryland to Canada guided by the stars and signs people would leave, a gourd ladle with the handle pointing the way. She walked herself out of slavery and into freedom. I had the advantage of a bicycle and would soon be on a bus. Piece of cake. Pedaling on the deserted street, catching strobed images through windows of illuminated rooms, the picture blooming on a wall-mounted screen as the TV goes on, a kid's head bent over an open book, a mother sticking an oblong casserole dish into the oven. I'm different from them now, unscripted, a pedaling person defined only by that action, the flying pedals, spinning wheels. I create myself out of revolutions, going back to the last place I remember feeling like myself when I looked into the mirror. All of this, the life with Randall, an aberration we won't speak of again once I explain it to her. I'll explain and we'll not speak of it again.

I thought of home, the huge ash tree overhanging the porch with its gray paint chipped to show the concrete, the screen door where I used to look in and find her standing at the kitchen sink with her back to me, and that old table where we peeled and chopped and snapped and rolled every bite of food served in that house. We'd sit there to visit, too. Anyone who was really a friend would join us at that old table in the kitchen for a cup of coffee and something hot from the oven if it was baking day. Home. The word alone so freighted with throat clenching memories, one syllable like a sob. I think of it printed and see four-square solidity, the posts of my bed, the fenced-in yard, a daily round of life, routine, a carousel ride, two peaks so steep the stock market would be rocking, the seismic tremors that mother brings to it, and last a turnstile, easily slipped through. I want to slip back in, hope the return will be smooth as my way out.

I sat up, rode straight-backed because the bike has old-fashioned handle bars, not the kind that curl down like ram's horns but the level kind. I sat up and took my hands off the grips altogether. Such a feeling of lightness, as if I've slipped my skin, turned to pure spirit, immaterial as the stars, a heart's disembodied yearning flying home for Mother's Day.

I flew down a gentle slope in the moonlight, the breeze like a jolt of gin or a kiss, and I wondered why it had taken me so long to finally do it, to break away, to go home. I heard the liquid babble of the creek, felt as if I were one with it, slipping irresistibly toward the sea, la mer, la mère. The arrest, when it came, I felt as a sharp shock, a vault out of the saddle, as if the pleasure of leaving had given me wings, sent me flying into night air.

For June, the month of brides, a wedding serves as our holiday. Unfortunately, in the case of Corina Acosta, the nuptials never came off.

# The Bride Wore Duct Tape

S ATCH TERRY HAD put it off for six weeks, but on a rainy afternoon in late June when the Padres were traveling between out of town beat-downs, he found he could put it off no longer. With heavy reluctance, he dragged the box from the back of the closet and lifted out the two manila file folders crammed with case notes as cold as Feldman in his cemetery plot. All the information on the Acosta case, even scanned copies of handwritten statements, resided on a hard drive somewhere, but Feldman had never really believed in electronic records—so much smoke and mirrors, as prone to corruption as a Jersey union boss.

The contents of one file slipped out and cascaded across the carpet. "Jesus, Feldman, you ever hear of a rubber band?"

Feldman, tucked 'neath a neat patch of sod since April, uttered not the ghost of a reply.

Satch, a six-four frame, mahogany in both hardness and hue, did not stoop easily. He groaned as he reached for a Xerox of a news clipping that featured a grainy photo of Blanca Casteneda in a tiara—homecoming queen with the street smarts of a ten dollar whore. "Jesus, Feldman," a strangled refrain. Dan Feldman was always at his elbow these days, closer even than when they'd partnered on the force. *"I shoulda listened to my mother and found a nice Jewish girl."* Feldman's comment on being charged with statutory rape. It ended up a he said/she said that never went to court unless you figure the court of public opinion, all that ink that got Feldman kicked off the San Diego police force. Satch had never been able to talk to Feldman about his fall from grace, not the why of it. All that unresolved mess was what weighed on him now. Satch studied Blanca Casteneda's taunting, obsidian eyes. Cops were supposed to be smarter than that, cynical, weighing up time and crime, cost and benefit. She'd taken Feldman down like a spark takes a dry hayfield. Seventeen years ago.

But the Acosta case wasn't about Blanca. It was about the disappearance of her mother Corina Acosta, accountant employed by one Diego Fuentes, aka El Cirujano, a Barrio Logan drug lord who had a number of businesses, all restaurant related, so the paper trail of their fictitious receipts and expenses made a nice Gordian knot. There was enough real commerce to foster an appearance of legitimacy while laundering Fuentes' drug money. Corina had kept all the balance sheets straight and managed payoffs to several key San Diego politicians. Acosta's accounts had come under scrutiny during the reelection campaign of then State Congressman Brad Paisley whose campaign spending records included receipts for hookers who accepted government credit cards. But that wasn't what got Corina killed. The drug boss came out squeaky clean. What sealed her fate was the discovery, by said boss, that Corina had siphoned off some of his assets to build a nest egg for herself in a number of bank accounts set up using the names of persons Corina had met in the parish assisted living facility, Our Lady of Divine Peace Home for the Aged, where she did volunteer work preparing taxes for inmates who had no living relatives. It was presumed that her skimming had come to the attention of her employer because the day before she was to be a June bride, the bank accounts were all cleaned out and Corina went missing. Corina's daughter Blanca Casteneda filed the missing persons report, but in the absence of a body the official position was that the bride had gotten cold feet about the impending wedding and left town. Two months later a skeletonized body was found in the Sonora Desert. Dental work matched that of the missing mom from San Diego.

But Congressman Paisley's self-destruction took the heat off the investigation into Fuentes' political connections, an inquiry that had all the earmarks of a dry hole. When the Fuentes matter was quietly dropped a cadre of DOJ special investigators heaved a collective sigh of relief that resonated in the halls of the SDPD. The Acosta case slid to the back burner and then into oblivion in spite of the fact that it never made any sense. Running out on a wedding indicated panic, as if she'd found out somehow that the boss knew she'd been ripping him off. Okay, so she flees San Diego without a word to anyone and goes to … the Sonoran Desert? "How's that work?" Satch muttered. The lack of a reply from Feldman didn't seem to bother him. Feldman, even while alive, had never held up his end of the conversation. The terse margin notes he'd left on the transcription of an interview with Gina Gastelum, the last person to see Corina alive, didn't help much: *NOT about $—Cartel accountant would never have gotten caught—find insurance.* Then farther down the page and underlined twice: *green monster.* The last time he'd opened the file on the Acosta case Satch had verified that Corina Acosta had no insurance policies apart from auto. He felt like a disheartened rat, having once more run the maze to a dead end, but continued shuffling the papers till he found the post mortem report.

The ME had given a verbal summation in his usual laconic prose. "A dame getting dolled up for her wedding day don't usually accessorize with duct tape." The deceased woman's hair, recovered intact after it had sloughed off the skull, still had a couple loops of the gray tape stuck tight. When situated on the cranium with the lower mandible in place, it was clear that the tape had been stretched across her mouth and wound around her head. "Fingerprints on that tape?" Feldman asked, in spite of the improbabilities.

"No. Scorched and scoured to a holy relic. I'm surprised it hung together at all. Good stuff, duct tape. Indestructible." The way he said it Satch knew he meant "fuckin' indestructible," but it wasn't in the doc's WASP genes to put it that way.

Having examined his dead partner's files to a fare-thee-well, Satch headed downtown to police headquarters at 13th and G to see Glenna Sawyer, one of the few cops still on the job who had known Feldman. She was whiling away the months before retirement in the evidence room where she had her own coffee pot, refrigerator and microwave set up in an armoire behind the counter where she registered the receipt of articles in prosecution cases from across a county four times the size of Rhode Island. "Well, well, well," she said. She heaved herself up from her chair when she saw Satchmo and advanced on stiff pins to bear hug him. He explained the promise he'd made to Feldman, the thing about the Acosta case.

Glenna threw a skeptical glance over her bifocals. "You want to paw through that stuff again? Geez, what's it been fifteen years?" She admitted him to the cage. He followed her back through the shelves, reminded of his mother, that same painful walk. Mom Rose, her knees shot from scrubbing and praying, enjoyed a sublime misery, her very bones aching for the Lord.

She pointed to a battered box on a high shelf. "Seen better days," He said, lifting it down.

"Ain't we all," she replied. "This section here got damaged during the reorganization they did a few years back. They were moving everything with one of those little yellow tow motor things and it crashed into this here and everything spilled off. Oh, God. I'm glad I wasn't down here then." A buzzer sounded to summon Glenna to the counter up front. "There's a table you can use," she said, and left him to it.

The first thing he saw upon lifting the lid was a five-by-seven color photo of Blanca Casteneda covered in shards of glass from a shattered frame. His brain flooded with images of The Three Pigs, one of Fuentes' restaurants where Corina Acosta had kept a small office. At the foot of the Caesar Chavez Parkway exit, it crouched near National Steel and Shipbuilding in the shade of the span crossing the bay to Coronado. The Three Pigs was the kind of joint that sidetracked men with grit embedded under their nails as they made their way to and from work the way a filter feeder sifts morsels of sustenance from the mud stirred up by a flowing tide. As they drove to the interview all those years ago Feldman had said, "All I can think about is how I should have gotten the CD player with the removable face." The streets on that September day had been as depopulated as a David Hockney painting, suggesting that all the meaningful commerce in the area proceeded under the cover of darkness. Or maybe you just needed to know the signs and countersigns to be admitted to wherever it was the inhabitants went to do business.

At The Three Pigs the lunch rush was over. A waitress in a flouncy orange skirt and a white drawstring blouse, Gina Gastelum by name, was at the counter filling hot sauce bottles. Smoke drifted past her ear from a cigarette burning between her lips. Her shiny makeup accentuated the hard lines of her face. "I dint know Corina very well. We weren't big buddies." Gina screwed the lids back on the refilled bottles and stuck one in front of every other stool.

"So you didn't get along with Mrs. Acosta?"

"Elle es algo especial."

"What?" Her street patter left their Spanish in the dust.

Gina sucked on her cigarette and snorted some smoke. "She was one of those goody-goody types—looks down her nose at anybody who shows a little cleavage. You don't show a little cleavage around here you don't make out too good on tips, know what I mean?" She flipped the spent end of her cigarette into the oblivion below the counter. "Sangrón."

"What does that mean?"

"Sangrón, it means it kills her to give up even a penny. Corina loved the smell of money better than anything you dab behind your ears. Why she liked keeping the books. Sat on her fat caboose in the office at the back with those half glasses stuck on the end of her nose. Thought she was big shit with her night school accounting degree. Tiramierda."

There'd been no need to ask about that last expression. Gina's manner of speaking couldn't be confused with flattery. She led them through the scullery into a small storeroom. Gina flicked on the overhead light and parked her God-given assets on the edge of a carton of tortilla chips. In the cramped space was a desk with a metal chair on casters in front of a walk-in freezer, a big steel trash can, a bale of paper napkins, a gross of plastic film gloves, sacks of beans, shelves stacked with cans emblazoned with red tomatoes and green chiles. A little TV perched on a five-gallon tub of lard. On the corner of one shelf, an old-fashioned record player and an innocent blue and white box of forty-fives seemed out of place— ballerinas at a teamsters convention. On top of a number fourteen can of chorizo was a framed five-by-seven of a pretty girl. "That's Blanca," Gina had said, after Satch had picked up the photo.

As he stood in the evidence room, the look of the sixteen-year-old girl staring up through the shards of glass was still as sharp as a slap across the face. She favored Elizabeth Taylor in that movie where Montgomery Clift murders Shelly Winters, except her hair was long and straight a raven's wing and she wore a pleated plaid skirt and blue pullover with 'OLDP' embroidered on the youthful rise of her left breast, the uniform of Our Lady of Divine Peace, or "Old P" as she was wont to say. Between the hem of her skirt and the top of her Nikes a disconcerting length of leg suggested a Vegas floorshow might be in her future, but her eyes glowed with the polish that comes from being tutored in Greek after school by a priest.

The frame fell apart when he picked it up, leaving only the five-by-seven print in his hand. The print, upon closer inspection, turned out to be a bi-folded eight-by-ten. The part folded under in the frame showed a second person, a thirty-something man Satch had seen before—Chad Bliss, the man Corina Acosta was supposed to have married. Bliss was striking a jaunty pose next to a motorcycle. The bike was mostly obscured except for the license plate. Satch had a feeling the DMV database would turn up an owner in Imperial County. It did.

The next day he was driving east on Interstate 10, the sun shafting into his eyes through an early morning haze that reminded him of the last brownish montage he'd seen before he passed out once. *The color of failed romance.* He drove for a couple of hours thinking of a woman he'd almost married, her hair the color of the sun-blanched hills in the San Joaquin. Just west of Blythe the exit sign for highway 78 hove into view and he left the freeway.

He checked in with the cops in Blythe who sent him on to Palo Verde, a euphonious scrap of civilization stuck in a bend of the Colorado River about thirteen miles south, below the Chocolate Mountains among the Algodones dunes. Palo Verde took up less than five hundred yards of frontage. On the right hand side of the road were four bars, a bait store, a museum, the market/post office, a rock shop and Wheelie's, a gas station and convenience store. Satch stopped at the closest bar, a shack called The Station. With a Dale Jarrett banner flying over the door flanked by Confederate battle flags, it didn't look like the sort of place where people would smile in warm welcome at the sight of Satch Terry's African-American face. But such thresholds had to be crossed. *If you don't, one day you'll find the line is the edge of your counterpane and you dare not stir out of the bedclothes.* Mom Rose whispering, an urgent hiss.

Three ceiling fans kept the patrons at the L-shaped counter and the pool table cool in spite of the ninety-degree heat outside. There were three TV's too, all of them showing the second game of an American League contest between Seattle and Cleveland. Even if the other patrons had started after him with broken bottles, Satch wasn't about to walk out on that. In truth, they looked benign enough—dry, whispy creatures mostly, cigarettes held in knobby, tobacco-stained fingers. He took a spot on the short leg of the L. A woman with gray hair and glasses came over without delay. "What'll you have?"

"I'll take a Bud out of the bottle."

She brought it and let him alone. Satch unbuttoned his collar and loosened his tie. The beer was good and cold. To his left a wiry guy with tattoos and a face graven as a tire tread said, "That damn Ichiro." He was with a woman with a complexion like pickled pigs' feet.

"You know where the Harkness place is, by any chance?" Satch asked.

The tattooed man perked up. "You looking for Constance?

"It's kinda off the beaten track," his lady friend said. "Might be you'd want to ride out there with the deputy."

"He ain't the deputy no more," the tattooed man groused.

"Who's that?" Satch asked.

"Ozzie Grand," the woman said. "He retired quite a while ago, but he was the resident deputy for twenty-two years. You want to know anything that goes on around here, talk to Oz.

Satch smiled. Ozzie Grand was still the man to see all these years after Satch had originally sought him out to show him where Corina Acosta's corpse had been found. Oz was a beefy guy in a cowboy shirt and jeans, pretty much what Satch had expected, except for the wide brimmed straw hat and the hand with a middle finger that seemed to have been refashioned from the basic design with a sledgehammer. Blocks of bone jutted under the skin in a way Satch had never seen before.

"Don't mean to be rude," Oz explained at that first meeting as he held up his strange digit for examination. "That finger just don't bend anymore. I got shot there and through the side. Guy by the name of Mort Hawk had a place in the Smoke Tree Valley. He was dumping old tires. Had a contract to dispose of 'em, but he just stacked 'em up around his trailer till people complained about it and the EPA sent a crew out to clean it up. He went off and got drunk and when he showed back up he started making trouble. They called me out there to calm him down and he started shooting. Got me right through the finger and in this side. I pretty near bled to death. Took forty-five minutes for backup to get there. By the time it was over, there were cops from two states, four cities and three or four Federal jurisdictions. Had to have a swat team take that trailer down. They finally got me a MEDEVAC helicopter to Yuma. I told them I knew my rights and I'd refuse medical treatment if they tried to send me to the hospital in Blythe. They about killed me there once before. I wouldn't surrender my weapons till I saw that chopper."

Fool's errand, Satch reflected, that first trip to the site where the body had been found. A corpse two months old—anything the killer left would have been scattered by animals, washed out by rain or blown away. Besides, the crime scene investigators had taken the soil that was under the main group of bones, leaving a hole the size of a steamer trunk hoping to find some trace evidence. A local weirdo by the name of Roy Andreeson had got wind of the excavation and pitched a fit about it. Roy Andreeson had been concerned about the destruction of spadefoot toad habitat— Couch's Spadefoot toad, to be exact, *Scaphiopus couchi*. That part of the Sonora Desert where the chubascos come up from Mexico along the Colorado, Andreeson had explained, was their breeding ground. Explained in person and at length, as it turned out.

That night Satch had stayed over in a motel in Blythe. He'd ordered a pizza and thought the guy in the Padres hat and the camouflage windbreaker was bringing him his dinner. Otherwise, he'd never have given the toad enthusiast the time of day.

"They spend all year underground but come out to mate during thunderstorms—July, August and September," Andreeson had blurted out before Satch had closed the door behind him. "That's why I was out there that night. I was checking breeding sites. You know, it's like ten-thirty/eleven o'clock at night. This year the storms started in June, kind of early, but every season's different, know what I mean?"

Satch tried to humor the guy. "So the spot where the body was found is a breeding site and you didn't want it disturbed. That's why you didn't want them to dig up the body."

"Yeah. But some of those deputies said maybe I had something to do with dumping that body there. They said if I didn't leave them alone and let them do their job they'd run me down to the police station in El Centro and make me sweat bullets in a cell until I calmed down. Pissed me off, man." He shook his head and focused his disgust on the coffee table. "I coulda told them stuff about that night, but since they pissed me off I didn't say anything."

"What night? The night the body was dumped?"

"Of course that night. The night of the storm. The toads were coming out of the ground like popcorn!" Andreeson had a ratty, rolled-up sheaf of papers that he'd dug out of his jacket pocket. "Okay," he said, "look here. This is my species distribution data." He spread out the disreputable roll and bent over to decipher the pencil markings that filled a spreadsheet grid. "Here it is," he said.

His grimy index finger pointed to the first cell in the chart. "See, it says, 06-29-01. And see the location?" He moved his finger to the right. "Creosote scrub wash 1.2 miles below Milpitas Wash Road. I was leaving there and going to my next site when these two people drove by on the motorcycle. I didn't think anything of it until like fifteen minutes later the same bike goes by me again, this time heading south with only the driver. He got rid of the passenger, see. I didn't think much of it at the time, but when they found that body I put two and two together. It was that lady from San Diego who was supposed to get married but got popped in the desert instead."

"How do you know the bike heading south was the same one you saw with two people going north?"

"There aren't that many panhead FHL Duo-Glides running around," Andreeson had said with a smirk.

Seventeen years later Satch was back with a picture that matched Andreeson's description of the bike he'd heard that night. "Shit," Ozzie Grand said, once Satch had made contact and asked about the Harkness place. "So after all this time you think that nut job was onto something?"

"Too much of a coincidence to be any other way," Satch said as he climbed into Ozzie's pick-up. He didn't say anything more about it until they were sitting at Constance Harkness's kitchen table. She'd just poured them cups of coffee and had sat down herself.

"This is about Chad, isn't it," she said. "My husband's nephew? Only time the law ever shows up here it's about Chad. I haven't seen him for fifteen years or more, so you're wasting your time."

"We're interested in a vehicle registered in your late husband's name," Satch replied unresponsively. "It may have been involved in a crime."

The woman looked confused. "A vehicle?"

Satch passed her the photo showing Blanca, Chad and the motorcycle.

"Oh, that old Harley," Mrs. Harkness said. "My husband loved that old thing. Kept it like a museum piece. After he died Chad rode the hell out of it."

"Is that right," Oz remarked. "You still own it?"

"It's in the shed out back," she said, studying the photograph again. "This was taken about the time Chad went away," she added. "What ever happened to the girl?"

"Who?"

"This girl." The widow pointed to the photo. "The girl he was supposed to marry."

Satch had to concentrate to keep any sign of a reaction out of his eyes. "When was the last time you saw Chad?"

"Like I said. Gotta be fifteen years at least. Showed up here late at night, then a couple days later some friends of his stopped in. He said they were going for a ride. That was the last I saw of him. Didn't even take his clothes. I gave it all to the Salvation Army."

"His friends, do you know their names? What they came to see him about?"

"I say friends, but I don't know. They were Mexicans. Could have been people he knew from his job or something. Kind of people I wouldn't want to get involved with. I always told my husband that nephew of his would come to no good."

With a glance at Ozzie, Satch got to his feet and thanked Mrs. Harkness for her cooperation. The two of them strolled out to the truck and climbed in before Oz said, "Sounds like the cartel came after the boyfriend. Musta thought Chad had the money Corina had stolen."

"It does sound like that," Satch agreed, "like he went away permanently."

"Six feet under."

"Yeah."

"So it really *was* the money that got Corina Acosta and her boyfriend killed."

"The killer set it up so we'd think so."

Oz shook his head. "You're gonna have to spell it out for me."

"Feldman said all along Corina Acosta wasn't killed over the money. Satch paused, trying to remember Feldman's scribbled notes. "He wrote 'green monster' in the file. I thought he'd been daydreaming about Fenway."

"What does Fenway have to do with it?"

Satch smiled. "Nothing. Say, you feel like some Mexican food? I know a good place in Barrio Logan."

"What? You want to go all the way to San Diego for lunch?"

"We need to go back to The Three Pigs."

"I'll go if you quit talking in circles."

"I'll explain when we get there," Satch said. "Quit griping. I'm buying."

The waitress had changed—the new girl appeared in threadbare jeans and a San Diego Chargers tee shirt—but the menu had not, except that dinner prices went into effect after two. Satch said he and Oz were from the Board of Health and asked to see the freezer. The waitress shrugged and took them through the kitchen into the storeroom where the walk-in unit looked the same as it had seventeen years ago. All of Corina Acosta's things were gone, except for the wheeled office chair and a few pictures that had once hung on the wall at one end of her desk. "So give," Oz said, once the waitress had returned to the front.

"Corina Acosta is a single mother who goes to work at night and earns an accounting degree. She goes to work for a drug boss and manages to make a good living for herself and her beautiful daughter Blanca. Kid goes to Catholic school, has all the advantages. But there's something off with her. You look at her and you see something behind the eyes, like the look of a poisonous snake. Something beguiling. About the time the girl is ready to graduate high school Corina takes up ballroom dancing and meets Chad Bliss. He's one of the professionals who takes turns with the new students, making them feel light on their feet and lighter in the wallet. Corina goes all out with the private lessons, the costumes, the competitions. Then, after about a year of cha-cha-cha Corina shows her boss a rock on her left hand and hands in her notice. Chad put all that in the statement he gave the cops when they questioned him about Corina's disappearance."

"But Mrs. Harkness said Chad was going to marry Blanca."

Satch nodded. "That's what made me realize Feldman was right. Mother and daughter were involved with the same guy. Somehow Blanca and Chad got rid of Corina and made it look like the mob killed her. Feldman never bought that because he said accountants who work for crooks always keep something, like a duplicate set of books. You tell somebody you trust where they are, that if anything untoward ever happens to you the incriminating stuff goes straight to the DA. Feldman called it insurance. He never found Corina's." Satch sighed. "Since they got rid of her office, I guess we won't find it either."

"The cops already went over this place with a fine tooth comb anyway," Oz said.

Satch gazed forlornly at the pictures on the wall, mostly ballerinas and waltzing couples.

"I haven't seen one of these things in years," Oz said, pointing to a cross-stitch sampler amongst the dancers. "My daughter did one when she was about ten." He reached up to take the sampler off the wall to get a better look. As he lifted it something fell on the floor.

Satch bent to pick it up. "Holy shit!" he said, as he showed Oz a small recorder.

Oz looked at the back of the needlework. The fabric backing was stapled around a stretcher about two inches deep, enough space to hold the device. "I seen some neat ways of hiding a wire in my day, but none as good as this."

Satch peered at the small recorder. "High end piece of equipment. Voice activated." He ejected a cassette tape hardly the size of an old Zippo lighter. "We need to get some batteries so we can play it. Can you wait for lunch?"

"We'll call it dinner. You'll buy me a steak at Mr. A's after we hear what's on the tape."

Twenty minutes later in Satch's car they stuck the double A's in and hit play. The click of the recorder turning itself on occurred simultaneously with the sound of a phonograph needle hissing across the edge of a record. The throbbing of Elvis Presley's voice. "Don't, don't that's what you say/ Each time I hold you this way . . ." A woman's voice, Hispanic. Corina: "Oh, now I've smudged my mascara." Small sounds. The creak of a chair. A drawer closing.

"Don't" plays on.

Again, the creak of the chair as she rises. "I thought you weren't coming."

A man's voice. Young. Not Latino. Chad: "No, you didn't, chica. You know I can't stay away from you." A rustle, a pause. "You have the money?"

"In the backpack. Nearly two hundred thousand. Just like I said."

"Why are you so jumpy? Everything went like we planned, right?"

A pause, soughing, rustling, perhaps an embrace, a kiss. "Yes. I worry too much. I just want it to be perfect. Everything must be done very carefully."

"Just a few more days and we'll be walking on a Hawaiian Beach. Now get undressed."

"What? No, no. We don't have time! You need to take the money and go before somebody sees your bike out there. Somebody could come along and see the license number."

"Relax, the plate has a good coat of mud on it. Go on. Do what I said. Strip. Sit down and close your eyes."

Corina, giggles. The chair creaks. She asks coyly: "Why? What are you doing?

A ripping sound. "How do you feel about a little bondage?"

"Chad, stop playing. Take this tape off me!" More ripping sounds. "Chad stop it. This isn't funny! I don't—" A muffled scream.

"Stop kicking, damn it! Jesus. You look ridiculous."

Corina's screams are muffled, but the one syllable is barely discernible. "Chad!"

Chad laughs. "I should get a picture of this."

Sounds of a struggle, the chair creaking, something banging on hollow metal, Corina's inarticulate screams. More ripping sounds. A door opening, then a heavy thud as it closes.

The needle scratching. Chad goes to move the tone arm. Elvis begins "Don't" again. Halfway through the second rendition, a new voice. Female. Blanca: "Hi, Chico. Is it done?"

"She's in there. I don't know how long it will take. When I was taping the trashcan between her legs the cunt tried to kick me in the balls. I felt kind of bad till then. Now, fuck'er."

"By midnight she'll be stiff as a board and you'll whisk her away on your bike. Just like she always dreamed. Ride with the backpack between you and her. You don't want frost bite."

Laughter. The tape ends abruptly.

"So Blanca and Chad killed Corina by taping her to her chair and shoving it into the walk-in freezer," Oz said. "That's cold."

"You can add duct tape to the list of household items considered lethal."

"Why freeze her? Tape over her nose and mouth would have killed her anyway."

"Remember what Andreeson saw? Two people on a bike. Frozen, the corpse sat up straight. Chad posed her with her knees apart so she'd slip right on the bike. Probably used something like a bungee cord to tie the two of them together."

"Not exactly the togetherness Corina had in mind," Oz said.

"Then Blanca Casteneda put the Mexicans onto Chad. Told them where to find him and the money. Left her sitting pretty without any loose ends."

"Sitting pretty?"

"In good with the cartel. Made her bones, so to speak. She's probably married into the top dog's family by now. Living high on the hog in Mexico. Untouchable." Satch shook his head. "Feldman knew. He had it figured out, so Blanca had to get him off the case before he found a way to charge her. So she accused him of rape. He got suspended. It all makes sense."

"But why?" Oz asked. "She couldn't have been in love with Chad if she put La Familia onto him. Why'd she kill her mother to get the guy?"

Satch shrugged. "Feldman thought it was jealousy, the green monster. But I think Blanca just couldn't stand the thought of her mother getting dressed up in white lace and living happily ever."

Oz chewed on that for a while. "You think she seduced Feldman or was it the other way around? Or was the rape charge a total lie?"

Satch thought about Mom Rose for a minute and sighed. "I think the devil hath the power to beguile."

For the protagonist of our story for July, memories of Independence Day in a small West Texas town are inevitably comingled with scenes from a funeral, a fire and the death of a child. Such is the setting for a tale of vengeance spawned of envy and exacted regardless of whether the person to be punished for the tragedy is in fact guilty or not.

# Unknown Assailant

I HAVE A MEMORY of Jack Flynn riding down the main street of Coleman in the Fourth of July parade in his Ranger uniform, the hat with three dents in the crown and a wide, flat brim. He was easy to spot because he sat tallest on his horse and because he was the sort of man you instinctively sought out in a crowd, the one you wanted to steer clear of. The irony sits heavy, how it came to pass that the Flynns and their kin all died right around Independence Day. Jack was laid to rest at the beginning of July in 1952 and Barbara Anne, his grandchild, died that same day. Valeria, Jack's daughter, was shot this Fourth of July past. Unknown assailant, paper said. And Scrub Thompson gone only a few days before Valeria.

I count Scrub Thompson as kin to the Flynns because Jack and Valeria was all the Thompson boys had on this earth above sod. Floyd, Hap and Scrub rode in on the gusts of a blue norther' in the bitter winter of 1939, a set of three like a run of bad luck. They showed up lean and wary as the wolves that howled down from the hills to steal sheep. The ranchers got together and hired a trapper to take care of the wolves. Come spring, the wolves and the trapper were gone, but the Thompson boys stayed, all but Hap. Hap said what Jack Flynn paid wouldn't keep a snake in shoe leather, so he was off to Alaska. Last anyone heard of him was the slap of the kitchen door as he stalked out of the house.

Floyd and Scrub stayed in Talpa but came to regard each other as not much more than nodding acquaintances. It must have been that the middle brother kept them glued together. Or maybe the trouble was Valeria had come between them. Jack's daughter had her fourteenth birthday around Easter and parted with her virginity that spring with no more a backward glance than Hap on his way to Anchorage.

It was generally rumored that Floyd had her before Scrub, and Scrub never forgave him. And as most rumors do, this one probably had a grain of truth in it. Floyd was a tall, broad-shouldered man whose word pretty much went with the rest of the boys. He was the first to cross the floor to ask a girl to dance, the first to fling a saddle on a horse that needed to be broke, the first to enlist after Pearl Harbor. First with Valeria Flynn just stands to reason. There's no way of knowing exactly how it played out, but Valeria Flynn left enough male wreckage in her wake to leave no serious doubt in the matter.

Scrub, on the other hand, was small by west Texas standards. He was quick and dark, with perpetually amused eyes peering out from behind a hank of black hair. Right away folks assumed he was part Indian. He just grinned at that and said, no, he was made of the orts and peelings of the stuff used to make Floyd. He dressed kind of fancy to make up for what he felt he lacked in natural endowments, shirts tailored to fit without a wrinkle, boots tooled with a flower of his own design. The army rejected him for flat feet. By our senior year in high school, it seemed like Scrub Thompson was the only man left in Coleman County who didn't wear bifocals. And I was in love with him and knew he didn't love me, knew I had to get out. All I wanted was to get me a class ring and a bus ticket.

I joined 4-H and raised a white-faced calf with the cold-blooded intent of selling the wet-eyed baby off at the county fair for as much cash as his future in hamburger would fetch. But instead of cash they gave me a check. And since I had no bank account, I had to rely on my mama to cash it. She worked part-time cooking for Jack Flynn and put in as many hours as they'd give her at the switchboard. She never had the money for a warm robe. I should've known there wouldn't be any for a class ring.

"But I raised that calf myself. I earned that money. It's mine. You can't take it!"

"It's gone. We were short this month because I was sick those days. Remember when I couldn't go to the telephone exchange? They were going to cut off our fuel oil. That's our heat, honey. I'm sorry, but it had to be done. When you're older and have a house to run, you'll understand." Mama's lips hugged a narrow line. I knew she wasn't about to change her mind.

"You're a liar and a thief. I hate you!"

What I said to my dying mother haunts me to this day, but there was no taking it back. Coat flying open, books clutched to my chest, I charged out, head down, murdering crystals of hoarfrost under my feet as I ran to school. How I hated her. I hated her for reasons I couldn't even understand back then, a vague notion about her and old Jack, the thing that hangs in the air after the deed, a whiff of sweated bedding and cold cigarette ash underneath the tang of that aftershave he always wore. I don't know how she missed it when she dressed to come home, that smell that betrayed her. Her nose was beginning to fail. I can see it now. Death puts things into perspective. You walk back from that terminal point, noting all the signs you missed before, reordering the days to reflect that all-defining end so it comes out inevitable, rational even.

When I got to school I joined the others, huddled together on the playground like cattle, our breath steaming the frigid air. Little kids raised two fingers to their lips to puff pretend cigarettes. Valeria Flynn and her cronies congressed between me and the door. Her voice pounced just as I reached for the door handle to go inside. "Remember your ten dollars, Cat?"

"I remembered." No lie, in fact. Remembering was one thing, having quite another.

Before algebra the teacher said if anyone had money in the cloak room they ought to go get it, because some people weren't above rifling the sack lunches and jackets. I got the idea of going back there and claiming somebody had already stolen the money I'd left in my coat. But I felt my cheeks heat up at the very idea of carrying off such a performance and lost my nerve.

I spent all morning worrying. How was I going to face everybody without that ring money? Counting on the full price of that calf, I'd bragged about getting the fancy one set with a red stone. I'd sooner have taken a whipping with a wet rope than admit I didn't have it.

When we were dismissed for lunch Valeria said, "Let's see your ten dollars, Cat."

I told her to mind her own business. We went to different ends of the schoolyard like boxers to opposite corners. I don't know how, but Scrub Thompson knew I was in a jam. He must have seen me bolt out of the house with a homicidal look on my face. A few minutes before the bell rang to call us back inside, he pulled into the parking lot in his old dust-covered pick-up. He dug two fives out of his jeans. Told me I was a fool to be such a nervous wreck. Grinned at me like I should have known he'd show up to save the day—the way God must look at sparrows.

Right after history the man from the ring company came. He called out our names one by one. Kids paraded by him and dropped off their money. When I passed Valeria's desk with my head up and cash in my hand I could see it just about killed her. Later on I think Scrub told her he'd rescued me. I reckon she decided to ruin his life right then and there.

He was my champion, like in those pictures of knights and ladies at tournaments. That's how I thought of him—even after he ran off to Las Vegas with Valeria—even after I brought him back to Talpa fifty years later to die. I remember the morning he left me, him in the bed with the side rails, me sitting next to it, the two of us locked in amber.

"Scrub?" I pressed the button on the morphine pump one more time for good measure. A jolt of oblivion coursed down the tube. "Scrub, honey?" I said again.

His eyelids fluttered. He mumbled some garbled nonsense to somebody in a dream. He was out, all right. I reached for the rubbing alcohol on the bedside table and soaked a cotton ball. He hated it when the visiting nurse pulled the tape off without softening the glue with alcohol first. "Never mind," I said to him. "I won't let her manhandle you anymore." I bent my mind around the biting scent and went about my business in spite of Death standing in the corner, waiting to have the last dance with my man.

He moaned, poor soul.

"Don't worry, honey, I'm doing it right." I stroked the tape where it clung to the flaccid whiteness of his inner thigh, peeling it back easy, first one end then the other, until I got to the place in the middle where the needle penetrated the skin.

I slid the needle out and put it on a Kleenex, then stroked the cotton across the puncture wound, wondering if all those years in the saddle had worn his leg bald, or if hair had never grown there in the first place. "Kind of thing a wife would know about a man," I said, "but if you had one of those, I wouldn't be doing this, would I?" Out of respect for his modesty, I pulled the sheet over his naked frame. I sat down in the chair next to the bed, rolled up my sleeve, and prepped the vein inside the crook of my elbow. I have a knack for popping the needle in. It's one of those things you can't teach, like being able to fuck good.

I gave myself a dose of the painkiller.

Scrub had fought the cancer almost a year, but gave up something to it every few weeks, as if his body were not his anymore and he was just renting. He lost his job at the casino. Then he couldn't walk as far as the store. Then he couldn't remember what pills to take when. He was moon-faced from steroids and his teeth had shifted in his jaws like a salmon on its last trip upstream. He stopped eating. Then one morning he stopped halfway through getting dressed, his pants on, but not zipped, defeated by the necessity to stand up and get his shirt. That's when he called me to come up to Las Vegas, to come get him and carry him home.

I've always had a weakness for morphine and cowboys, morphine being the easier of the two to handle. I know how to take it, how to get back. Same as learning how to hold your bourbon, not that many people would agree. Don't have to go any farther than Cory Vaughn to get an earful of self-righteous disapproval. "What you gonna do when he dies and the last of it runs out?" Cory makes it sound like I might start a crime wave in Talpa, Texas.

Oh, Cory means well, and he's right, of course. Morphine is the Mop'n'Glo of drugs. Mop'n'Glo gives the linoleum a nice shine, but just glazes over all the grit and grime. Morphine didn't do a damn thing to alter the steady creep of the cancer consuming Scrub, but it tuned out the hiss and suck of the oxygen machine, the drip of the catheter and the sickroom stench of baby wipes and fading posies.

It was barely 10:00 a.m. and already the flannel shirt that felt good in the chill of dawn was damp with sweat. I picked up the *T.V. Guide* and fanned my face. A few strands of hair tickled my neck in the manufactured breeze. "It's her birthday next week, honey," I said to Scrub. Funny, the way I kept talking to him, as if he could answer or even hear me from where he stood looking into the great void we must all face at the end of our days. "Course, she's not fond of birthdays, being an actress, but I got her a card anyway. I knew you'd want me to. I put everybody's name on it and sent it yesterday." I gave a thought to that heavy, lilac envelope and the card inside with the big 7-0 on it. She'd have a fit. Made me feel a little better, imagining it might spawn a new crease on her forehead and send her running off to get it botoxed.

Scrub moaned and lifted his arms over his head.

"I know, honey, I know." I grabbed the washrag that hung on the rail of the hospital bed and dunked it in the bucket of cool water I kept on the floor by my chair. I was twisting the water out of the rag when all at once, stuff came crashing down off the nightstand—the lamp, my can of Sprite, the box of Kleenex and the clock. The phone clipped my ear as it jangled to the floor.

I bolted up. "Easy, hon." I caught his flailing fist still clutching the tablecloth. "Easy," I said, the way you'd talk to a skittish horse. I got his wrists crossed one over the other so I could hold them on his chest with one hand. The fight left in those wasted limbs surprised me. They had grown so thin they made his hands look oddly overlarge. That made me want to cry. Scrub had always been a dandy, small and elegant. Even his feet. He'd been downright vain about his boots, always shod in custom-mades.

When the tension left his arms I let go of his wrists, hoping no one would think the worse of me when he came up in bruises. I pulled the needle from my arm and retrieved the phone to call Cory. "You better come on," I said. "He just had a spell of what they call terminal agitation."

Cory said he'd be right over. I hung up and went to get some paper towels to take care of the Sprite puddled under the table. The roll hung underneath the cabinet to the right of the kitchen sink. I stood there for a minute and looked past a pile of dirty dishes out the window. Cows grazed in the field across the street where the Flynn's house used to be. There hadn't been a house there since

Jack's funeral, the day of the fire. The rubble of the chimney was still visible through the spiky growth of weeds. And there was Barbara Anne casting jacks in the dirt, my beautiful, long-legged child. She loved her jacks and that old Zippo lighter. It hadn't worked for years, so I gave it to her to play with, something to keep her quiet. Hadn't worked for years.

I shook my head against the effects of the morphine. It was really only cows I saw through the kitchen window, no phantom child. I ripped three towels off the roll and headed back to the bedside. Halfway down the hall, I missed the ragged rasping of his breath. I stopped and listened hard to make sure. I couldn't hear a thing.

"Scrub?" I couldn't help myself calling to him as I ran. When I picked up his wrist I felt nothing, nor any ebb and flow of air on the back of my hand as I held it in front of his nose, nor any glimmer behind the pot metal irises with their disjoint stare. My stomach took an elevator shaft drop. I grabbed the bed rail and tried to steady up. I don't know how long I stood there. It makes no sense, because I knew it was the end. I knew after the end there's nothing next. But still you wait. You hold your breath, listen for the refrigerator to run, the bawl of a cow—any anchor in the here and now to keep from being swept away with the departed soul. You look away from the corpse, as if death were an eye-borne contagion.

I switched off the oxygen machine, withdrew the cannula, moved his eyelids down.

That melancholy fiddle tune in three quarter time lilted through my head, the one I always saved for him at the Saturday night dances all those years ago. I saw him standing over by the punchbowl, punch-lining two or three old boys, all grinning in their string ties and western shirts with pearl snaps. My heart took a giddy leap as he started across the floor, slow and easy, in time to the fiddler scraping the strings. I sniffed and dabbed behind my glasses with a tissue.

I didn't stay to see him buried. I'd promised him I'd take a letter to Valeria Flynn as soon as he was gone. That's how I came to be driving to San Diego, to the address on the envelope, the last thing he'd written in his shaky hand. He'd paid somebody to find her, get her address so he could send his last words. But he didn't trust the mail. "I know I've asked a lot of you, little sister," he said, "but if you ever cared for me, take this and make sure she gets it."

The first day driving I got as far as El Paso. Slept in the lot of a big truck stop. About first light I pulled myself together and went into the café to wash up and get some eggs with a big pile of grits and coffee strong enough to wake Lazarus.

I wanted to stay at that table in the truck stop, just sit and listen to the long-haul semi drivers hashing over the fastest run ever in the long ago time before fuzz busters. Seems like I'd been tired ever since I left home. Maybe even before that. Sleep didn't touch my weariness anymore, just postponed it until the next time I opened my eyes.

Somebody plunked a few quarters in the jukebox and 'Sweet Dreams' started playing. Why is it I love those Patsy Cline songs so much when they burn like iodine in an open cut? Only thing I can think of is when you love somebody you can't have, all you got is the pain of it. I let myself sit there and listen right to the end. I left a couple dollars on the table and went to the bathroom. Caught sight of a condom dispenser on the wall. A buck a throw. I looked in the mirror, ran a brush through my hair. "So much for romance," I said. Made me feel a little better.

As I put my brush away, I saw the letter in my purse, the address in his craggy scrawl. I had a powerful urge to tear it open then and there, but as my mind was fussing with the edge of the flap I stopped and ran my fingertips over the writing, as if the ballpoint depressions in the paper were a kind of Braille that would link me to him. "You've got no time for this," I told my reflection. Then I started to feel really bad.

Under my clothes sweat slipped down the creases of my body. I didn't dare take a deep breath or I was sure my breakfast would come back on me. Sometimes when I go too long without a shot of morphine it feels like I'm in a small boat heaving on a big sea. But this was different. The room tipped. My head sloshed like a jug half-full. I had to get out, get air, but my legs wouldn't work. I braced my arms against the sink, tried to hang on till the spell passed.

Clutching the porcelain, I wondered if I was dying, because of the clouds. Instead of the restroom mirror I was seeing a blue sky and high clouds. Reminded me of that painter who used to have a show on public television. He taught how to make landscape paintings. After he put in the blue for the sky he'd show how to make wispy white clouds. Always made me sleepy. His voice, better than Valium. Three clouds? Thirteen? Put in as many as you like.

Then everything took on a dingy tinge. The sky muddied to that brownish gray of a blue norther'. I felt the grit between my teeth and the numbing cold. I smelled the manure and heard the bawl of the cows rolling on and on like the sound of surf. I picked Scrub out from among all the drovers and ponies and cows and dust, the way I always did. His nose and mouth were covered with a bandana, chaps cocked behind his hips, all dust-covered with his quirt in his hand and his hat tipped back off his brow. I could see his face, the right angle jaw and eyes so amused at the adoring way I looked at him.

"How could you do it?" I asked.

"What do you mean?" he said.

I showed him the Mexican marriage license and that photo of them starting out on their honeymoon, leaning on the fender of that '46 Ford that took them up to Vegas. Every time I looked at it I knew the answer to my own question. Hell, it was plain as day. She had the long stems, the blond hair, the face. "She loves Floyd," I said.

He pulls down his kerchief. Flashes a smile. "I was always better looking than Floyd."

The only times we ever argued, it was because of her, even after she left him—hell, even as he lay dying in that hospital bed in my front room. I was okay as long as he didn't flaunt her in my face. But when I saw him mooning over that eight-by-ten glossy, I got good and mad. She was posed like Lauren Bacall, the ingénue looking back over her shoulder with her pageboy smooth as a blue note and mockery in her eyes. An autograph was penned across her neck: *To my darling Scrub, love Val.* I told him if I ever saw that picture in my house again, I'd burn the place down. I never laid eyes on it after that. After the mortuary van came and I rolled up the mattress of the hospice bed and sorted through the stuff in his box, I never found it. You'll sooner find brains in a turnip patch than a lick of sense in people when it comes to love.

I had the darnedest craving for a Lucky Strike. Got a mental picture of myself waiting for the voice of God to call me up to the pearly gates and getting some oily old radio announcer instead. *Lucky Strike Green goes to war. And now we have a member of our studio audience chosen at random. Come on up here and account for yourself. Speak into the microphone.*

It's an old microphone, radio call letters in an arc over the big boxy thing on a pole. I want to talk about the lighter. Jack Flynn gave Zippo lighters to Valeria and me for high school graduation presents. They were just alike, silver with that heavy lid you thumbed back, turning the wheel against the flint to make the spark. Hers broke right away. Wouldn't light, so she left it when she and Scrub took off for Vegas. When Scrub brought the baby back to Talpa, I gave her Valeria's broken lighter to play with. I figured when Barbara Anne was old enough to understand I'd tell her the lighter was like her mother: shiny outside and not a spark of warmth inside.

*You gave the child the lighter?*

I came to flat on my back, felt the cold, gritty tile under my palms, managed to get to my feet and walk out to where my car was parked. A rattle of palm fronds in a breath of air made me think for a minute it had started to rain. I looked up and squinted hard against spears of glare flung from the low point on the horizon where the sun was hanging red and angry. Jack Flynn died at just this time of day, during the slow-ticking hours of morning in the first week of July in 1952. He took down with influenza and never got up again. It was wretchedly hot. He was laid out in the parlor. We had to wait to have the funeral because Valeria was on her way to pay her last respects. The air was sickly with the smell of lilies and the sweet stink of death.

Valeria arrived, sore as a yellow-jacket, as if she blamed us for Jack's up and dying. She was having a little success acting in Southern California and talked to us if she was playing to the cheap seats. After a couple drinks she let it all hang out. "Such a bunch of nobodies. You walk around like martyrs, moaning because life is so hard. In winter the sheep freeze. In spring it floods. By summer it's so dry anything that catches fire burns to the ground. Not one of you had the brains to get out of here. But I did. That's what sticks in your craw, isn't it."

"No," I said. "What sticks in my craw is you. Why'd you come back if that's how you feel? Why couldn't you've just left us alone?"

She spoke softly to the toe of her shoe. "You don't know what my father meant to me."

"If he meant so much, why'd it take you so long? We were afraid of maggots."

She lifted her eyes, as if she was doing a close-up of somebody reminiscing. "Talpa's hellish in July. I'm burning up inside my clothes. I can't go to the funeral. I have a fever."

Floyd came over with Eula and Mrs. Hale. I rode to the burial with them. I remember Valeria out on the porch saying she'd stay with Barbara. I wondered where you'd go for mourning as fine and fashionable as that outfit Valeria had on. She turned to check her seams as we got in the car, showing off her legs. Then she went inside and we drove to the cemetery.

About the time the minister got to the part where they lower the casket I saw black smoke rolling up into the sky back in the direction of town. I don't know who finished burying Jack because everybody ran for the cars. We all had a horror of fires. There's no water, no irrigation. There was never but one outcome, only a question of whose place it was.

It was the Flynn place. We found Valeria on the ground out front, covered with soot. She'd come out the second story window, crawled across the porch roof and jumped. Turned her ankle when she hit the ground. Tears muddied the dirt on her face. She was crying out,"Barbara Anne! Barbara Anne!" Every square inch of the house was afire, flames spurting from all the windows, smoke just pouring out. It was impossible for any living creature to have survived in there, but a couple of the men were going to try to raise a ladder to the second floor. The whole house collapsed before they even got the ladder out of the barn.

I never should have gone to Jack's funeral. What good's a funeral anyway? It's got nothing to do with sending the dead man to the afterlife, cajoling the gods with song and prayer and tears to take his soul to its rest. It's all about convincing the people left behind that the dead man's really gone. You watch them close the casket, lower it into the ground, throw the dirt in, clods clattering down on the coffin lid, one last try at waking the man inside, but it never does. If I hadn't gone, Barbara Anne would still be alive. Scrub's baby girl. All I ever really had of him.

Everybody said I mustn't blame myself for leaving the baby with Valeria. Most natural thing in the world for a mother to look after her child. You can't carry on as if the whole thing's your fault. Why don't you go on down to Forth Worth, visit your cousin for a while? You should get away, Cory Vaughn said, even though he'd never traveled farther than you could spit.

I don't remember driving the rest of the way to San Diego, don't remember much of anything before that moment when I stood on the brakes. The freeway traffic was at a dead stop, brake lights as far as I could see, people laying on their horns, threading through the snarl of cars toward the off ramps. I showed the address to a motorcycle cop and he told me which exit, said it was the second one down, not more than a mile if the traffic would ever start to move again. He asked if I was all right, said I looked a little off-color. "There's nothing for it," I said.

I got off the freeway and stopped at the first service station I saw. The man pumping gas sent me across a vast park full of flowering trees, long Spanish arcades, buildings covered with decorations fancy as icing swirls on wedding cakes, people wearing shorts, pushing strollers, babies with pinwheels spinning, fountains throwing water in big gushes three stories high, lily ponds, pools with orange fish hovering. All that water just running like there was no end to it. Water noise, rushing liquid sound that made me think of gold coins falling in a stream through your fingers, hypnotic like a chant that made me forget what I came for.

I saw a guy press his lips tight around a cigarette, cup his hands around a flame and light up. It came back to me.

On the street on the other side of the park, I asked a girl walking a miniature collie how to get to the address. She pointed to an intersection, said to turn left and go three blocks. As I pulled up to the house a plane came over, flying so low I thought it would clip the peak of the roof. It filled my ears with a blast of engine noise as I walked to the front door.

She answered the door, all pretty like she was expecting company. Had her make-up on and her hair done up. Stood there in gold sandals and painted toe nails and a shiny green dressing gown, color of a chameleon. "You got your nerve pretending to be blond at your age," I said.

"It galls you that I'm still an attractive woman, while you … well, if I didn't know better I'd say you slept in those clothes."

A plane flew over just then, and I was already mad enough to wipe the smile off her painted face, but I wasn't done with her yet. I waited till the jet noise passed then I opened my bag. "I came to bring you this."

She looked at the writing after I handed it over. "From Scrub Thompson?"

"He died. Made me promise to see you got his last words."

"My God, old Scrub. He was a sweet man."

"He was a fool."

"You're one to talk. Still running to do his bidding at the drop of a hat, still a slave to whatever it is you want to call it— unrequited love."

"Some people would say I was faithful. True. You wouldn't know anything about that."

"Deluded is more like it. You've got no use for what's true, the way it really is."

She took a pack of cigarettes from the pocket of her wrapper, held it toward me for a second. I shook my head. She lit up, took a lungful of smoke and blew it out again, dragon hot. "Too good to smoke, now? Well aren't you the virtuous one. When did that change?"

"The day we buried Jack."

"You mean the day she died. What's wrong, can't you say her name?"

"Barbara Anne."

She looked at me funny. It occurred to me that all those years of acting might have taught her a thing or two about people, how to read them. "That's what this is really all about, isn't it. You want me to make it right. You want your pound of flesh."

"I want you to say what really happened."

"I don't know what you mean. What is it you think you need to hear from my lips? Why mine? When did you ever care about anybody except your precious Scrub?"

"You need to admit what you did."

"Admit what? That I'm the devil incarnate? Source of all your misery? My God, you're such a bitter pill. A walking, talking Greek tragedy. You poisonous soup. You brew up your own bitterness, mix it up in your liver and feed on it like a bear lives off its fat in winter. What do you want from me? It wasn't me who made you stay in Talpa. It wasn't my fault you fell for someone who never loved you. You made all those choices. And it eats at you—envy—that I dared to have a life. You're sick with it. Why, you're—"

That's when I showed it to her. She stopped talking to gawp, then pretended she wasn't scared at all. She clapped her hands together slowly. "Bravo. Nice scene. What do you intend to do with that thing?"

"Say what happened to Barbara Anne. Say what you did."

"Or what? You'll shoot me? I don't think so. What would you be without me? How would you name your reflection in the mirror without cursing mine? What's there, once you take away the monster's wail for vengeance?"

"Say what happened."

"You won't shoot. That old piece probably hasn't been fired since Jack died. It's probably as useless as that lighter he gave me. There were two lighters. You remember. Two Zippo lighters just alike except that mine didn't work and yours did."

"Say what happened."

"That morning I felt sick with the heat, like I was smothering. You showed up with Floyd and Eula and Mrs. Hale. You were all out on the porch, having a smoke, waiting for me. I remember looking around for Barbara."

"She was upstairs."

"No. She was out on the porch with you all. She was sitting on Mrs. Hale's lap. Mrs. Hale was sitting in one of those old wicker chairs, flicking the ashes from her cigarette over the railing. There was a pitcher of tea on the table next to her, some glasses. Nobody took any. Pitcher was sweating, getting warm. Barbara was whining for some, but you all wouldn't let her drink tea. You took out your cigarettes and lit one, last one in the pack. Crushed the pack in your hand and said you were going inside to find an ashtray. 'Take the tea in,' I said. 'No use letting it sit here and get warm if nobody wants some.' So you put down your lighter and grabbed the pitcher and went in. Little later Floyd said it was time to go. I said I was staying at the house. There was a to-do about it, but I put my foot down. I called to Barbara to come and go inside with me. She hung back, clinging to Mrs. Hale, so I grabbed her arm and pulled her to me. You said, 'Don't treat her like that.

She's not used to being treated rough.' And I said 'She needs to learn to mind her mother.' And you said, 'She doesn't know you is all.' I pushed back through the screen door, dragged her away because I knew it made you sore. Saw your used up cigarette pack in the kitchen trash later, thought about that ashtray, seeing it with the other stuff on the table on the porch." Valeria smiled. "Easiest thing I ever did was take things away from you.

"I took Barbara upstairs because she was being so whiney and sulky. Told her she'd stay in her room until she could act right. I went across the hall to my room and stretched out on the bed. Next thing I knew I was gagging on smoke. I went to the door but I couldn't open it. The knob was red hot. I grabbed a sweater or something and managed to get the door open. Got a face full of fire and smoke, unbearable heat. Hell on all sides. There was no way to get to her. It was too late. I barely got out on the roof. Jumped with the fire right on my heels."

"You let her die, your own child."

"You're the one taught her to play with a lighter."

"One that wouldn't light."

"The two of them looked just the same, you damned fool."

Terrible thing about the truth is that ring; that clear, undeniable ring. Anybody asked me after the funeral what had happened to my lighter I said I slipped it into Jack's casket before the lid went on. I said I quit smoking because I couldn't bear to replace it. Practically a full carton I had back at the house I gave to Cory. He said I'd take it up again before long. He was wrong. I blotted it out of my mind, the whole thing: the spot on the table next to a ring of water where I'd left it, the little girl tugging against her mother's grasp, clutching something in her fist, how the child vanished into the dark doorway, the hollow slap of the screen door. Just like when Hap left and we never saw him again.

Valeria Flynn crossed her arms below her breasts and gave me that smart look with one eyebrow arched higher than the other. "You know I'm right. I can see it in your face."

Jet noise started rolling up the canyon as another plane approached the runway. I squeezed off a round and watched her fall, watched the life run out of her as that roaring filled the air and then receded again and left me standing in the silence of a waning summer afternoon. She lay where she fell with the letter scattered across her body. I didn't read what was in the letter because in the end it wasn't about him, not really. He was a symptom, a weeping gall on the trunk of an ailing tree. I stood very still, held my breath to see if it had eased, that pressure in my chest like an iron band around my heart. I stood there looking down at her, pretty even in death, her face more youthful as she lay on her back with the flesh drawn back toward the floor, wrinkles erased. I should have shot her in the face. If I let my eyes blur, the crimson blood, the chartreuse kimono and the pages bright with yellow sunshine reminded me of a stained glass window. It made me so blessed mad.

Our story for August commemorates Women's Equality Day, an observance of the day women in the US got the right to vote. To assert her rights, our heroine needed more than a ballot.

# Strangers

MYRT VAUGHN FINGERED her gloves, fiddling up the nerve to come out with what was on her mind. "They say everybody finds Jesus in jail," she said at last. She watched Claire unpin her black felt hat, hang it on the peg, and slip her white apron on over her black dress. "Haven't you had enough for one day? Shouldn't you go upstairs and rest?"

"No rest for the wicked," Claire replied. "They say that, too." She stepped behind the counter and shoved her glasses on. "Besides, we need the money. The store will be open every day from now until we move. I'm marking everything down."

"Maybe I'll take a look around." Myrt stuffed her gloves into her handbag and headed for the fabric shelves. "Way I feel about it, those two boys shoulda been no-billed. Everybody in town thinks so, too, I reckon. I thought about killing your husband myself a time or two. Much stock as people put in horses around here, it's a wonder he wasn't shot down by the railroad tracks when he put that black and white filly down."

"Poor Skunk," Claire said. "She was high spirited. Adam couldn't abide that in a female."

Myrt pulled a yellow print from an array of chintz and held it before the window in the natural light. "What do you think of this color for my kitchen? I just need two lengths for the window over the sink. I think it'll make up nice, don't you?" Myrt plopped the bolt onto the counter and ran her hand across it one more time.

"I do." Claire pulled a couple of yards off the bolt and smoothed the wrinkles out of the place she meant to cut. She opened her shears and snipped about an inch in from the selvedge, then pushed the blades, going with the straight of the grain to the other side. Left an end as square as a Kansas cornfield. "No charge," she said. "Adam would want you to have it, for being a good neighbor all these years."

"If he ever knew how much I heard of what went on in here— not that I intended to, but living next door it was hard not to—I don't think he'd be disposed to make me a present."

Claire pulled out a hunk of brown paper from the big roll at the end of the counter and ripped it along the cutter. Myrt watched her put the folded piece of fabric in the middle and wrap it up with twine. "I sure will miss buying from you, Claire. You make the neatest job of things. Never a frayed end or a short yard."

"I use a steel on my scissors and knives every week." Claire wound the fabric around the bolt again and went to put it back on the shelf.

"You should stay here," Myrt said. "Go on running this store. You're good at it. Especially the way you do the front window. I declare it sure brightens up our dull old main street. I always looked forward to seeing how you'd change those two girls with different clothes and hats. Remember that one Christmas they were Santa's elves? This year we'll be lucky if we get a few shiny balls stuck up there."

Claire glanced at the mannequins, poised on the point of moving, with vague intentions caught on their painted faces. Setting up scenes with their dead limbs, she had tried to tell stories: a confrontation on the street between two women wearing the same outfit, typists conspiring against the boss at an office party, one woman giving her friend a manicure while burning her hair with a perm. It was challenging, thinking up situations. There were only female figures to work with, in the store window. "Maybe the new owner will get in a better line of hardware. That's something Adam had intended to do."

"A hammer's a hammer to me." Myrt shook her head. "I just don't know how you can go out to the old James place. Sam says it's a quarter section if it's an inch. He says you'll never work so much land with only two little boys. You taking them or leaving them with your mom?"

"When I'm settled I'll bring them home," Claire said. "We'll be all right. I grew up dry farming."

"Won't you be lonely out there with no one to talk to?"

"I reckon I'll be too busy to notice."

That night Claire lay in the middle of the double bed eyes wide open, waiting for him to walk through the door like he always had, drunk, mean, dangerous. She knew in her head he wouldn't, that he was beyond all that now. But at the core of her, she couldn't believe it. A person of faith would say God had looked down and seen what only He could see and laid a Judgment on Adam as sure as the gravediggers had laid a stone over his coffin. But Claire was not of a righteous bent. She had never been able to convince herself there was an Almighty with His eye on the sparrow. All she could do was whisper in the dark. "It's over. It's over."

She lay there wondering how Adam might stand at Judgment Day, if there were such a thing. She imagined how he might plead. *Yes, I raised my hand to keep order in my house, but as long as I lived I never turned away a beggar.* She remembered the first time she had tried to shoo a bum off the porch, Adam's lecture on the ancient Greeks who believed a wanderer might be a god in disguise. Refusing hospitality could bring down a curse on the house, he'd said. Highfalutin nonsense, she'd said. Unthinkable, such rash frankness in light of what had come next. She'd tasted her own blood that day, ladling out to such vagrants as might have caught the whiff of her stew from twenty miles off. She'd wondered how they found the place, but knew better than to speak a word. In time, one of the tramps had told her about the runes, the signs the hobos left by the road that pointed a way from the railroad station along by the feed store and up to her door. So she fed every sooty scarecrow that clambered up the back steps, but Adam found other reasons to beat her, up until that night he got his throat slit.

She thought of those two sorry bums who'd be going upriver for Adam's murder, the way they'd appeared at the back door, peering in through the screen. She had just picked up her knife to start peeling potatoes for stew, slipped it into the pocket of her apron when she went to speak to them. The taller one had worn a battered straw hat, tugging the brim as she stepped out onto the porch. "Morning, madam," he had said, his smile flat on one side beneath a drooping eye, like maybe his face had been stove in once. A good sized man, but narrow in the shoulders, made more for running than working, in spite of the grease-stained denim coveralls and the sweaty bandana around his neck. "I'm Philip Prendergast and this is my companion Leonard Frye." The shorter, pigeon-chested and hook-nosed companion had worn a fedora and a dusty pinstriped suit. In his hand at the end of the frayed sleeve he carried a small canvas grip that held, surely, everything they possessed in the world between them. "We understand that this house is kindly disposed to persons such as Frye and myself who are on the road." She remembered how Prendergast had flicked his tongue over his lips. "You're a charitable lady. You have a kindly eye. You could spare an apple, a glass of water, perhaps."

"Sit down on the step and I'll bring you each a cold plate and a glass of milk."

It's only a few cents worth of crackers, a spoonful of beans, Adam would have said. But he had gone dove hunting that morning. She spoke her thoughts when he wasn't around to hear. "You'd feed the devil himself." They can tell you don't mean it kindly, Adam would have said. "I never yet had one refuse to eat because they thought I gave surly service." Claire remembered dishing up pigs knuckles and putting a thick slice of bread on each plate, thinking about vagrants who came by day to beg a meal and look around for valuables to steal by night, how sometimes they'd kill the householder sleeping in his bed. She'd felt for the knife in the pocket of her apron before putting the plates on a tray and pushing out the screen door.

Prendergast had stood to receive his. "This looks fine. See here, Mr. Frye, trotters."

\* \* \* \* \*

S HE REALIZED SHE had slept only when she woke with a gasp. Her terror shimmered in the dark though the room was empty of any person save herself. She swung her legs to the floor and toed the boards for her slippers. Somewhere Adam's ghost was gnashing his teeth, thwarted once more. Often as he might rush out of the bathroom with the porcelain top off the toilet tank she would always wake before he brought it down on her head. She pulled on her robe and went downstairs through the store and back to the kitchen to put on coffee. Her hand shook as she struck the match to light the gas. Through the kitchen door she could see no one had come up to shelter on the porch in the night. The tramps had stayed away since Adam was killed.

Waiting for the coffee, she took up her knife steel and began flicking the long blade of her favorite carving knife along its length. That first time Adam had wrapped his arms around her and guided her hands with his as he spoke in a voice like the center of a dark chocolate truffle, "a twenty degree angle to the steel."

She felt the rhythm of the flashing blade falter and put down her tools, steadying herself on the counter. His sweetness, even in memory, could still melt her, the image of them spooned together in bed, his gas-jet eyes, his deeply fleshed hands that knew her body's cravings. She dropped into a chair and covered her face with her hands, stifling sobs until she felt she would strangle. How was it possible those same hands could rain down such blows as would cow a man his own size, much less a woman who had scarcely felt the sting of a rough word in her father's house? What set him off? She remembered facing contusions in the mirror, wracking her brain to discover her offense. The irrationality of it more than the beatings themselves had steeled her to the deed— that and pure fear, wondering what new form his wrath might take as day by day his gentle side lost ground to the monster. She hugged herself, rocking like an abandoned waif till she got her grief tamped down again. Then she rose unsteadily and poured a mug of coffee.

Hands clamped around the mug, she climbed back upstairs to dress. Her funeral clothes lay across the chair where she'd left them the night before. Such black things. So new. She felt of the fabric as it lay there, inanimate, waiting for her to put life into it. But how? How to start again, face another day with the blood stain at the foot of the stair? She'd scrubbed her fingers raw, but she could still see the outline that showed where his life had gone after it leaked out of him. She put on her faded calico house dress, left the mourning on the chair to be dealt with later. She drank the coffee down and plodded down the stairs to another day in the store.

She flicked on the lights, took up her dust rag as she did every morning before opening time, and started wiping the tinned goods on the next shelf over from where she'd stopped the day before. Sardines from Portugal. Pictured on the lid of the oval can, a smiling, black-eyed woman in a red dress that hung a little off the shoulder. How lovely she was. How much to be envied—untouchable, young, laughing. She held a platter of fish fillets, offering them to anyone who might glance at the tin. How generous she was, how much better than Claire felt herself to be. Claire felt that she'd held herself back from charity because that was what *he* wanted, what *he* prided himself on. She had taken the opposite position if only to hold on to something of herself, a tiny spark. But it hurt her that she had taken the role of the miser. It had cost her. "No more," she said, as she wiped the tins of sardines, "No more."

There came a pecking at the door a good hour and a half before she usually raised the shade. It was Jasper Weiss, the sheriff. He waved at her through the front window. She put down her dust rag and smoothed her bobbed hair. With a moment's hesitation to remind herself who he was and what he might want, she answered the knock.

As he entered, he swept his hat off his head with a blunt-fingered hand. "Mornin', Claire. Hope I'm not botherin' you, but I saw you up and doin'. Wonder if we might have a word 'fore you open up."

His newly razored cheeks were pink and tender-looking, his eyes red-filigreed under drooping lids that would have been rakish if it weren't for the rest of his face drooping, too. "Sure," she said. "I've got coffee on."

He followed her through the racks of clothes and tables of speckled porcelain cook pots, crockery bowls, and canning jars. "How's Marjorie?"she asked, over her shoulder.

"Declinin'. Doc says she likely won't make it through another Thanksgivin'. Marjorie likes that Thanksgivin' dinner they put on at the home. They put a feather headdress on her, like the Indians who come to eat with the Pilgrims. Makes 'er happy."

"She still don't know you?"

"Naw. They tell me she won't get her memory back." He sat down at Claire's kitchen table and watched her lift the coffee pot, fill a cup and bring it to him.

She sat down across from him. "What did you want to talk to me about?"

"Awful lonely out there on the James place. Don't know why you've got a mind to leave the store here. You like to make up the display window and stock shelves, don't you? An' you're good at it. I've never seen anythin' like it, how you can dress those dummies up and make 'em look like they could walk right out of the store and down the street."

"I can't stay here, Jasper. I can't even close my eyes at night for thinking of what happened right downstairs while I was asleep in bed. I feel like if I'd waked up I might've run 'em off somehow before they…"

"We never found that money," he said. "Buried somewhere most like. They shoulda buried that knife, too."

"I got no hopes of seeing that money again," she said.

He fingered his cup, took his time with the words. "You know, Claire, I care for you. Many evenin's I've seen you workin' late, busy in that front window playin' with your big dolls, the light shinin' from behind you. Occurs to me since Adam died the two of us should marry when Marjorie's gone. It only makes sense. You're young, too young to be without a man. I'm not young, but I ain't old enough to live without a woman."

"Jasper…"

"Let me finish."

She cast her eyes down on the oilcloth.

"I got no illusions of romance. I'm not of an age to sweep you off your feet. I'm of an age to not want to appear foolish, though I often do."

"That's not true," she said. "Not at all."

"I have an honest proposition to make you. I want us to go upstairs right now. I want to show you, Claire. I'm not as old as you think. I can make you happy."

"Jasper, I got my boys to think of." She rose to her feet, turned away.

He came up behind her, put his hands on her shoulders. His lips brushed her ear. "Claire, I know."

A drop of sweat rolled down under a spit curl on the side of her face. Her voice barely scratched out a sound. "What?"

"Those two old boys said they found that knife wrapped up with two wedges of pie you give 'em to put in their bag 'fore they left. Must've hurt you to part with it, much stock as you put in your knives."

"That's a lie. One of 'em took my knife while I was out waiting on a customer in the store. When I left the kitchen it was next to the spuds I was peeling. I shoulda taken a minute to latch the screen door, but they were standing up to leave. I was in a hurry. Sure enough, when I got back to the kitchen the knife was gone and so were the tramps."

"Why didn't you tell me right away when you saw it was gone?"

"I didn't want Adam to know. He'd have taken it out of my hide twice." She summoned up a frown of irritation and turned around. "I gave you my statement. I don't see why you're standing here making me repeat myself. You still want that coffee?"

He backed off and sat down, touched the side of the mug but made no move to pick it up and drink. "How you think those boys feel? Sent up for ten years. A lousy knife. Coulda been anybody's. Don't matter. They say they never took it. Say they was never in your house, just outside. Jury's a strange animal. Not always swayed by reason. Sometimes swayed by a pretty face. A young widow's tears. Those two didn't have a prayer, even if all the facts was on their side."

"But the facts are on my side."

"Say ten years from now they come outa prison. What you gonna do out there on that old farm all by yourself? Imagine two little black scratches at the end of the lane. Your eye picks up the gait, somethin' between a gimp and a lope that comes from walkin' long miles and sleepin' rough. Even at a distance, you know they've come for more than a meal. You feel a chill jump up your back. What happens then? Who's gonna care ten years from now when the farm's wrung all the sap out of you and your hair's the color of dust?"

"A woman alone never sees strangers coming that she doesn't feel dread hanging in the air. But you learn not to make trouble if they don't bring it. You check the load in the shotgun and wait and see. That's what happens."

Weiss drew his fingertips across the oilcloth and thought a minute. "I'm gonna tell you plain how it is. I don't think you appreciate your position here. You don't see what I'm sayin'."

"You're saying you don't believe those tramps killed Adam."

"I'm sayin' you gotta make me believe it. I'm sayin' you got the means to make all my doubts disappear. Now I already told you what that is. All you gotta do is decide. Do I want to take old Jasper upstairs or do I want him to keep workin' this case, lookin' for new evidence.

Claire felt her skin stiffen. "What new evidence?"

"S'pose I found out what happened to that money? S'pose I could show that those two old boys never took it, that you stole it yourself. That would put the rest of your story in doubt, wouldn't it?" He smiled. "Money ain't no good 'less you can spend it. The take from this store that Adam had squirreled away is a damn sight more than you could ever put by workin' the old James place. You'll be lucky you don't starve out there. So tell me, Claire, how you ever gonna spend that money without people askin' how you got it? How you gonna support two kids without you have a little extra to use for gas and groceries? But let me tell you somethin'. You spend a dime that ain't egg money and I'll bring down the law on you so fast you won't have time to change your panties.

"See, Claire, there's lots of criminals a lot smarter than you who still haven't figur'd out how to put over a murder. They always make some sorta mistake. They tip their hand." He finally took a sip of coffee. "They got Capone on income tax evasion. You smarter than him? Hell, you're just a woman. Not even that. A little girl playin' with your store-window dolls. You think I'm gullible as a jury? Think you can arrange things to look a certain way and I'll buy it? No, sir, sister. I spotted the truth of it a mile off."

Claire pitched her voice low to keep the tremble out of it. "It hurts me that you think I'm capable of such a thing. I don't know how you can think that and want to have anything to do with me. You say we should marry, but how can we while you harbor such suspicions?"

"Easy. My needs get met in exchange for your stayin' outa jail."

"Won't it linger in the back of your mind that maybe someday you'll be sitting at the table and I'll get up to dish you a second helping and get my knife instead? Wouldn't you be afraid whenever I picked it up to cut you a slice of pie?"

"I thought about that," he said. "I got what you might call insurance."

"What kind of insurance?"

"Lawman kind."

"If that's true, I got very little choice here," she said.

\* \* \* \* \*

MYRT VAUGHN SIPPED her coffee and glanced around Claire's kitchen. "You certainly fixed it up nice." She tugged the front of her dress several times to air it. "Every time I take a mouthful nowadays I get a hot flash. The change of life. I swear."

"How times goes by," Claire said. She stroked the fine wrinkles around her eyes that had deepened some since she and Jasper had moved out to the James place. She had aged, but there was no privation there, nothing to suggest life had been as hard as everyone had predicted.

"And every year seems to bring a new misery. It started when Elmo Tate and Ola got killed out on the railroad track at the first grade cross. Then the next year old Mrs. Rose fell and died waiting for somebody to find her. And Doc Jones overdosing." She sighed and shook her head. "And I surely didn't expect to see you widowed twice in less than ten years."

Claire half smiled. "This rate I'll wear out my mourning."

"It's terrible to think he spent all that time as a sheriff only to retire and then get himself killed. And worse to think he waited all those years for an invalid wife to pass, God rest her, so's he could marry again, only to have it all end before he could comb gray hair. Course, some folks say he changed from what he was and that's what did him in. Flashing all that cash whenever he come to town. Never behaved that way when he was a lawman. But I expect he never had it back then." She paused to read Claire's face. "No disrespect intended."

"Of course not."

"You did well dry farming," Myrt said. "Still, with the price of wheat these days I always wondered how Jasper could afford that silver Cadillac. Used to peel off tens like they was toilet tissue. I told Harry he must've got an inheritance from Marjorie, or had some insurance on her."

"Jasper wasn't talkative about where his money come from," Claire said, "and I never asked. I never have been good with money myself. Adam kept the accounts at the store. I never knew how much we made or what those tramps took when they cleaned out the safe. It was foolish, I guess." She gazed at the brown hairline crack on the side of her cup and remembered doling out Adam's money, Jasper holding up a wad as thick as your foot saying it wasn't enough. *"I don't care if it's all gone tomorrow. These two kids of yours are of an age to start working. Let them take care of you if you run short."* She couldn't recall precisely when it struck her, maybe something she'd heard at the Saturday night dance, talk about drifters and dangerous men and hiring somebody to clean out the wolves that had been taking so many sheep.

"So what will you do now?" Myrt asked. "I sure would move back into town if I was you. Your two boys will be grown and gone soon. It don't make any sense to try to hold onto property for children nowadays. Folks is too footloose. That's changed since I was a kid. We always expected to stay on the homeplace, but that's not how young people think. You ask me, that's one reason why there's as much violence as we have now. Nobody knows their neighbors. Strangers wander into town and go to the dance on Saturday night and see a rich guy driving a fancy car. They get him to buying drinks and first thing you know the car's nosed over in a ditch and the poor man drug out on the road and killed with his own tire iron. They find out anything about who did it?"

Claire studied her coffee cup and shook her head. "I don't hold out much hope."

"So what *are* you going to do?"

"The boys want to start a feed lot," Claire said. "They've been talking to Jack Flynn about it. He might go in on it, being a cattle broker. It makes sense."

"I s'pose," Myrt said. "But what about you? What about the company of a man?"

It was on the tip of Claire's tongue to say something cautionary about company and strangers, but instead she sipped her coffee and looked down toward the end of the lane, half expecting to spy two little black scratches coming toward the door— tramps, with that gait they have, something between a gimp and a lope that comes from walking long miles and sleeping rough.

Labor Day marks the end of the tourist season in many a vacation spot, and the opportunity for owners of restaurants and inns to enjoy a little down time to rest, reorganize and, in the case of our next narrator, get rid of some excess baggage.

# Baggage

WAITING AT THE gate at SEATAC, I heard my flight was delayed another two hundred hours. A woman wearing Ugg boots and an off-the-shoulder leopard sweater rolled her eyes at me and said, "If only I hadn't checked a bag I'd have rented a car and been home by now." Not one to strike up conversations with animal impersonators in airports, I didn't say what I was thinking: *This boy never checks a bag. I'm outa here!* I actually reached down for my carry-on before it occurred to me that I'd never be able to convince Frederick that throwing away half of a round-trip airline ticket made good sense. I fiddled with the band on my left ring finger—it has three diamonds and the date of our commitment ceremony engraved—and thought of Frederick, the old bawl and chain.

He had elected not to accompany me on my latest junket to flog a dismal whodunit with all the market potential of a swooning soufflé. I pictured him with his bathrobe sashed below his Buddha belly, and wondered why I was in such a hurry to get home. He was no longer welcoming. His vitriolic taunts were no longer even interesting. Our love nest had gone cold and acerbic, and, worse than that, Laz-E-Boy trite. The hot roistering of our early days had degenerated into housekeeping, and our soul-baring wee hours pillow talk into the frank and functional (weighing the merits of various air fresheners) or the vaguely sports-related (dissing Bill Belichick).

Times like this when I've read all the cartoons in the *New Yorker* and there's nothing else to distract me, I fantasize about leaving him. But in that besotted past when it seemed like forever couldn't possibly be long enough, we had merged our finances, bought a B&B with a fat mortgage and indulged in every form of conspicuous consumption in the name of sheer joy. So now money is tight, especially since there's no living on love any more—from hard-on to hard up in only eight short years—and walking away from our joint investment is out of the question.

The podium attendant, clad in airline issue white shirt and navy trousers, speaks: "I hajus recie anu status on flie fiefiesenfie to Medfor. We wiobe bodding in twenty-fie mint. I woo lie addis tie to ass is anyone interess in volunteereen to tay a layta flie in retun for a free ticket on Unite Airlies to any destination in the US essep HawaianAlask. Anyone interess in giveen up hissea, plea come tooda podium."

I left the molded plastic seat I'd come to regard as an integral part of my anatomy and, quicker than you can say hemorrhoid, exchanged my boarding pass for a free flight voucher. *Free. Not even Frederick could find fault with free.* As I headed off to rent a vehicle I felt exhilarated, playing it fast and loose without even a reservation. A weary Avis clerk handed me a set of keys to what I imagined was a subcompact inspired by *Under the Rainbow*. But when I got to the rental lot, I discovered I'd drawn a blue RAV4, just like Frederick's, only brand new. *Weird.* I hopped in, showed my Visa at the gate and a minute later I was merging onto I-5 south.

The sky was murky with rain. The freeway lamps were illuminated, bent over the slick highway like concerned parents over an ailing infant. I flicked on my headlights, though sunset was hours off. Better safe than sorry. I fumbled out my cell phone to give Frederick a call with my new ETA. But as soon as I touched the screen, it beeped, signaling the end was at hand. I'd forgotten to recharge the battery. *Shit.* I tossed it on the passenger's seat and wondered if I'd even remembered to retrieve the charger from the wall socket near the head of the bed in the hotel room. I didn't remember packing it. Frederick would have a field day. Not only hadn't I called to say I'd be late, I'd fucked away another charger.

About that time I felt a soothing warmth in the small of my back. Heated seats! And the rental company had even left them turned on for me. Now that's nice. It struck me how much nicer we are to strangers than to the schnooks we live with. For the next thirty miles I pondered the ironies of relationships, with special attention to common courtesy, saying please and thank you, opening doors, waiting patiently while the other person puts on his scarf and gloves instead of storming out and sulking by the car. The catalogue of Frederick's offences against my sensibilities expanded to include the thermostat wars and his habit of always, regardless of the subject, having the last word.

At Portland the rain was heavier. Passing a semi was like going through the brushless carwash at sixty-five but never coming out through the dryer. The puddles that sprayed up white reminded me of the ocean, those gray waves crested with foam that swallow whole tankers without a burp. I white-knuckled it to Eugene before I had to stop for a coffee and a whiz. In the gas station convenience store I asked the cashier if there was a pay phone anywhere. She shook her head. "Everybody has cells."

On a good day it's three hours from Eugene to Bradford, aka Bardford, the southern Oregon theater town where we'd set up as overnight hosts to playgoers. That night it took over four. My eyes were so bleary I almost missed the sign by the hedge that marks our drive. I pulled in under the porte-cochère, dragged my bag out, and left the car. Frederick hadn't bothered to turn on the outside lights. He evidently wasn't expecting anyone. Though it was only September, business was so slow it felt like deep winter. We used to close for the entire month of February, go skiing or to the islands. We hadn't done that for years. Major renovations followed by a couple of seasons when occupancy was off all over town had sapped our savings. Seems we're too *un*busy to get away.

I used my key to let myself in. At the foot of the stairs I called his name. He didn't answer. I climbed to our second floor quarters.

Frederick was lying on the bed in his bathrobe with our dog Lucy cuddled against him. He had a scotch in one hand and a wad of Kleenex in the other. As I crossed the threshold, he blew his nose and threw the tissue on the floor. "Nice of you to call and let me know you weren't dead in a ditch somewhere."

"My flight out of Seattle was delayed forever because of the storm. Finally I just said fuck it and rented a car." He was already pissed, so I didn't bother to explain about the free flight voucher. Maybe I wouldn't tell him. Maybe one fine day I'd just play pin the tail on the map and fly away.

"Why didn't you call?"

"My cell was dead. I forgot to charge it. I forgot to pack the charger, too."

If you cared anything about me you'd have found a pay phone at the airport. It's that simple. You just can't be bothered. Meanwhile I sit here in tears playing Angry Birds." He held out his phone and shook it at me the way you shake a rolled-up newspaper at a bad dog.

I stood with my hands hanging out of my sleeves. Lucy took pity on me and slunk over, weighing the urge to befriend me against being judged a quisling by Frederick. I got down on the floor and lavished her with affection from ears to belly. Frederick blew his nose with a honk of finality and stood up. As soon as he did, Lucy deserted me and fawned at his ankles. "No, no more treats," he said thickly. "Mommy is going to take a shower." He cleared his throat and said to me, "How many of those fucking chargers have you lost, anyway? I don't know why I keep talking to you about this sort of thing. You're completely oblivious. You make me insane."

I watched him turn on the water in the shower. He stood on the bathmat feeling the temperature with his hand as the glass door steamed up. His feet were wide and flat, digited puddles of the stuff he was made of. He turned and took a step toward where I stood in front of the towel cupboard. He stepped into my space and opened the cupboard as if I wasn't there at all—just moved me over by taking my spot on the floor. As he reached for the towel, I shoved him. I said, "Can't you say excuse me?" I shoved him with both hands on his chest. It wasn't hard, but it unbalanced him. Maybe it was because his one arm was up and reaching into the cupboard. I don't know how it happened exactly, but he staggered backward and fell. His head hit the tiled edge of the Jacuzzi enclosure with an unwholesome crack like when a hitter gets jammed and takes a pitch on the narrow part of the bat and it breaks.

He slipped to the floor and sat straight-backed against the tile, his legs splayed out like a doll with no knee joints. I was sure he was dead. His eyes had frozen on two different focal points. I was already thinking about how it would look to the cops. No one knew I was home. There were no guests. I backed up to the bathroom door and studied the scene of Fred's fatal accident. The water was still beating against the shower wall. I left it on and withdrew down the hallway, thinking. Lucy came out of the bedroom, sat down next to me and looked up, her eyes full of questions that made her brows wobble. Had the neighbors seen me pull in under the porte-cochère? So what? So someone says the blue RAV4 was parked in the driveway at 11:15 and was gone thirty minutes later? Perfectly plausible to imagine Fred had parked there and unloaded something or gone in to pee before he put the car away. The cops would find the RAV4 in the garage and shrug their shoulders as to what errand had taken the deceased out on a foul night.

I grabbed my bag from the bedroom and carried it downstairs. Lucy trailed behind me. I tried not to imagine her nosing Fred's body, perhaps lapping at the blood that would surely puddle around his butt. I went into the kitchen and grabbed the pint bottle of tequila I keep for making barbeque sauce. I unscrewed the cap and took a gulp on my way to the door and then closed the bottle and slipped it into my jacket pocket.

I locked the door as I retraced my steps to the rental car. I exited our driveway and drove back to I-5, northbound. I had to be delayed in reaching home. Mechanical failure wasn't a plausible excuse since the rental car was new and its working condition a matter of record. So was my starting mileage and the amount of gas I'd set out with. But maybe I'd stopped for a drink. I checked my watch. 11:48. Fred's accident had occurred about 11:30. I had to stay out of the house long enough to be outside the window the cops would estimate as the time of death. Not safe to go back for a couple hours at least.

I got off the freeway at the first Medford exit and cruised down to Riverside Avenue looking for a gin-mill where I might lay low. I turned into the Shamrock Bar and almost got out of the car when it occurred to me that I didn't have much cash, certainly not enough for more than one drink. Not a good move to sit and nurse a single drink for two hours. That would look suspicious. If I used a credit card, the time of my stop would be fixed on the receipt. More room for mischief there.

I hit on a much simpler idea—a rest stop. I had a specific rest stop in mind. It was just north of exit 24. There was usually a trailer pulled in there giving out free coffee. Some service organization ran it for donations. I'd hang around a while, chat up the codger manning the coffee urn so he'd remember me when the cops got around to verifying my story.

When I pulled off at the rest stop I didn't see the coffee wagon. I parked near the cinderblock building that houses the restrooms and waited. A beat-up old Honda pulled in and a couple of teenagers got out. They staggered to the men's room, giggling and obviously drunk. After them it was a wagon with Idaho plates. A mom took two little girls into the loo. She'd want nothing to do with a strange man on a dark and stormy night. Besides, even if I did manage to engage her in conversation she'd be in the next state by the time the cops needed her to confirm my alibi. What was I going to do? Ask her to be my pen pal? I needed a rest stop regular, somebody who hung around like the coffee wagon guy from the VFW or the American Legion or what the fuck. Then I got it—hookers. Don't hookers work these places? But there was the money issue again. I fingered my Rolex. Was it worth it? And if it was, could I pull off a performance on the other side of the tracks? I rolled down my window for some air.

Then I saw him—a guy wearing jeans, a denim jacket and a cowboy hat. He was young, spare and had no shirt on under the jacket. He eyed me as he took a pack of cigarettes from his pocket and lit up. "You like to watch guys go in and out of the bathroom?" His voice was too loud in the rain-patter of the night, like the TV when you've nodded off and you wake up to some blaring infomercial.

"No, no. I just—I need some help."

His lip twisted in an expression I remembered from high school. "What kind of help?"

He was a bad boy, all right. I felt my confidence returning. "I've had a rough night. I was stuck in the airport in Seattle for hours and then I said fuck it and drove down. I pulled in to catch a nap. But I can't close my eyes. I need to relax. What's your name?"

"Brad. What's yours?"

"Simon." I pulled out the bottle of tequila. "Want a drink?"

He strolled over and grabbed it. "Shit, man. This is barely enough to wet my whistle." He drank the pint down by half before he handed it back. "What else you got that I might like?"

"Plenty."

He grinned. "That so. My truck's just over there if you'd like to back that up."

"You mean put my money where my mouth is?"

"Put your mouth wherever you like."

"I'm more of a hammering man myself."

"You wear the pants, huh? Well, come on over. I'm accommodating." He turned and started back toward where the semis were parked. Gave me a good look at his ass as I scrambled out of the car. I followed him to a big rig with a deep purple cab. There was curly script on the door. Brad Stevens Trucking, Medford, OR. "You're local," I said.

"Local talent. How about you?"

"I live in Bradford."

"Small world." He nodded at my ring. "I got a old lady, too. She's okay, but I like a little variety." He opened the door to the sleeping compartment.

"I know. Me, too."

He insisted on my using a condom and after we were done he dropped it into a bottle of bleach. "No footprints," he said. "No little blue dress. Know what I mean?"

"So if it ever came up you'd say you never saw me here tonight?"

"You got that right. I never even stopped here."

I played it cool. My mind was racing, but I pulled on my pants like everything was sweet and felt around the floor for my shoes. My jacket was down there with the tequila bottle in the pocket. In the process of retrieving my stuff I stashed the bottle under the bed, quick and quiet.

I left the rest stop at about six-thirty. The rain had stopped. It was a bright, clear morning, one of those times when you look at the blue sky and wonder if you really did what you knew you'd really done. At home there were cop cars in the driveway. Flashing lights. I felt like a giant fist was squeezing my chest. I pulled in and ran to the door. "What's going on?"

A uniformed cop guarded the back door. "Are you Simon?"

"What's wrong?"

He keyed the walkie-talkie on his shoulder and said a name. "Stand by for a minute, sir," he said. "Detective will be here shortly."

A plain clothes cop came to the door and badged me. "I'm Stan Kramer. We're investigating a homicide at this address."

"Homicide! What?" I couldn't get my breath. My knees went mushy. The detective pulled me into the kitchen and sat me down at the dinette. From the chair opposite he penciled my story into a tiny notebook: how the storm had delayed my flight from Seattle, so I rented a car. He asked for the rental slip. I retrieved it. He frowned at the time the car was logged out and did the arithmetic. "How come it took you so long to get down here?"

"I stopped at a rest area around eleven. Spent the night." I was reticent at first. Spilling too much information right away would look calculated. "Please tell me what happened here."

"Your partner, Mr. Lindstrom, called 911 at eleven fifty-six last night. All he managed to say was 'Pushed.' By the time the EMT's arrived he was dead. Massive head wound. His skull struck the corner of the tub enclosure. You got any idea who might have done it?"

"Done it?"

"Pushed him. Your partner have any enemies?"

"No. I have no idea. Maybe a thief."

"Nothing was disturbed. His wallet and a bank deposit were in the study in plain sight. No sign of a break-in. Doors were locked." He paused. "I have to say, it looks like a domestic flare-up gone wrong. You came home. Had an argument. You pushed him. He fell. It was an accident. That right?"

"No! Absolutely not. I wasn't even here last night."

"You were in a rest area."

"Right."

"Which one?"

"North of exit 24."

"Right up the road here?"

I nodded.

"Why stop so close to home?"

"To take a piss."

"All night?"

"I—I met someone."

He looked at me, trying to read me, or maybe curious about how the other half lives. "Someone have a name?"

"Brad."

"You're gonna have to do better than that if you expect me to corroborate your story."

"Stevens. He's from Medford. Drives a semi. We spent the night in the cab."

Kramer wrote in his little notebook before poking it into his breast pocket. "Okay. We're done here. You might want to stay somewhere else tonight."

"I'll be all right," I said. "My dog is here, right?"

"Yeah. Black lab running around."

"Is it okay if I clean up?"

His eyes went predatory. "Clean up what?"

"I mean can I take a shower?"

"You can do whatever you want. I'm releasing the scene. There's some blood in the bathroom upstairs, stains in the grout. You might want to take some bleach." He passed me a card and said to let him know if I planned to do any more traveling.

After the cops cleared out I made breakfast and waited for the call I knew was coming. Kramer came over instead. He told me Brad Stevens had said he stopped some time after eleven to take a leak at exit 24 on his way home to Medford. "He remembers seeing you on the way into the bathroom, but he isn't vouching for the rest of the night."

"I don't understand," I said. "Why would he lie?"

"For one thing he has a wife. But more to the point, maybe he isn't lying. Maybe you're the one who's lying."

"No, I swear. I was with him." I gave it a couple of beats before I took the shot. "I can prove it."

"I'm listening," Kramer said.

"We were drinking some tequila I had. I kicked the bottle under the bunk when I was putting my shoes on. It's probably still there."

Kramer deputized one of his minions to revisit Brad to find the bottle. "We got PC if you need a warrant," he said. He cast a stale glance at me as he left. "I'll let you know."

I ate pâté on toast around one and took Lucy for a walk. We went down to an irrigation pond where wood ducks congregate.

She splashed across the shallows and flushed seven of them. I found myself crying at the sight of the birds winging out of sight. My abandoned inner child missed the solidity of Frederick, the anchoring predictability of his ill humor. The sky was thickening to rain again. I turned toward home, calling Lucy as an afterthought.

I made tea, twitchy with foreboding as the digital display on the stove gave me a slow count to sixteen minutes after three. I started when the doorbell rang. It was Kramer, once again, followed by a beefy boy in blue. "We found your tequila bottle. It had Stevens' and your prints on it. After we confronted Stevens about the prints he admitted you were with him till morning."

"That's good news," I said. "You could have phoned."

"No, not really. You see, we need you to come downtown with us."

"Why? You have all the information you need to rule me out as a suspect."

"What we got is information that rules you in," Kramer said. "There was a third set of prints on the bottle. Frederick's prints."

I shrugged. "So what? So he used to raid my cooking tequila."

"That means the bottle came from the house here."

I saw the problem but I couldn't let them see that I saw. I brazened it out. "Of course. I took the bottle with me on the trip. I stuffed it into my bag at the last minute. I didn't want to run around looking for a liquor store as soon as I got to Seattle."

Kramer shook his head. "Impossible. You wouldn't have gotten through airport security. We checked with the airline. We know all you had was a carry-on. Too bad. It would have worked if you'd checked a bag."

All right, sure. The TSA got me with their stupid rules. But I reserved my most bitter regrets for Frederick. The plan would have worked if Frederick hadn't shot off his mouth to 911. "Pushed." The old blister had gotten the last word in for all of time and eternity.

In October a group of Classics students at a small Northwestern university join their professor at his annual celebration of a Roman Holiday. The Julio-Claudians were notorious poisoners. At the professor's latest bash, it seems someone took a page out of their book.

# Meditrinalia

BARNES SHUFFLED HIS shoes through the fallen yellow leaves on the sidewalk as he walked to the house next door, a Tudor with crisscrosses of brown half-timbering. Shrouded in ivy, it hung back from the street behind a screen of pine trees as if it didn't want to be noticed lest someone stop and bang on the door. He climbed the front steps with the heavy footed gait of the reluctant messenger. It seemed like such a big pie plate, a great wheel of custard. Ironic to be carrying food of any size to the house where a young man had died of food poisoning. He recalled his wife's counter to his objection. "Don't be silly. Home cooking is always welcome at times like these." Marjorie spoke with authority on all matters domestic. He believed she was right but it felt awkward all the same. His knock upon the heavy door was as tentative as if he expected a troll to answer.

When the door opened, Wilfork stood with drink in hand, blinking in the sunlight like a prisoner newly emerged from a dungeon. In spite of a general unkemptness, Wilfork had a cool, put-together look. Barnes assessed his neighbor's insouciant chic and thought of the people that feature in small town lifestyle pieces in the Sunday supplement. *University classics professor Peter Wilfork enjoys the many cultural offerings of this Northwest theater Mecca as well as its shtupping opportunities...*

"Hello, Wil," Barnes said. Peter Wilfork was called Wil, a small irregularity that annoyed Barnes as much as his neighbor's firm belly, his ample prematurely gray hair and his steel blue, heavy lidded eyes. Louche, those eyes. Marjorie had called them bedroom eyes once, prophetically. After Wilfork's wife died, Marjorie and the widower had an affair. Marjorie had never told Barnes, but he knew because when it was over and Wilfork had moved on to his next conquest, all that was left of his wife was as hollow and frail as the broken eggshells discarded in the sink during the making of the offering he now held in his hands. The glass ovenware was still warm, and reminded Barnes that it was in fact her warm beating heart that he carried to present to the man next door. "Marjorie baked a quiche." Barnes held out the gift that betokened his wife's sympathy but Wil made no move to relieve him of it.

"Come on in," Wil said. He stepped aside and Barnes dropped off the quiche on a table in the foyer. "Have a drink?"

"Sure. Whatever you're having. So how are you bearing up through all this?"

"I'm half in the bag at ten o'clock in the morning," Wilfork said. He led Barnes into the dining room with a breakfront where a dozen place settings, each a different pattern, were displayed. Wilfork poured Scotch into two glasses from a ship's decanter on the sideboard.

It was her own fault, Barnes thought, as he examined the floral border of one dinner plate. Marjorie had not stumbled blindly into Wilfork's arms. She knew him for a cad. Faculty wives snapped up such information—their husbands' career ups and downs, infidelities, moist fetishes hidden beneath tweed and corduroy— with the alacrity of Indians swapping vast tracts of North America for handfuls of blue beads. Indeed *she* had lured *him*. That spring before it was really warm enough, she had donned her favorite cut-off jeans and torn tee-shirt to work the long row of rose bushes that separated their two back yards. The outfit that harked back to her grunge period gave her such a careless youthful air that she seemed, that year, with the sun-kissed streaks in her hair and the scent of steaming earth about her, to embody spring itself. As the season ripened, she drew him, with her glad rags and her brown limbs, as surely as the bursting buds of her roses drew the honeybees. Thick as thieves by fall, swanning around with her invented excuses to pop next door, helping with Wil's annual dinner for his Classicists. Hah. Not this year. Wil had snuffed the affair by Christmas.

Wilfork handed Barnes his drink and led the way to a great room with a stone fireplace that could have accommodated a side of beef on a spit. "I feel lousy about it, as you can imagine. Responsible to some degree."

The two men positioned themselves on opposite sides of a hatch-cover coffee table on facing worn leather sofas littered with pillows and cigarette ash. As they sat down, Wilfork fished a pack of smokes out of his pocket. "Adrian called and gave me a bunch of crap first thing this morning. The caterer. Said his business has disappeared faster than a fart in a gale. The police still have his kitchen closed down. Poor bastard says he can't understand why they aren't after the person up in Eugene who supplies his vegetables." He struck a match and lit the cigarette. "Says he won't be catering my annual dinner next year." He blew a lungful of smoke into the sun-shot space where the dust motes danced. "I hate to see our little Meditrinalia celebration go by the boards. It was Barbara's idea, you know. She detested Columbus Day and thought that in as much as October 12 is fixed in the Federal canon of holidays, we should observe the Roman holiday dedicated to the goddess of healing."

"Meditrina?"

"Exactly. She was sort of a parvenu who was incorporated into the festival celebrating the new wine. A crap goddess; but, there she is, all the same."

"A convenient alternative, in any case."

Wilfork raised his glass and sipped. "I fear the principle of healing went right off the rails at our latest gathering."

Barnes tasted his scotch. "You remember those awful lang and lit parties we used to attend so faithfully?"

"Quite the scene from Who's Afraid of Virginia Wolfe, weren't they. Thank God we Greco-Roman types got transferred to the history department."

"Marjorie would always tell me the next morning who was sleeping with whom." Barnes chuckled. "Was always the ones who seemed to be feuding. The hotter the argument, the hotter the sex, apparently."

"Spare me." Wilfork flashed a bleak smile.

"Marjorie says I'm inattentive to innuendo, deaf to double entendre. I tell her she's alert to alliteration."

"Spoken like a true English weenie."

Barnes paused to give his next statement space to land. "Marjorie says she knows how Patrick Dexter was killed."

"Oh, yeah? How's that? She some kind of mycophile or something?"

"I'm serious," Barnes replied. "She knows who did it."

"Oh, stop."

"No, really. She reads a lot of true crime, detective fiction. Claims she always knows 'who done it' before the end of the book."

"So has she been to the police?"

Barnes shook his head. "Heavens no! She would never tell on one of the good ones—you know how the wives refer to other wives they like as 'one of the good ones'—especially since Dexter had it coming as far as Marjorie is concerned."

"So? Who is it?"

Barnes cut his eyes toward his host and gave him a sly smile. "Deborah, of course. Marjorie says it's nearly always the spouse."

"That's bullshit. Deborah Dexter could no more murder someone than…"

"But it's poison, remember," Barnes continued. "That's a woman's crime. Think of Livia, Agrippina."

"Yes, yes; but this isn't ancient Rome."

"All of you Classicists know about them," Barnes said. "That's the point. It's a copy-cat crime."

Wilfork considered the premise. "It was a kind of joke around the table each year, the fact that Claudius's death date was only two days after Meditrinalia in the year 54. Sometimes John Chapman would get into a food fight with me about what kind of poison killed him. There's a contrary school of thought that says the emperor's symptoms are indicative of muscarine poisoning because that toxin acts quickly. Trouble is, it's not usually fatal. So, I go along with the theory that Agrippina—she was also Claudius' cousin, incidentally—offered him a mushroom from her own plate at dinner. This was a harmless mushroom known as Amanita caesarea, but it was laced with extract from the highly poisonous Amanita phalloides, the Death Cap. And consistent with Amanita poisoning, Claudius didn't die right away, but began having the green apple quickstep the next day. A physician by the name of Xenophon was apparently Agrippina's co-conspirator. When he was called in to relieve the emperor's gut pains, he administered an enema laced with the poison of a plant called bitter apple. That dispatched the old boy within twenty-four hours. I tend to think it suits Agrippina's style to deal the final blow in the guise of a cure. After Claudius was proclaimed a deity post mortem, Nero, his successor, called mushrooms 'the food of the gods' in reference to their having launched Claudius into eternity. Nero was a nasty little shit."

"There you have it," Barnes said.

"But why would she…Deborah, I mean."

"Apparently he beat her. According to Marjorie, Deborah confided in Carly Nash that she wanted to leave Patrick, but couldn't find the courage. So often the way with abused women. Lately people said she was seeing someone else. I expect having another man waiting in the wings might have given her the nerve."

"I don't believe it," Wilfork declared.

"Put yourself in Deborah's shoes. You're saddled with an abusive husband who is your academic inferior. Common knowledge that the only reason Patrick got his job at the university was because you and he came as a package deal. You're his lifeline. He'll never let go of you. Now what's out of the question?" Barnes lifted his eyes to the ceiling for a second. "Of course you'd have to have a reasonable expectation of getting away with it. Whether you're stealing a candy bar, diddling someone else's wife or killing your husband, the key is not to get caught."

"I still say it's out of the question. Deborah Dexter couldn't drown a kitten. She's so thin a stiff breeze would blow her into the next state."

"Again, I hasten to point out that physical strength has nothing to do with the crime in question."

Wilfork crushed out his cigarette in an overfull ashtray. "All right, smartass. Go on and make your case. Give me the facts. How did she do it?"

Barnes savored a swallow of scotch. "Nice single malt."

"Quit stalling."

"Right. The first thing to note is that Patrick and Deborah Dexter had been to your Meditrinalia dinner—what, three or four times, I should think?"

"Three before this year," Wilfork replied.

"So Deborah was familiar with your way of putting it on. She knew to expect a formal invitation with the menu printed on the back. I assume you still do that?"

Wilfork rose from the sofa. "I have one right here," he said. He shambled through an open set of French doors into an adjoining room. Barnes could see a cluttered desk and a computer from where he sat. His host pawed through a stack of papers and emerged a minute later. "Here it is," he said. He handed Barnes a long, skinny card formally lettered on one side, then went back to the couch and sank down into the depressed cushions. "Carly Nash volunteered to do the calligraphy this year. Not nearly as pretty as Marjorie's hand, but I could hardly refuse."

It was a five-course meal that made Barnes long for an early lunch.

Course 1: Button mushrooms in burgundy sauce with Crater Lake Blue Cheese on Crostini served with Zéfiro All'ombra del Prosecco

Course 2: Warm Potato Salad with Feta and Honey Mustard served with Palais Kesselstatt 1999 Reisling

Course 3: Poached Salmon with Polpettas and Olive Tapenade served with Henri Bourgeois 1999 Petit Bourgeois Sauvignon Blanc

Course 4: Rock Cornish Game Hen, Brandy Glazed and Halved, with Porcini Wild Rice Stuffing served with 1999 Folonari Shiraz

Course 5: Torte Regina with Cinnamon Ice Cream served with Épervier's 1996 Barilé

When Barnes looked up, Wilfork was eyeing him. "You're wondering about the Shiraz, aren't you. The pairing was a little unconventional, but I thought in as much as it was a game bird and that particular vintage has wonderful forward fruit ... It's Sicilian. Cheap, too. Came off quite well, I thought."

"Right," Barnes said. He couldn't tell a Côte du Rhone from a cotillion and couldn't have cared less. "Okay," he continued. "So, everyone would be required to appear in party attire. The caterer, Adrian, cooked and plated each course in the kitchen then served two plates at a time, giving you ample time to pour the accompanying vintage and lead the faithful in swirling and sniffing. Oh, and I almost forgot the most important detail. Each guest would dine on a unique set of china. Upon emerging from the kitchen with a course Adrian would match the plates he was serving to the bread and butter plate already on the table. Is that accurate?"

"To a tee," Wilfork replied with an exaggerated emphasis on his consonants.

"Oh, and one other thing. The women would go into the kitchen before time to be seated at the table as it was their job to pass around the canapés during the cocktail hour. Carly told Marjorie she thought it was chauvinistic, but she did it anyway out of a spirit of largesse."

"Yes, yes. Guilty as charged," Wilfork said. "So what?"

"Well, that gave Deborah an opportunity to peek into the warming oven where the dinner plates were stacked. She could see the order in which the entrees would be served. Then she went to the dining room and rearranged the place cards to make sure she and Patrick would be sitting at the places that would receive those last two plates."

Wilfork rolled his eyes. "So where does the poison come into it?"

"Oh," Barnes said. "I forgot that part. Well before the date of the dinner Deborah collected some Death Caps. It's common knowledge they grow locally in wooded areas. In fact, the Parks and Rec issues a warning every autumn about them. Deborah likely cooked them in butter and then pureed them in a blender to achieve a consistency that could be injected into the stuffing of a Cornish Hen using something as simple as a turkey baster."

"A turkey baster? I don't remember seeing her schlepping a turkey baster around."

"Yes, well that's where Deborah's particular style of dress comes in. How would you describe her wardrobe?"

"Sort of a peasant vibe—long, full skirts and boots and blouses with puffy sleeves."

"Exactly. The sort of clothes you'd wear to conceal as much of your body as possible."

"Because of the bruises?"

"Yes, and because she was painfully thin. Easy enough to shove the poison apparatus into her boot, I should think."

"Go on," Wilfork said.

"Once the dinner began, Deborah bided her time until the main course was being served. Adrian emerged from the kitchen carrying two plates at a time, you said, each with half a hen. Sometime into the process, perhaps when the first four plates were brought out, Deborah came up with an excuse to leave the table." Here Barnes looked expectantly at Wilfork.

Wilfork scratched his head. "Yes," he said. "There was some ruckus, some wine spilled. She said she needed to put some water on her skirt so the stain wouldn't set."

"Perfect. So she knocks over her wine then loiters in the laundry room adjoining the kitchen until Adrian has gone to serve and only one bird remains to be split and dished up on the remaining two plates. Deborah quickly injects the stuffing of the last bird with the mushroom poison and retreats to the guest bath where she does splash some water on her skirt."

"But then her meal was poisoned just as Patrick's was."

Barnes smiled. "That's the genius of it. She ate her portion of the poison just as Patrick did. She had to be prepared to do this since the hen would be whole when she had the opportunity to inject the poison. Adrian split each bird immediately before plating it." He raised his hands in the air. "Voila. That's how it was done."

"But why wasn't Deborah poisoned?" Wilfork asked.

"She was," Barnes said. "That is, she would have been if it weren't for the fact that Deborah is bulimic. Marjorie says she periodically takes a leave of absence to get treatment at some private clinic."

"I always thought it was for depression."

Barnes shrugged. "So after consuming the main course she doubtless excused herself to go to the powder room where she vomited."

"My God!" Wilfork exclaimed. He got to his feet and went to the mantle where he pondered what Barnes had said. After some time he spoke. "But you can't prove any of it."

"It isn't my theory to begin with," Barnes said. "Marjorie would probably kill me if she knew I'd told you about it. She explained it to me in strictest confidence. You won't say anything."

"Of course not," Wilfork said.

"Well," Barnes said, "it's getting late. Marjorie will be home from the store soon and I have to help her with the groceries. Try to take it easy. Let the police sort it out."

"Of course." Wilfork saw Barnes out and watched him step lightly down the sidewalk. When Barnes was out of sight, Wilfork closed the front door and locked it. He looked at the quiche on the side table, deliberated for a moment and then carried it into the kitchen.

Wilfork thought about motive, about self-preservation and spite as he cut the quiche into eight pieces and then fed each light, perfect wedge down the garbage disposal. After that he ran some water into the empty glass pie plate and added a splash of bleach. When he was finished, he pulled open the door of his refrigerator freezer and extracted a Marie Callender's frozen dinner. Marie, he was confident, had nothing against him.

Fifteen minutes after Barnes got back to his own home, Marjorie returned from running errands. When he heard her car pull into the garage, Barnes jumped up to help her with her grocery sacks. "How is Wil?" she asked, as she shucked off her coat and hung it in the closet.

"Hard to tell," Barnes answered. He put the sacks on the kitchen counter. "Seems like water off a duck's back one moment, then the next he's raving about how he thinks Deborah killed Patrick. Quite bizarre. He really thinks she did it."

"Oh, my," Marjorie said. "And I suppose he'd been drinking."

"Greeted me glass in hand at the door," Barnes said. "I had one to keep him company."

Marjorie sighed and shook her head. "That man will drink himself to death." She lifted a box of pasta out of one of the brown bags. "Did you tell him to call me when he's finished with the quiche so I can collect my pie plate?"

"Yes, of course. You don't think I'd forget about your favorite pie plate, do you? He'll call you. Don't worry."

"Of course you didn't forget. You never forget anything."

By this time Wilfork's frozen dinner had heated in the oven for the number of minutes prescribed on the box. The minute minder went off. With a pot-holder he lifted the aluminum tray out of the oven and set it on the counter. He was assembling a napkin and silverware on a tray table in the TV room when he heard the phone ring. The electronic noise blasted through the empty house with alarming insistence, yet Wilfork remained rooted to the spot where he stood, making no move to answer. Eventually the machine picked up. Barbara's voice invited the caller to leave a message. "Peter?" Deborah said, breathy and tentative as if she thought she may have called Mars by mistake. "Are you there? Please pick up. I need to talk to you. I need to see you. I miss you, Peter. Desperately. Call me as soon as you get this. Any time. I'm so alone. Please call me. I love you."

As soon as the call ended Wilfork dashed to the answering machine and erased the message. He was frankly horrified to have the voice of this murderous woman in his house, encoded in some electronic apparatus. He felt directly threatened, even terrified, as word for word his brain replayed the pleading message. It was worse even than the quiche.

After the Veteran's Day parade in the upstate New York town of Zymo a well-heeled matron goes missing and turns up dead. Her best friend flies in for the funeral and stays to see that justice is done.

# Justice in Zymo

S HE WAS LATE and gave the cabbie too much money because she didn't want to wait for the change. The sidewalks were iced and the atmosphere thick and white. A few stragglers scuttled through the freezing fog and picked their way delicately up the glazed steps. She followed them, cursing herself for wearing high heels as if she were parading down the street in Dallas. No one lingered on the steps of the chapel to say hello to an approaching acquaintance. The mourners scurried inside with a kind of cockroach haste, eyes cast down, mouths hugging a grim, tight line. It didn't look like sadness to her. She couldn't decide whether it was simple discomfort or the habitual expression of country folk who got by on grit and determination.

Inside an astounding number of mourners jostled for position in the pews. Amazed that so many had turned out on a raw December day to pay their respects to Lettice Morgan, she smiled, remembering the girls at college. Those who liked her called her Letty, those who didn't dubbed her "Lettuce."

She settled into an unoccupied space next to a broad-shouldered man in an olive drab uniform dabbed over one breast with an array of colorful ribbons. She was still thinking of meeting Lettice in those first days of freshman orientation at Cornell. Letty was attending out of family tradition while she, Jayne, had managed by cobbling together a scholarship from the Coleman County chapter of the American Legion, a whopping student loan, even for 1969, and some money her mother had put by from her sewing business. Lettice, with her fashion sense and that way she could navigate any situation as if she'd been born with a social road map along with her silver spoon, had loved Jayne's stories about armadillos and luckless cowpokes. They had shared a double room in Balch Hall.

The war hero next to her cleared his throat and it occurred to her that he had already spoken to her once. "Friend of the family?" he asked, again.

"Oh, I'm so sorry. I'm just overwhelmed is all. This place." She turned her palms up in a gesture of appreciation toward the interior that Louis Comfort Tiffany had created for the Morgan Memorial Chapel. It was overwhelmingly green. Green glass beads around the paintings, swirling green tinted art glass in the window panels, a green pattern reminiscent of a Celtic cross on the altar. The mosaics, the chandeliers, the decoration of the apse were all in shades of yellow or smoky purpled milk glass that complemented the primary color—green. She felt shaded and subdued, as if she were in a garden bower, secluded and sequestered, on the verdant bank of a creek whispering in tones sibilant and sylvan. "Poor Letty. I can't believe it."

"Yes," he said, soberly. She noticed that the somber tone of the occasion didn't stop him from casting a sidelong glance at her nylon clad legs. He was a square-jawed type, nicely aged with silver woven through his honey-blond hair. "I suppose one always thinks, at these times, of one's own last rites," he continued. "I'm Bryce Harper, by the way."

She clasped his beefy paw briefly. "Jayne Justice." She rearranged her legs, feeling his appreciation. She was well north of fifty, looked a fabulous forty and knew it.

They fell silent as a chord of organ music flared into the expanse of the chapel. Jayne surveyed the crowd, all colors of collar and race, who had turned out to say goodbye to Letty. It must have been through her charitable and civic work that she'd engendered such affection. For the first time that day Jayne wept into a hankie, thinking of Letty's great goodness.

She turned her attention to a wall-mounted flat-screen displaying a montage of photographs showing Letty at every age: black and white snapshots of her as a baby, a faded Polaroid of her in a flannel nightie and red velvet bathrobe hanging her stocking over the mantelpiece on Christmas eve, a newspaper shot of the high school cheerleader posing in her abbreviated skirt and letter sweater with pompoms, a shot that could have been a postcard of the perfect girl on the perfect day soaking up the Italian sun with Trevi Fountain in the background, a professionally composed wedding shot of the happy couple poised to cut the multi-storied wedding cake sharing the grip of a bright, lethal-looking knife, Letty a lithe Grace Kelly look-alike in a satin sheath dress and cascading veil, Sam in that very dress uniform worn by those large hunks of manflesh who now occupied the pew behind the grieving widower, a forbidding formation assuring his privacy. She wondered why Bryce wasn't up there with the others, pictured them swilling hard liquor neat and talking about choppers, Viet Cong and Napalm. But she didn't really want to think about that. She wanted to think about Letty and try to find some remnant of her here amid all these strangers. *Closure. Such a trite word these days. But there it is.* She wanted closure. If not closure, just a respite from a dozen nagging questions and imagined horror scenes of what the gnawing animals had left of her friend's body.

Jayne concentrated on the organ music and began to feel more at peace, as if the chapel had lent her its great green soul for a time certain. She felt, with sudden clarity that being in Zymo was not only a chance to find out what had happened to her friend, a chance to make amends, but an opportunity to understand the past, the greenness of youth, the salad days. She felt there was a huge revelation just on the threshold of conscious thought.

A figure in a surplice climbed to the dais and the mourners fell silent. He began to speak of Letty in that ritual intoning voice that all real preachers have, a hypnotic delivery, a cadence more than a series of words. The sound of his voice washed over her. "She is with God," he said. "She is at peace. It is for us to adore her always, but to let her go to this rest and not to charge her with our sadness, our loss. She would not wish it. She would want us to rejoice in her freedom, her joy." *Freedom. Why do women walk out of their secure houses, that all so safe round of the everyday routine? Freedom, the wild thing. Freedom, a word from the seventies.*

Her eyes wandered back to the photo montage again. It had progressed to the more recent past. Letty standing in a sundress beside a vintage convertible with huge tail fins, Letty giving out a prize to a little scarecrow at a children's Halloween party, Letty in that cream-colored suit, the same suit she had on in the newspaper photo that accompanied her obit, but in this shot she filled it out better. Jayne hadn't noticed it before, but in the photo taken on Veterans Day, the day Letty went missing, she looked thin and wan.

The preacher concluded his remarks and invited Letty's family and friends to come to the dais and share memories of her. A silver coifed woman stepped to the microphone and introduced herself as a friend from the garden club. She talked about how Letty loved to get her hands into the dirt. She told about how the two of them had tried to exterminate moles using things that looked like fire crackers that you lit with matches and then as the fuze spit sparks all over the place, you shoved it into the mole hole and this rotten egg gas came boiling up out of the ground. She had everybody laughing and crying by the time she was done. The next person stepped forward. A line had formed along the aisle to the right of the center section of pews, twenty people at least. Jayne considered possible escape routes as she did a quick calculation of how long it would take to get through all these testimonials.

The next speaker to take the dais was one of the men in uniform. He cleared his throat and adjusted the mike as he drew himself up to his full height. The undercurrent of chatter that had begun during this less formal part of the service stopped dead. "I'm Master Sergeant Hal Barton," he began, "and I've been a friend of this family since Sam first laid eyes on Letty. In fact, I saw her first." He paused to give the joke time to land. "I don't need to tell anybody here that besides being a great gal with a big heart and enough brains to keep Sam on his toes, she was one beautiful lady. Women like Letty never really get old. Just look at the photos on these monitors. She always had that thing that gave you goosebumps whenever she entered a room."

As he went on Jayne found herself stuck on that point. *Letty never got old?* She wasn't so sure. It was that photo in the newspaper again, one that didn't appear on the monitors, as it turned out. Letty didn't look well in that last picture. What was it that had worn her down? Maybe that was the sixty-five thousand dollar question, the key to why she had walked into the woods that afternoon. Jayne kept coming back to that same question. *Why? Why? Why?*

"I remember when Sam told me he'd proposed to Letty ..." Master Sergeant Barton droned on. All Jayne could think was how she couldn't stand it when guys got tapped to speak in honor of someone else but instead told long, lame stories about themselves.

She stood to sneak out before the next tedious anecdote, but just as she was about to make a break for it, a crazy woman in an open trench stood up and started yelling. The wild-eyed woman was of indeterminant age with short hair dyed blond, a blocky face and chunky jewelry. She waved an eight by ten photo and screamed, "How about Joey Zealand? Anybody remember him?

Joey never got a nice funeral. He never had anybody stand up and speak for him. Joey got shoved into a hole in the ground and forgotten!"

The uniformed figures sitting near Sam Watson swarmed to the crazy woman and dragged her, squalling like a scalded cat, out of the chapel. Jayne turned to look at Bryce Harper. "What was that all about?"

"Search me," he said.

"She had a picture of a soldier with the flag in the background—like they show on TV when a soldier is killed in Afghanistan."

Harper shrugged. "Maybe she lost her son or a grandchild. Or maybe she's just one of the crazy women of Zymo. There was a women's asylum just outside of town, you know. Some years ago the inmates were all released. Budget cuts. You'll see them wandering the streets, all ragged and raving. One old gal spat on me once."

"Maybe," Jayne muttered. She felt for the protesting woman, violated by the olive-drab tribe. "I need to get out of here." She tried to get past him to get to the aisle. He stood and inflated his chest to impede her progress or maybe just to feel her body as it wriggled by.

She emerged from the over-warm chapel into the sleeting chill of late afternoon and stood on the steps thinking of her shoes, the icy footing, the realization that she had no hope of getting a taxi unless she walked a long block up to the main drag. As she reluctantly stepped off the porch, Bryce Harper hastened out and called to her. "Ms. Justice! I'm glad I caught you. Look, I ... I have a confession to make. I don't know exactly why, but I lied to you inside when you asked about the woman with the photograph. I don't know her personally but I know of her."

She found his admission sympathetic.

"It's a long story," he continued. "Listen, would you consider joining me for a drink. I know we just met, but I could use one. There's a spot a couple blocks from here, on the way to the mansion. You're going to the reception, aren't you? At least let me give you a lift."

"I appreciate it," she said. "I could use a drink, too."

He led the way to a low slung vintage XKE that no woman in a pencil skirt could possibly get into without compromising her modesty. Jayne clicked the old fashioned seatbelt, the kind that only went across your lap but had no torso restraint. "Nice car," she said.

"I'm a collector," he replied and slammed her door. He got in behind the wheel, reached behind the sun visor for the keys and started the car. The engine surged to life with a satisfying rumble engineered to cause a spike in testosterone all over town. He backed out of the parking space and threw a wave of slush as he turned onto the street.

"So that gal in the chapel?"

"She's the widow of a guy who was with our unit. He died a few years ago. She's had a screw loose ever since, a real wacko-bird. All of us avoid her like the plague."

"Us?"

"The guys, our unit."

"I see," she said, as he got the rear end under control. "So you live around here?"

"I live in Ithaca, but I spend a fair bit of time up at this end of the lake, enough to know my way around Zymo at any rate."

Harper pulled over to the curb near a street door with a black awning and flickering gas lamps. The carpet beneath the awning was blood red. "This is The Skeleton Key," he said.

In a day in which Jayne had already devoted a good deal of time to contemplation of death in grizzly detail, any reference to skeletons, however metaphorical, was hardly appealing. But often life offers no choice in these matters. And even if she did want to turn away from that door on grounds of grim reaper overload, the smell of greasy burgers and fries that wafted from a vent over the door was enough to tempt her inside. Her stomach was empty and not nearly so picky as her brain with its finicky notions of low cholesterol and high fiber.

And so, with a feeling that she would look back on this day as one of the more macabre in her life, Jayne walked the carpet as Harper heaved open the brass handled door. Boldly she entered, in search of that solace that only deep-fried food and red meat can provide.

Though her eyes took a minute to get accustomed to the dimness of the interior, Jayne was immediately aware that this place was a one-off. Just inside the door was a primitive therapeutic device about the size of a shoeshine box with a hand crank on the side and leads coming out that attached to a helmet thing. The contraption was evidently an early means of delivering electroshock treatment. Sitting next to it was a whirligig that featured a swordsman who would lop off a kneeling prisoner's head when activated by a breeze. She also noted a flying pig kite overhead, and a chair with arm and leg restraints next to a miniature guillotine. The walls were covered with purloined street signs: a state route shield emblazoned with "69," and plain rectangular ones with the words "Nowhere" and "Perdition," as in 'the road to.' Her favorite object was a porcelain head used to illustrate phrenology with different character informing areas mapped out: the loci of acquisitiveness, tune, destructiveness and amativeness, for example. On the face of the poor mannequin with the dotted black lines and words all over his skull, someone had tied a Mardi Gras mask of yellow, green and purple feathers, adding insult to injury. The weirdness went on and on, as every available horizontal surface and square inch of ceiling space was crowded with more stuff of this genre.

Harper led her to a booth across the room from a U-shaped bar where a lone female was polishing glasses and staring fixedly at a televised ice hockey game that had degenerated into a plain old brawl. "Hi, Audrey," Harper sang out.

The barmaid put down her towel and reflexively grabbed a shot glass and the bottle of Wild Turkey. "Hi, Bryce," she sang back. "How you doin'?"

"Oh, middling." He shucked off his army greatcoat and scooched across the bench seat, pinning Jayne next to the wall. Audrey brought Bryce's drink and looked expectantly at Jayne.

"Mine's scotch on the rocks. Glen Morangie. Love your décor."

"At the Skeleton Key the distinction between Halloween, penal servitude and mental health facilities is blurred as you can see. All this junk is from Morgan State Hospital, the Zymo Penitentiary and a costume shop that was on the premises before the bar opened. The electric chair was used for the first time right here at the Zymo Pen," she added with a nod in that direction. "Some guy who'd murdered his lover. We've had electrocution since 1890."

"Progressive," Jayne said.

"Oh, and just in case you're going that way," Audrey continued, "I should warn you that in the Ladies' there's a life-sized wooden carving of a South Seas islander buck naked and fully erect, standing just next to the paper towel dispenser. You've gotta see it. Makes a trip to the can worth the effort."

After Jayne had her drink, Bryce clicked his glass against hers. "To Letty," he said.

"To Letty," Jayne replied and sipped. She found herself craving a cigarette, though it had been thirty years since she'd quit. "So did you know Letty and Sam in Germany?" she asked, trying to take her mind off the urge.

"Sam and I served in the same unit in Vietnam. It was all guys from upstate New York. Sam was our CO before he got shot. Most of us who got out of combat alive came home to this area to live. I stayed in the Reserves, got my retirement."

"That explains why your uniform still fits," Jayne remarked.

"We're Special Forces," Bryce said with a smile of unabashed pride. "We tend not to go to seed." On the other side of the room were a couple of pool tables where one lone player lazily stroked his cue, sending the white ball to kiss a colored one with a desultory click.

Jayne did the math. Thirty-some years since America's Vietnam adventure had ended, here they were, with their flat stomachs and hair cut high and tight, as if no time had passed at all. *Who lives like that? Who are these guys?* She didn't want to go there. She wanted to think about Letty, not about a handful of throwbacks to a time and place that had never brought out anything but the worst in most of those who had lived through it.

"So what's your story? Where are you from? How do you know Sam? Are you married?"

"Dallas. I don't. I was, but Roy got drunk and drove into a tree so I'm not anymore."

"What do you do, besides run off at the mouth?"

"I'm an art dealer. No gallery at the present. I've been preoccupied."

"With what? Kids?"

"In a manner of speaking. So far I've spent my life taking care of men who never got enough attention from their mothers."

"I'd say you're due for a change of pace."

She assessed his grin. *What do you have in mind? Fast and loose?* "You know, I'm starving. Any chance we could grab a burger or something?"

"Why don't we just go on over to the reception. There'll be plenty of food there." He knocked back his drink and she, somewhat disappointed, did the same.

The Jag cruised through the historic district of Zymo, a nineteenth-century enclave of old brick and new money amassed by the industrialists of that day. Though her family fortune had no doubt dwindled since the heyday of her ancestors' starch company, Letty would have been a dependable supporter of charity Christmas craft fairs, ice-cream socials to benefit animal and human shelters, and garden bazaars featuring the work of starving artists. Jayne knew Sam Watson had been shot during the war and had come home paralyzed. She thought of the invalid husband and wondered if Letty had occasionally slipped out of sight for what she would sotto voce call an "indecent weekend." Letty would have returned tan and fit to wink at direct questions as to the exact nature of the most recent escape, saying something like, "Young men really are boring after three days, just like house guests." That's all she would have admitted to.

Some of the old cats in her garden club would call it comeuppance, what had happened when she dropped off the radar for the last time that November. Why had she left her home for a long cold walk into the densely wooded hills above Cayuga Lake, this girl who had so loathed exertion of any kind? Jayne remembered their first day together in their dorm room, watching Letty unpack a rainbow of cashmere sweaters and coordinated skirts from elegant leather bags. Her luggage tags were printed with quips like, "Of course I want room service!" and "Camping?

Do I look like a cub scout?" She had reported to her first phys ed class with a letter from her family doctor specifying that she was cleared only for square dancing.

Two days. Why had it taken so long for anyone to notice that she'd left without taking her purse or keys? And why was it Lettice's maid who notified the police that something was terribly wrong at the Morgan house? Why not Sam, her husband? What did that say about their marriage? Was Sam among those Zymoans wringing their handkerchiefs in distress or among those crowing with delight? And which of the two groups outnumbered the other?

Letty's three-story Greek revival home on Zymo's main drag was a white painted brick structure with a slate mansard roof punctuated by dormers. Bryce dropped her under an old fashioned port-cochère and went to park the car. A grizzled old patrician stepped out onto the porch and lit a cigarette. She stood on the steps of the family mansion swathed in an alopecic mink and wearing dark glasses. Her arms crossed over her meager breast and the smoke clutched between two talons, she regarded Jayne with an acipitrine glare and spoke in a voice like tires over a blue stone drive. "I'm Lois, the mother," she said. "You must be the college roommate."

In the old dame's features Jayne recognized a resemblance to a studio photo that had been perched dutifully on Letty's desk. Lois must have been about forty when the picture was taken. She had Garbo eyes with high arched brows, the angles of her face unsoftened by prematurely gray hair brushed straight back. Lois Morgan might never have pinched a small child to make him cry when his mother's back was turned, but from the moment Jayne first laid eyes on the old harpy she found it hard to give her the benefit of the doubt. When Bryce trotted up, Lois looked knowingly at them and said, "You'll want to get to the buffet before the ham's gone." She languidly motioned toward the front door. Jayne and Bryce went inside.

The walls were painted a rich creamy yellow that reminded Jayne of egg custard. The woodwork was bright white. A crystal chandelier reflected colors from the stained glass panel in the front door, a motif of vines and grapes in green, aqua and deep purple. A winding staircase seemed to wait for the queen of the ball to make a stunning entrance. The hardwood floors gleamed almost as brightly as the ormolu framed wall mirrors that repeated each other into infinity. Jayne identified an elevator behind a pair of pocket doors in a recessed alcove only a moment before the doors retracted and a man in a wheelchair emerged followed by a twenty-something Asian beauty. Sam Watson navigated his power chair with his svelte assistant at his side. He was swathed from hip to ankle in a plaid lap robe, leaving her to imagine legs wasted to sticks since he'd lost the use of them.

Sam stopped in front of Bryce and extended his hand. "Hello, old friend," he said with a smart nod of salt and pepper curls that brought to mind a bust of Caesar. "Thanks for guarding the rear at the chapel." His face had a flush of hypertension, as if his necktie were too snug, but he was too stiff-necked to loosen it. "I see you brought a date. Who is this charming lady?"

"I'm Jayne Justice," she said, unwilling to be taken for a silent partner. "I came by invitation of the family. I was Letty's college roommate."

The young woman behind Sam bent and whispered in his ear. Sam slapped his forehead. "Of course you are. I told Marcia about you myself. My wife spoke of you so fondly. I'm sorry we never had the chance to meet before today." He gestured over his shoulder. "Marcia Strong, my administrative assistant. Marcia, I believe you spoke to Ms. Justice on the phone."

Marcia Strong nodded at Jayne and smiled. Her gleaming black hair, exotic features and pale, gold skin suggested a Eur-Asian hybrid. Her low-pitched voice was at odds with her petite frame. "We're so glad you were able to come, though I wish it were under more cheerful circumstances. Did you have a pleasant trip?"

Jayne made the predictable response while Sam urged Bryce to accompany him upstairs. "Can you get the elevator? Do you have your key?"

Bryce dug in his pocket for the Jag fob. "Excuse me," he said to Jayne.

"Shall we get a bite," Marcia suggested, taking over escort duty.

Jayne readily agreed. The funeral baked meats included a whole ham, a roast turkey and a steamship round, something she hadn't seen on a buffet table since the days of cheese fondue and bellbottoms. Guests were camped out all over the downstairs with plates on their knees and drinks in hand. The true extent of the infestation of Zymoans was not evident until the cleaning crew went through the next day and found discarded plastic ware and olive pits even in the broom closet under the stairs where they'd never have looked had it not been the storage place for the vacuum.

Flushed with the nose paint from The Skeleton Key and a couple of glasses of champagne offered by white-gloved waiters who buzzed around attentively as bees in a zinnia bed, Jayne wandered the ground floor in a haze. It might have been a pleasant way to pass the wet afternoon except .... *The trouble with the whole affair is that I'm troubled.* She drifted to a window that looked out on a bare rose garden, thorny plots all box-hedged, and gave herself over again to the puzzle of Letty's demise. She didn't even notice him standing behind her until he spoke. "Jayne Justice," he said with a note of expectation in his voice, as if he were calling the roll on the first day of class.

She managed not to respond *Mr. Dorfmann?* as if she were still nineteen. Instead she turned, shook her head in a worldly way and said, "Howard. How time goes by."

Dorfmann had been an adjunct professor in Comp Lit. Letty and Jayne had signed up for his class sophomore year. Letty was taking extra hours and said she found the reading too much so she dropped it. Jayne had stuck it out through the Odyssey, Oedipus, and Joyce, the sum of which made for a perfect cultural progression in the opinion of Mr. Dorfmann, though the connections eluded most of his students. It didn't matter to Jayne whether the syllabus made sense or not. Dorfmann was the incarnation of every coed's dorm room daydream; six feet tall, rope thin, long blond hair and a fascinating manner of speaking. He used his hands in a way that got more intimate the longer he toked. She was infatuated. So was Letty, it turned out, which was the real reason why she dropped the course. Letty wanted to be his lover, not his student.

Jayne had wanted to be his lover, too, but lacked the imagination and the courage to pursue that as a goal. Only once did she screw up her nerve to go to his house with a late paper, hoping to be asked in for a beer.

The house on Eddy Street where Dorfmann lived was called the white elephant, a dilapidated three-story hulk with a mansard roof, unmarketable at any fire sale price. It was never quite certain how many students it housed. They came and went with the drafts that swept through the cavernous rooms. In early fall when classes commenced at the university on the hill flocks of undergrads would settle in. In winter more still would huddle in against the high-drifted snow. Then in the first warm days of spring, out they would fly into the clear bright air. Dorfmann was a shadowy figure amid this ebb and flow. He had leased the whole building and sublet the rooms. He himself lived in a dead Chevy Step Van parked behind the house.

If Dorfmann was regarded as possessing a romantic panache, it was because so little of what was suspected of him could be positively verified. It was said he was a PhD candidate in philosophy whose degree was being held ransom by the bursar's office until his university parking tickets were paid off. Another rumor had it that Dorfmann had decked the chairman of his department in a fit of rage and had been chucked out of the program as a result. Some of the younger faculty mentioned Dorfmann to friends who needed to score dope, but only if their usual sources had dried up. He was said to overcharge. Dorfmann was a boxer and the fact that he appeared from time to time with bright magenta crescents under his eyes added credence to the story of his assault on the chairman. Another version of how he fell from grace with academia had it that he simply quit in order to work with the inmates at the Morgan State Hospital, a mental institution where he was doing independent research on the relationship between speech and ideation. (Could thought exist in the brain without a word with which to make itself known?) In this version, Dorfmann's father, a prominent New York psychiatrist, played some angst-engendering role. Dorfmann's friends were Marxists. His dog was addicted to fresh squirrel meat, hence the firearms and the tufts of fur stuck to many of the appliances in the big kitchen where the dog's dinner was skinned and gutted. A variation on the squirrel theme had it that Dorfmann had been drafted and had done a tour in some war-torn country, honing his killing skills, his sour political views and his combat-themed wardrobe. A trickster, an aesthete, a Byronic warrior. Dorfmann was all of these, if only in the imaginations of coeds and the wives of his colleagues.

When Jayne had contemplated going back to upstate New York in the wake of Marcia Strong's phone call, she had thought of Dorfmann in the same instant as Letty. The three of them would be forever braided together, Letty the bright strand, he the deep jewel color, Jayne the compliment to both.

"I wondered if you'd turn up," Dorfmann said. He was a little stooped now, his hair white, his features sagging, his eyes still full of amusement at some joke only he would ever understand. "Wasn't it Texas where you went to disappear?"

"Spoken like a true New Yorker," Jayne replied. "How are you?"

He shifted his gaze out to the wintery rose garden. "Old."

He still talked like a Jewish comedian. "Come on," she said.

"Well, let's see … how to catch up on thirty years in a cocktail party kind of way … I did the Canadian exile shtick preferred by draft dodgers of my day, came home at some point and tried to resurrect my academic life. But that was a bust, so I went to work at the asylum, which I found quite rewarding, by the way, but then the state closed the hospital so I returned to the earth and got a job tending the vines on a winery estate not far from here."

"A vineyard!" She couldn't quite feature Dorfmann in an agricultural role.

"I was seduced by a name. The winery is called Thyrsus, another riff on ancient Greek culture. I'm sure you noticed long ago that upstate New York was loony for the Greeks at the time they named the towns. Syracuse, Utica, Seneca Falls, Aurora, Ilion, Rome—and, more to the point, Zymo. It's a learned borrowing from the Greek that has to do with fermentation. How appropriate, then, that wineries populate the shoreline of Cayuga Lake like jewels studding a necklace."

"You're lecturing," she said.

"A habit left over from long ago," he replied. He looked at the watch on his wrist with white rabbit haste. "You know, I have to go. But we need to talk. Can you come out to the winery tomorrow?"

"I'm not due to fly out until Tuesday," she said.

"Good. Just ask at the tasting room. The guy pouring will tell you where to find me. Wear walking shoes."

"All right." She felt bad, wondering if she'd said something wrong, something to drive him away. "I'll see you tomorrow."

The moment he was gone she realized she had to find a bathroom in the worst way. She set down her flute and climbed the grand staircase in hopes of finding a loo somewhere among the bedrooms on the second floor. It was, predictably, the first door on the left at the top of the stairs. She found it unoccupied. Upon emerging and turning to the right to go back down to the reception, she noticed a door ajar and a slice of light falling across the carpet at the end of the hallway. She went to the cracked door and nudged it open a little wider. There was Lois sitting on the edge of the bed holding an oversized volume on her knees. From the big block letters embossed on the cover, Jayne recognized it as the Cornell yearbook from the year she and Letty had graduated, 1973.

"Ms. Justice, you shouldn't hover in doorways," Lois said. When she looked up Jayne saw her eyes for the first time. They were reddened and strained, so very tired that it was hard to say what pale color they were. Lois patted the bed next to her. Her red painted nails stood out against the spread patterned with pale green willow leaves. Jayne sat down and saw that the yearbook was open to Letty's senior picture.

Lois seemed unbothered by the intrusion. "This is the picture we used when Letty and Sam announced their engagement." She reached to the bedside table for a rocks glass with an inch of whisky neat and took a swallow. "It ran in the New York papers. Very like her, don't you think?"

Jayne did. It had a spontaneous quality, a quickness about the gently smiling lips that brought out Letty's humor. Her large eyes shivered with mischief like heat marcelling the air on a hot day.

"I'm quite put out with her," Lois said, "for breaking me out of my condo in Palm Springs to come back up here in the dead of winter. I moved south for a reason, you know. This is her room. Shades of green." She took another sip of her drink. "She absolutely wouldn't be toilet trained. Almost four and still in soggy diapers. Dear god, I thought she'd never get her act together. I don't think she ever got over the divorce. But I had to do it. Carlton spent us into the poor house. He bought a winery with the money from the sale of the starch company." She barked out a laugh that degenerated into a croupy cough. "He was going to introduce good Bordeaux to the Finger Lakes. Oh, yes. Trouble is most of the folks around here grew up on Catawba and those sweet reds. Besides which Carlton didn't know beans about winemaking. The stuff was swill." Another sip. "My God, before he was through this house was crumbling around us. We couldn't afford to have the brick repointed because all our cash was tied up in oak barrels. In seven years the winery was bankrupt. I said good riddance. But Letty was crushed. She was eleven when Carlton bought it—a bundle of emotional nonsense like all girls that age. Spent every waking moment in the vineyard. Begged and begged us to keep it. Said she'd go to school to learn enology, become a winemaker, salvage all her father's plans. Even after it was sold she used to go over and help the new owner tend the vines and top off barrels. I'll bet you never imagined Letty as a cellar rat."

"Thyrsus?" Jayne asked.

"Yes. How did you know?"

Jayne had to smile. It explained why Dorfmann had sought out the place.

"Such a dreamer," Lois rattled on. "Always out of touch, wasn't she, even as an adult? There was something about her, a distance. She seemed to have no idea what the rest of us were about." Lois paused to consider this for a moment. "After we divorced, Carlton married a rich widow in Charleston. Letty took her friends to her father's house because if she brought them here they'd find out we were living on peanut butter sandwiches. Stony broke. That's why she had to marry Sam. It all worked out, from a financial point of view, anyway." Lois fell silent, reflecting on the ways it hadn't, Jayne suspected. "There was someone else, someone from Cornell. You must know. Tell me about him. I never could get Letty to say much except that he was brilliant and didn't have a sou. She was madly in love. So I wangled a loan and dragged her off to Europe."

Lois waited for Jayne to spill the beans about Dorfmann, but Jayne shrugged and shook her head.

"Uh-huh," Lois muttered. "Letty could be very closed mouthed, too. And stubborn. God help me, I just loved everything about her. I hope she knew that." She sighed and finished her drink. The conversation took another hairpin turn. "Tomorrow I'll show you her garden. Some of the roses have been dying off for some reason, just going dead in the middle of the shrub. She wrote me about it last summer. You can't tell now. They all look dead at this time of year. I guess we'll pull out the dying ones in the spring and plant more roses. Is that stupid, planting the same thing that just died? Do you think the new plants will fare better? I don't know. I was never a gardener myself."

"Bone meal," Jayne said. "You might try bone meal."

"Oh?" Clearly Lois was never expecting an answer. "Were you one of those horticulture people at college? Letty called them Aggies."

Jayne shook her head. "Art history."

"Really! How fascinating. What did you do with your degree?"

"Went back to Texas."

She gave Jayne a blank look.

"A sick friend. I had to take care of him."

"Oh, I see." The subject of sickness cast a pall. Lois closed the yearbook and stood up to put it back on the shelf.

Jayne got to her feet. "Mrs. Morgan," she said, "do you think it was a suicide? I can't quite believe that myself." She hesitated. "I have to tell you something, something I feel very guilty about. Letty wrote to me a couple of months back. A letter, the old fashioned kind. She said she wanted to see me next time I was on the east coast. I guess she'd been on my web site and seen the dates I had down for New York. She asked if I knew any book people. Said she needed help with something she should have done years ago. I put off answering and then finally I called her and left a voice mail. I made up some excuse about being too busy. Then I get the email about her death. I feel like if I'd come when she asked …"

Lois sank to the bed again, as if her knees had weakened. "My daughter was very ill," she said woodenly. "She was diagnosed with ALS earlier this year. It was such a shock. There's never been any such disease in our family. Letty was … she spoke about making amends before dying, taking care of things she'd neglected. I thought maybe she meant to leave Sam, but … she was quite weak toward the end, not able to walk very well."

"Why would she have wanted my help? Why book people?" Jayne asked.

"Oh, my dear," Lois said, switching off the bedside lamp, "what the Christ do I know? She was very close to the stage of needing help with everything. I'm quite glad she chose to end it when she did. My poor darling."

That night in the motel when Jayne finally turned off her light to go to sleep, she lay awake with her unanswered questions in a state of exhaustion that twice drove her to the mini-bar for a soothing nip of scotch. When she did finally drift off, she dreamt of Mrs. Rochester, the mad attic dweller of *Jane Eyre,* peering down from the dormer windows of the Morgan house with her hair on fire.

The next morning she made it down to the complimentary breakfast just before it closed. There she ran into Bryce. He was on his way out with a Styrofoam cup of coffee. "I didn't know you were staying here," she said.

He was wearing a sweater and jeans, looking much more like an average guy. "Yeah, this is where we always stay. Hey, I'm sorry for leaving you high and dry at the reception. I had more business to cover with Sam than I anticipated. I couldn't find you when I finally got back downstairs." He smiled. "It didn't feel right, that I brought you to the reception then left you to find your own way home. I wish I weren't always having to apologize to you."

"Don't worry," she said. "I should have thanked you for the drink and everything before I left, but I was tired. I hope you understand."

"Of course," he said. "As long as you're not mad …"

"Oh, no."

"So do you have any plans for today? I was hoping to make up for my rudeness by taking you to dinner, if you'll still be in town."

"That would be nice," she said.

"Great. I'll make a reservation. Why don't we meet in the lobby around seven?"

She agreed and he left her contemplating the waffle machine. After breakfast, she read a couple of newspapers on the computer in the business center then went back to her room for a long, hot shower. She was half-way in when she remembered the razor. She climbed into her robe again to rifle through her bag on a luggage stand at the window. That was how she chanced to see him getting into the XKE with the crazy woman who'd made a ruckus at Letty's funeral, a woman he'd denied knowing. *What the hell?* She stood there getting cold, feeling somehow betrayed until she made herself table the matter. She'd ask him about it at dinner, when, of course, Bryce would give her a logical explanation.

She put on warm slacks, a sweater, boots and her winter coat before braving the streets. Zymo's small downtown was just a few blocks from the motel. There wasn't much there; a handful of shops and a little independent bookstore, Books and Beans, just around the corner from The Skeleton Key. She dawdled in the bookstore, reading the flyleaves of best-sellers, before going to the bar for that burger she'd been craving.

It was around two by the time she arrived back to the motel. Crossing the lobby she chanced to see the crazy woman who'd gone off with Bryce that morning. She was nursing a glass of white wine. Jayne got a Bloody Mary and went to her table. The woman gave her a befuddled glance. "I'm Jayne Justice, a friend of Letty Morgan's. I saw you at the funeral. May I join you?"

"Suit yourself. Yeah, I seen you at the service, sitting next to Bryce Harper. You a friend of his?"

"Just met."

"Looked like you were getting along pretty well."

Jayne shook her head. "No, we just met, as I said." She sipped her drink. "I'm sorry, it's Mrs. Zealand, isn't it?"

"Sara Zealand. Did Bryce talk about me? What did he say?" Sara Zealand drained her glass and looked like she might run away.

"He told me he and your husband had served in the army together. A Special Operations unit. May I buy you another?"

"I don't mind," Sara said. "I drink for my nerves. My doctor says I need to relax, try not to get too excited about stuff. I haven't been right since my husband died. Bryce was friends with Joey. He's been there for me, ever since … I thought he'd be here this afternoon. He always stays here when he's in town. You know where he is?"

"Bryce? No. We're meeting later for dinner, but—"

"Bryce likes my cooking. He likes to eat at my place. He'd always stay for a meal when he came to see Joey."

Jayne sat silent and tried to exude empathy. "I'm sorry about your husband," she said.

Sara sniffed and swallowed some wine. "Joey was so young. They all were, but him especially. Immature the way he always believed in people, had these big ideas about coming home and going to college, being an architect, learning to fly a plane." She looked up with tears in her eyes. "He could have, you know. He was that smart. If he'd never gone over there and—" She stopped to pull a battered tissue out of her sleeve and blew her nose. "When we were in junior high school Joey bought himself this big, thick book, *Modern Airmanship*. He'd read it in his room at this drafting table—you know, one of those sloped desks with a T-square and onionskin paper and a kind of three-sided ruler. Oh, and you should have seen his drawings. He always used these really sharp-pointed pencils so it was all beautiful and precise like the drawings of airplane parts in *Modern Airmanship*. There was this one drawing I remember. It was a college pennant. Penn State. That was where he wanted to go. He made these real neat square letters with that back shadow and they got smaller and smaller as the pennant got down to a point. He said it was an exercise to teach him to draw perspective. He'd talk for hours about all that stuff, horizons and vanishing points. Sometimes he'd draw a picture of a town and there'd be a flat, straight road running down the middle of it, a road leading way off to nowhere like in the Midwest."

She stopped to blow her nose again and take a drink. Jayne waited for the 'but.'

"But then our senior year in high school it came up about this special unit the army was putting together with boys from Corinth County. Joey needed money for college and he figured if all these other guys he knew were joining up, well how tough could it be, you know?" A wistful smile appeared for a second on Sara's lips.

"So Joey enlisted," Jayne said.

"Yeah. He figured he'd gut it out and then come home with the G-I bill to get him through school. He said he could probably get himself a desk job even, sending out messages for some general. The army had other plans, though. Right after basic training they took the top half of the company and put them in Special Forces training. That's how The Brothers came about. They got home leave after they finished training. Oh, there was this big parade right here in Zymo. Everybody was so excited to get a look at what the army had made of our boys." She laughed bitterly. "What a joke. I didn't even recognize Joey when I saw him. It wasn't just that he was bulked up and bald, it was like he didn't see me anymore. Like he'd turned into this weird robo-cop. His mind was somewhere else when we were together. Before his leave was over we broke up. He said it was best that I didn't count on him for anything, like he was preparing me for if he didn't come back, putting on this big brave act. But later on I heard from other girls who been going with the guys in the company. Some of them had even been engaged. But all the guys broke up with their girls. It was like they couldn't be loyal to anyone outside the unit anymore. So I never heard from him while he was in country. I didn't know anything more about it than what anybody else did…just watched the news reports and read the papers."

"It?"

"The fight where he got wounded and sent home. One of those little villages over there. Hamlets. They always said hamlets. It was in a province up near the North Vietnam border and Laos. Quang something. I can't remember. I guess I tried to put it out of my mind." She swallowed the rest of her wine, but held onto the empty glass, fidgeting with it.

"Was that the same time Sam was shot? When he got paralyzed?"

"Yeah. Sam Watson got to be a big hero because he lost the use of his legs. Meanwhile nobody ever gave Joey a second thought because Joey came through it with just a limp. You couldn't see what was really wrong with Joey. But he was just as hurt as Sam, just as crippled. They make such a big fuss over Sam Watson. Goes to Washington so the President can pin a medal on him. Medal of honor, some shit. What a patriot! What self-sacrifice! Oh, the poor young wife, practically a newly-wed! What bullshit! Sam was no more a hero than my big toe."

Jayne sensed Sara was finally getting down to what was eating her. "How did he get wounded?"

"Joey? Shot in the leg. His unit went into that hamlet. It was infiltrated by the Viet Cong. There was a lot of confusion. A South Korean unit was providing cover, artillery fire. The South Koreans fired on some of our guys. Anyway, Sam was the one who made it over to their command post and got them to stop firing. The story is he had to pull himself across no man's land with his arms because he'd taken a round in the spine. Joey told me that was a load of horseshit. South Koreans!" She let out a bark of tipsy derision.

"Joey didn't fare very well after he got his disability discharge. He came back home, back to me. It was like a dream come true at first. He was so pretty in his uniform, and there was all this talk about what a great job the unit had done, along with Sam's heroics. I just couldn't believe he'd come back to me alive and well. It was too good to be true." She smiled that bitter smile of hers. "No, I mean that literally. It *was* too good to be true. He was an emotional wreck, in and out of one treatment center after another, hooked on heroin and booze, whacked out of his mind all the time. I couldn't get a straight story out of any of his doctors. They talked about shell shock, traumatic stress, addictive personality disorder … I don't know. The CO's wife tried to help me figure it out. She talked to some of the doctors, too. Helped Joey file paperwork for benefits, filling out forms on that old typewriter for hours. Shit. In the end all I know is he was fine before he went over there and he was fucked when he came home."

"How did he die?"

She shook her head. "I shouldn't be telling about that. Crap, I shouldn't be here at all. Yack, yack, yack, Joey used to say. You'll get yourself into trouble with your yacking. I thought Bryce would be here. Did he say something to you, where he was going?"

"What trouble?"

Sara smiled and whispered. "Trouble with The Brothers." She put a finger to her lips and did a drunken, "Shhh!"

"How did Joey die?" Jayne asked again.

"All those years he'd been in and out of the VA psych facility. And jail. There were times I couldn't even remember why I married him. He just seemed to slip deeper and deeper into depression. He'd do anything to escape for a while. Mostly drugs, like I said. It broke us. I was working two jobs and couldn't come up with the rent for a crappy single-wide trailer. Finally we moved into my mom's basement. I was just mortified. But it was better than living on the street."

"What happened?"

"My poor Joey. Always reliving the war, all that guilt." She burst into tears, trying to sop up all her grief with that same spindled Kleenex. "I don't know what happened, exactly. I was out that day. I remember I went shopping to try to find a dress to wear to a christening. My sister's kid. And when I came home I went down the basement like always and I found him. Looked like he'd been watching TV, sitting in his usual chair. There was a half finished can of beer on the table next to him. He OD'd is all. He'd just had enough, I guess. The doctor gave me something to make me sleep. I lost a week. Maybe two. We had a funeral. Just put him in the ground on a rainy day and went home. I couldn't take it in. You know, how when you don't know what to do with your hands?"

Sara looked longingly at her empty glass.

"One day at the Safeway I ran into one of the guys who used to hang out at the VFW. Joey used to go there and spend his afternoons talking about the old times. Truth be told he'd go there to get drunk on the cheap. But there was the companionship, too, I guess. Anyway, this guy I met at the grocery store, he said he was real sorry about Joey and all, and he said it was a shame no one would ever know the truth now."

"The truth?"

"About that hamlet, the one where Joey and Sam got wounded, Quang whats-it. Joey'd been talking to an agent, this woman from New York who said it would be a best seller, a real block buster. It took him years, sitting down the basement at that old manual typewriter. Not like people with computers, how you can just go back and redo. Joey thought that was a cheap way to write."

"Joey wrote a book?"

"He could have had it so easy; we could have had it so good. But he goes and kills himself. Fucked it all away. So here I am." She leaned in toward Jayne and spoke in a low voice. "It was about them. The Brothers."

"What happened to the manuscript?"

"It disappeared . Someone must have taken it."

*Taken it?* Jayne felt an overwhelming certainty that she knew who that somebody was. But there was no time to pull the thread. She needed to see Dorfmann and the afternoon was half over. Flinging some money on the table, she said goodbye to Sara Zealand, whose eyes followed her all the way outside to where a cab was loitering. "Thyrsus Cellars," she said. The driver nodded, giving every impression that he knew the way. She wasn't entirely sure he was legit until a vineyard came into view.

Against a backdrop of gray sky that threatened more snow, the vines stood bare, hardly more than gangly, crooked lines drawn by a pen-and-ink artist whose hand shook with the cold. Two score to a row, they stretched out their arms, cuffed to the trellis wire, like headless children holding hands. The tires crunched over frozen ruts banked with new drifts as her taxi approached the winery. She caught sight of a wooden sign with the name of the place, "Thyrsus Cellars" in simple incised gold letters. Carved next to it was a depiction of the object itself, a staff with leaves wrapped around it and a bulbous finial on top. Before she learned better, she'd thought the finial was a pineapple, that symbol of hospitality so often seen on New England door knockers and bed posts. But upon doing her reading she discovered the thyrsus to be a symbol of Dionysus, the Greek god of fertility, hedonism, and, of course, wine. The object itself, a staff made of the giant fennel, was wound with ivy and topped with a pine cone. Some construed it as a phallic symbol with the pine cone representing seed spurting from the penile shaft. Myth had it that the thyrsus when placed on the ground would produce a bubbling spring of wine. She smiled and thought of the maenads, the female devotees of Dionysus, who carried thyrsi in their dances. "Maenads," literally "raving ones." It was believed that in the frenzy of religious zeal brought on by dancing and drinking these women would go mad, losing all reason and control. They would hunt down animals, men and children, tear them to pieces and devour the flesh raw. Zymo, she thought, had its crazy women in more ways than one.

The taxi sped away once she'd shoved some money at the cabbie, again too much. She scurried across the rutted snow and entered a great hall with a stone fireplace where a cheery blaze jumped and crackled.

She loitered in front of the fire while a young couple finished tasting and selected a couple of bottles to purchase. Her eye was immediately drawn to a large oil painting hung over the mantel. It was a nice copy of a work by William-Adolphe Bouguereau, who had done the original in 1899. Bouguereau was a prolific painter of women and girls, shepherdesses in the tradition of Raphael, very pink and saccharine. He was criticized for a certain mannerism in his depiction of the female. Jayne had always thought that this work subverted Bouguereau's norm. Titled "Malice," it was a disturbing image.

The first time Jayne had ever seen it was on the cover of a printed copy of *The Bacchae,* the edition they were reading in Dorfmann's class. At first blush the female figure seemed childlike and gentle with her head shyly atilt, in her diaphanous white drape, exposing one breast and shoulder. Her dimpled hand holding her thyrsus, seemed innocent of any rough doing, her pale skin and softly curling hair almost too delicate, lit from a light coming from above in the foreground. But just as the back third of the canvas shaded to black, so the female figure became a darker image when examined more closely. Her eyes confronted the viewer with a frank, challenging look, seductive but also sly. The little finger of her right hand touched the right side of her mouth, as if she might be teasing a fragment of flesh from between her not particularly white teeth, somewhat pinkish, as if they'd been stained with wine or blood.

As she stared at the maenad, Jayne tried to parse the appeal of the raving women and remembered Euripides' play in which King Pentheus of Thebes banned the worship of Dionysus. The god's faithful handmaids then lured Pentheus into the woods and tore him apart. It was his mother who tore off his head, thinking, in her raving state, that he was a lion.

The couple at the bar slid off their stools, bundled themselves into their coats and left. Only then did the man behind the bar greet Jayne. "Welcome to Thyrsus Cellars. Would you like to taste? We're pouring our 2004 Super Alsation blend today. It's really quite special."

She went over to where he stood polishing glasses. "Is Dorfmann around?"

"You mean back of the house?"

She shrugged. "Anywhere?"

"Well, yes. He does odd jobs here and there," her host admitted.

"I want to talk to him," she said.

"I'll give him a call."

She returned her attention to the painting, involuntarily. *Why is the idea of a wild woman tearing men apart with bare hands so captivating? Do I hate men? Not all, or even most, surely. Those that look at me and see housekeeping or an invaginated space (a purse, a vessel, an ear, a cunt) I would gladly tear limb from limb.*

*But that's not me being a maenad. That's me being Jayne.* The maenads tore at men only in the service of Dionysus, only when they rose to a height of madness through ritual excess. On a calm day it was enough to drink and dance and beg honey from the rocks and milk from the furrowed earth and wine from where the thyrsus fell upon the ground. *Wine on demand—who can argue with that?*

*Now I'm being flip. I know there's a deeper channel here, something coursing through my subconscious, as blood courses under the skin. It has to do with he who taught me, with Dorfmann. A student is a teacher's devotee. Maybe I've always been his maenad. Maybe that's where the confusion comes in, my thinking of myself as a potential bed partner when all along I was an acolyte, a nun.*

*But don't tell me there isn't something sexual going on.* She considered the maenad's sagging eyelids, that finger between her open lips, probing between her teeth for something more sinister than a raspberry seed. *She poses for her painter and for the viewer of the piece. She bares one breast on purpose, arranges that marvelous back drop of light-tripped hair. This girl is no innocent caught tending her sheep unawares. She's a siren, a seductress. Come to me, Dorfmann. Come. I wanted to be your Waterloo, the one who'd burn you down to ruins.*

A bearded worker with hands dyed purple approached. "You looking for Dorfmann? He's working in a shed up in a stand of pines over on the south side of the vineyard. It's about a five minute hike," he said. "I'll show you."

They walked out into snowy yard at one end of the winery. He pointed up to where the weak sunlight was glistening the crusted snow between the rows. "You stay to the left of the vineyard. Go all the way to the top of the hill then bear off to the left maybe thirty degrees into the woods."

She thanked him, thinking it would be a miracle if she ever found the place. *Thirty degrees? Shit!* But the gods provide. She hadn't trudged past more than five rows of naked grapevines before a clear path of boot holes in the snow appeared to lead the way uphill. At the top of the vineyard where the woods began the boot prints ran off obliquely into the trees.

As she entered the wintery woods, she felt a claustrophobic shiver from being pressed all around by the dense growth. She heard a raven chortling but couldn't see him. She looked in the direction of the sun sinking behind the mountain top. The snow visible through the trees ahead was a bright clear blue. The light shining over the crest of the mountain was pure gold. The trees were black attenuated forms. It was as if she'd been dropped into a Giacometti dreamscape. All she could do was keep moving, following those holes in the snow. But then she heard falling water and realized her trail cut close to the edge of the Trinity Creek Gorge. That was where Letty's body had been found, at the base of Maiden Falls in the whitewater dashing along the rocks at the bottom of the ravine.

The raven laughed again. She felt an irrational terror seeping into her brain amid the old myths that held sway in this place. And suddenly God was on the tip of her tongue. *God let me get to that shack. God don't let the animals attack me. God don't let me lose my footing and fall to my death in the whitewater. God help me!* Her more rational self mocked. *It's like that, isn't it. You'll invoke any deity, make any kind of a deal with the powers that be if you can save yourself from whatever terror seems to be breathing down your neck.* She thought of Letty and a chill shuddered along her spine.

Then her brain recognized the scent of a fire. She looked up to see a pine grove not far off. Above the tops of the evergreens, a whisper of smoke lifted on a light breeze and was erased.

She trudged closer before calling out, "Dorfmann! Are you there? It's Jayne."

The shape of the shack emerged within the shadows of the pines. It was nothing more than a rabbit hutch, probably ten by ten. It had a window next to the door. Both were closed. "Dorfmann!" she yelled again.

As unlikely as clowns piling out of a circus car, Dorfmann opened the door and appeared standing there, his head scraping the frame. His eyes rested on her face for a couple of seconds before he said, "Kind of late. I thought maybe you weren't going to show. Come on in."

It was cozy inside, heated by a wood burning stove. A flannel-lined canvas jacket and a pair of overalls hung on hooks screwed into the studs. Near the overalls on the floor stood a pair of rubber boots. She dumped her jacket and handbag on the camp bed opposite the workbench. "This is a nice little hideaway," she said. "Warm."

"It's a pretty weather tight little shack. Stove works good. I pile up the canes we prune out of the vineyard and burn those. Fill those plastic bottles in Trinity Creek above the falls. It's good water. If I brought a squirrel gun up here I could eat game, but then I might not ever go back to civilization. I don't want to give in to my anti-social tendencies, so I never bring more than a few days' worth of groceries at a time. Forces me to go back into town, check my mail, get a shave, change clothes."

She felt a touch of the old jealousy rising. "Did Letty meet you here?"

"No, but she knew the place. Used to hide out up here when she was a kid. Left her books." He nodded toward the pile on the bench.

Jayne eyed the titles on the spines::*Freud's Interpretation of Dreams, Lolita.* "I don't know whether to believe you," she said.

She could imagine Letty stretched out on that cot, her long legs shining in the glow from the stove. Sure, it was only a narrow cot, but sexual congress has been accomplished in far more confined places.

"Listen, Jayne," Dorfmann said, "All that between Letty and me was a long time ago. I was in love with her when she was committed to ending the draft, racial equality, everything we talked about back at Cornell. But when the chips were down Letty Morgan went back to her roots. The revolution was just a debate to her. She paid it lip service. When push came to shove she was establishment all the way. Jesus, look who she married."

"What about me?" Jayne asked.

"You never had any political convictions at all, which I still find reprehensible, but at least you weren't a hypocrite."

"I went to the place where it happened," Jayne said.

"She must have been standing on the edge facing away from the gorge. Let herself fall backwards," Dorfmann said. "It doesn't make sense otherwise, how she cleared the shrubs and roots sticking out and landed face up."

*Unless she'd been pushed.* "I don't buy it," Jayne said.

"Why? You don't approve of suicide?" Dorfmann asked.

She knew he was being ironic, rubbing her nose in it again, the Vietnam War years when he'd led campus protests, burned draft cards with the Berrigan brothers and fled to Canada, losing Letty in the process, while she, so inaptly named Justice, had done nothing. It was a guilty patch that wouldn't scab over, even though in later years she'd joked about it, saying she'd left her social conscience out on the back porch and somebody'd swiped it. "Approve has nothing to do with it. I just don't buy it," she replied acidly.

"How do you see it? As an accident?" He laughed. "You still want everything easy. What you want is to think Letty Morgan put a foot wrong while stealing away to a tryst with a libidinous flush on her skin and scent behind her ears. It makes you feel better to think she'd been buoyed by anticipation, metaphorically anyway. It's such a romantic notion, so bourgeois, not to mention unsupported by any fact."

"There's no support for the opinion that it was suicide either," Jayne said. Her tongue had gone sour and seemed to resist every effort she made to restrain it. "Listen, Letty was trying to do something before she died, something that she needed my help with. She wrote and asked me to come see her on my next trip to New York. I think it had something to do with a manuscript. I think she'd come by a Vietnam story written by an enlisted guy. He'd entrusted it to her, made her promise to get it published before he OD'ed. She'd had it for years, but she was afraid to do anything with it. It was something on her conscience. She wouldn't have wanted to die before she'd kept that promise."

"And what did you do?"

"I said I was too busy. I didn't want to help her. I was still jealous. Over you."

"Vintage Justice," Dorfmann said. He gave her a scornful look. "If Letty had really had a book she would have shown it to me."

"You! Oh, please. She needed a friend, not a dialectical critique. She knew she was running out of time and she needed me." She looked up at him. "She was sick. Did you know?"

He shook his head. "She should have come to me," he said.

She felt heavy-hearted, burdened by the multiple ironies: she'd always thought she was in love with Dorfmann, she'd always thought Dorfmann loved Letty, and that Letty had always loved someone else. After all these years she realized the dual misapprehension: neither was her take on the triad true, nor did it matter. Not anymore. She gathered her things. "I have to go."

"Why is it, Justice," he said, "that you women today carry such gigantic handbags?"

She pulled on her jacket and slung the aforementioned gigantic object over her shoulder. "Fuck you, Dorfmann."

She was halfway out the door before he said, "Wait a second."

She stopped but didn't face him.

"The crowd you're running with," Dorfmann began, "They're bad news. You should be careful."

That made her turn around. "What crowd?"

"The Brothers. I saw you came to the reception with the one guy who drives that old XKE. Harris?"

"Harper." She waited for him to elucidate. "Dorfmann, if you don't start stringing subjects and verbs together in well reasoned fashion within the next five seconds I'm going to take this gigantic handbag and give you the hiding of your life."

"They were all in Vietnam together, Sam Watson and these guys that go around in their militia wear. They all convene at his house on the third floor, which is locked and inaccessible to those who don't know the secret handshake. They have an import business, supposedly a cover for bringing in heroin through Thailand."

She rolled her eyes. "Dorfmann you could find a conspiracy in a tub of margarine."

"They have weird ceremonies. They all dress up in Japanese kimonos and do these routines with Samurai swords. It's some kind of memorial to the ones who've died. They put up pictures of the dead guys and dance around with their swords."

"Dead guys?"

"You know, guys from their unit who bought the farm. People say they killed their own guys if they thought they'd brought dishonor to the outfit."

"Jesus, Dorfmann. Where do you come up with this stuff?"

"Come on, Justice," he said, as of old, "this is a group of Spec Ops guys, professional killers. You figure it out."

She gave him one last jaded look and left, but all the way back to the motel she thought about what he'd said.

It was well past five when she got back to her room. There was a message from Bryce on her phone. "I have to run Sam and Marcia to the airport. They're flying out of Syracuse tonight, taking some time in the Bahamas. I may be a little late meeting you."

She looked at her watch and calculated how much time it would take to get to Syracuse and back. Considering what she knew of Bryce it was a safe assumption that he drove wicked fast. Still, she had at least an hour and a half. She called a cab and had it drop her at the end of the block dominated by the Morgan mansion. She approached the house on foot, stopping when she saw Bryce heaving bags into the back of a black van with the license plate SWAT1. Marcia Strong appeared pushing Sam. The administrative assistant and Bryce maneuvered Sam's chair onto a lift at the side of the van. Once the invalid was loaded, they climbed into the front seats. Jayne hid herself behind the hedge as the van pulled out of the driveway. She saw Bryce's clean profile for an instant before the vehicle whizzed away.

She looked around to make sure she wasn't being observed, then trotted up the drive to where Bryce's XKE was parked in the driveway. It was unlocked. She slid behind the wheel and reached behind the sun visor. She held her breath. They were there. She sorted through the crowded ring on the Jaguar fob until she found a small key stamped "Otis."

She left the car and went into the house. There was no one visible on the ground floor. She crossed the foyer and stepped into the elevator. Once inside, she inserted Bryce's key in the control pad and turned it to the position marked "run." The doors swept closed. She pressed the button marked "3."

The third floor suite was a combination office and gym with a kitchenette and bedroom off opposite sides of the main room. She went directly to the desk, but found it clean of anything of interest except for a framed photo of twenty-something Sam Watson and five other young guys in jungle combat gear. She picked out Bryce with no trouble. He was right. They weren't the type to go to seed. She didn't bother to boot up the computer. Sara Zealand had said Joey wrote on a manual typewriter. The manuscript would be stuffed away somewhere if it hadn't been destroyed. She looked around and saw a two-drawer file cabinet with the lock button depressed. The key to the file cabinet was in Sam's middle desk drawer. Inside of five minutes from the time she'd entered the house she was sitting with a yellowed pile of Corrasable bond on her lap. She tried to skim, but found herself reading instead, pausing to mutter, "Dear God," once in a while. She watched the clock, saw she still had a ton of time, was hoping it was a maid when she heard the back stairway door click open, knew she was undone when it was not. Bryce stood in front of her. "I see my little mouse took the cheese," he said.

She set the manuscript aside and stood. "You played me? I didn't see that coming."

"You left us no choice after you talked to Sara Zealand. Sara called me right after you left her in the hotel bar and told me you'd been asking about Joey. Sam said we couldn't take the chance you'd try to find out about the book." He paused and stepped closer, stroked a strand of hair off her forehead. "I had to find out about you."

"Is it true?" she asked.

Bryce lifted his eyes to the ceiling briefly. "Quang Nam province. On the border of Laos. Viet Cong to the north.

There were reports that the Cong had the cooperation of the villagers. Ha My. I remember Barton started calling it Hammy and the whole unit took it up. Hammy. I gotta get me a Hammy Mammy. We wore ROK uniforms on the raid. It was—" He stopped speaking, absorbed in some horror show in his head.

"What about Joey Zealand?" she asked.

"He should never have been part of the unit. He was a big, strong guy, but he was soft inside. He wasn't up to it. He broke to the rear. Started running. Sam went after him. Nobody runs away. Don't you see?"

"You shot them?"

"If Joey had gotten away he'd have shot his mouth off to some journalist. The fucking reporters were everywhere with their cameras and their fucking questions. 'Who are these villagers? Do you know them? You say they're Communist fighters, but all I see here are women and children and old people. 135 people dead. You're saying these people were working for the Viet Cong?'"

He stopped as if it were too much to remember.

"So you ran after Joey and Sam."

Bryce came back into character then. "You see, my aim was off. I meant to take Joey in the leg. Just a shot to drop him."

"But you hit Sam …

"The first shot got Sam in the spine. I dropped Zealand with the second shot. We killed 135 innocent women and children and old men to scare the other hamlets, to send a message to anyone who might harbor the enemy. And I crippled the CO."

Jayne tried to keep her voice steady. "What happened to Joey Zealand?"

"We tried to talk to him. Gave him what he needed to feed his habit. We told him, we said, we all got to stay on the same page—that it was the South Koreans who killed every living soul in Ha My. We laid it at their doorstep and nobody in the US gave a rat's ass. Everybody back home was content to think it was gooks killing gooks. But Zealand…"

She finished his thought. "But Zealand was a loose cannon, trying to drink himself to death, writing to congressmen, badgering people on Veterans' Day. And even if no one took him seriously, he was an embarrassment. You couldn't stand it that he was dragging the unit through the mud. So you got rid of him."

"I had no choice," Bryce said. "There was an official investigation of the incidents in Quang Nam province. As a result of the investigation, the Army officially admitted that Ha My and other village raids were in fact massacres of innocent South Vietnamese civilians, but they laid the responsibility at the door of the ROK. The Korean general who'd been in charge of the ROK Expeditionary Forces during that time took the blame after years of saying Viet Cong had raided the villages wearing ROK uniforms. Joey really got spun up then. He got on the phone to any reporter who would listen and talked about how it was the US forces who had been wearing ROK uniforms, how this Korean general was paid off to take the fall." Bryce flashed her a grim smile. "Joey Zealand got it right. But we couldn't let that cat out of the bag. So I stuck a needle in his arm and made it look like suicide. We all chip in to pay his widow a monthly support check, enough to keep her from making a fuss. Because of that scene at the funeral we had to renegotiate. We came to a figure that will keep her quiet for a few more years before she gets drunk and drives off the road."

"And you killed Letty," Jayne said, "because she was going public with Joey's story. You tried to make that look like suicide, too."

"She was practically dead already. I don't even count that one." He walked over to a rack of free weights and ran his hand over the gleaming dumbbells in graduated sizes.

She watched his big, strong hands. *So this is how it's going to end—he's going to bash my brains out with a free weight.* But instead he took an automatic out of his jacket pocket and pointed it at her. "Get your stuff. We're going for a ride."

She pulled on her jacket and slung her purse over her shoulder. I guess I won't be needing the things I left back at the motel."

"No," he said. "You don't need to worry about that stuff. I'll take care of it."

He kept the gun trained on her as they rode the elevator to the first floor.

"What's it going to be this time?" she asked him, stalling, trying to imagine how she might get out of this. *Make a break for it? Run and I'll wind up like Sam Watson.* "How about a drowning? Or a mugging gone wrong. Maybe a sex crime. You can strip me and tie me up to make it look kinky."

"Don't say any more," he replied, "or I'll slap duct tape over your mouth."

Before they crossed the snowy driveway to the Jag he slipped the hand holding the gun into his pocket. It was full on dark but the area around the car was bathed in light from outside floods. Still, she felt the weapon trained on her and made no attempt to resist when he told her to get into the car. She climbed into the passenger's seat. He slammed the door. She saw a figure approaching from the dark side yard. As the person staggered into the light, Jayne recognized Sara Zealand.

"Where do you think you're going?" Sara yelled at Bryce.

Bryce spun around to face her. "What are you doing here? Go back to the motel."

"You said you'd meet me but you stood me up. You said you'd be there ages ago. What do you think I am, dumb? You think I don't know you been two-timing me? You can't do that to me and get away with it!"

"You're drunk. You disgust me." He walked toward the weaving woman. "Now get out of here, you crazy bitch."

"Don't you try to bully me," she yelled. "I'm not some weak kid. I'm not Joey. You can't tell me what to do while you go off to screw some fancy chick from out of town."

Bryce gave her a swift, sure backhand across the mouth. Sara reeled, but didn't go down. She pulled a gun and shot at point blank range. He flew straight back off his feet and lay still on the drive like somebody making a snow angel, except for the blood.

Sara Zealand just stood there with a red streak running from her busted lip and a vacant look in her eyes. Jayne scrambled out of the car and ran down the street. As she pounded on the door of the nearest neighbor, there was another shot. By the time the emergency vehicles arrived on the scene, Bryce had bled to death. They found Sara Zealand not far away in a copse of trees where she'd gone to blow her brains out.

Over the next year, there was an inquiry by the House Military Affairs Committee that exposed bribery of a former ROK General by an agent acting for a former Army Chief of Staff, one Harrison McAuley, who had been in command of US military operations during the Vietnam War. McAuley was charged with misappropriation of discretionary funds, falsifying official records and a host of other infractions of military law, along with abuse of the public trust.

Sam Watson was tried for conspiring with the deceased Bryce Harper to murder Joey Zealand and Letty Morgan. Sam would most likely spend the rest of his life in the Zymo Penitentiary.

Jayne caught a headline about the case on her way back to Dallas from Chicago. She'd been staring zombie-eyed at the TV monitor in her gate area when news of the verdict in the Watson case came through. It made her feel that the world was perhaps a little safer as a result of Sam's incarceration, maybe a little more just. She sighed and looked away from the screen. A guy in desert camouflage sitting on a stool in a wine bar across the way caught her eye. He was staring at her legs. He smiled a suggestion. She dropped her gaze and busied herself pawing through her oversized handbag, thinking of Dorfmann as she did. *Why, indeed.*

Made in the USA
San Bernardino, CA
06 October 2015